Mowzl's story takes the reader on adv
a child or a grown up, this tale, like a
ages. From the very start, you will fin
are transported into the magical world
The story is deftly woven between ou
of Mowzl, some long time in the futur
charms his human friends and brings c
confronting them with the painful real
much they have lost touch with nature
to a deep understanding of healthy, abu........ ......

This is a story of hope and encouragement. I most earnestly recommend it to you.

Rick Vick Artistic Director, Stroud Festival

Mowzl is ace and I wish I could meet him really truly and I want to learn purling, so I can talk to animals. I like stories of our world and Mowzl's all mixed up. It's lots of levels and fun and challenging. Thanks, Mowzl!

Will Beckwood Age12

Amazing! I slipped right into it and simply DEVOURED, I was so hungry for more all the way through! The story is deep, full of feeling and it made me think and sympathise more as the book went on. The story felt so real to me that I was shocked to be pulled out of it to find that I was not purling with the others, chatting with animals in the Glade.

Leela (A.K.) Age 10

This book inspired me – and hopefully others too – to do as much as I can to repair the wild web. It's great that it's addressing what we've done to the Earth, as so many people need to start helping the environment. I think the world would be a much better place if everyone read this book!

Charlotte Blue Age 12

I love the Mowzl books. I didn't read books but cos of Greta Thunberg I does now. We do climatestrike at school n I's worried for future.

Jim Keddle Age 9

Visit   www.mowzl.co.uk   to find out more and write reviews.

Also by Paul Thornycroft
The Adventures of Horatio Mowzl
Volume One: Little Humans

The Adventures of Horatio Mowzl

Volume Two
First Purlings

The Adventures of Horatio Mowzl
(Volume Two: First Purlings)

By Paul Thornycroft

First published in 2019 by MowzlPrint Publishing
ISBN: 9781916198128

All internal illustrations by the author
Cover illustration by L H Trevitt

***

MowzlPrint
PUBLISHING

For all children everywhere, for the wild web they share
and for those countless living things whose habitats are
disappearing . . .

Volume Two

First Purlings

Contents

Chapter One

Ocean

Springtime in Emmy's home world brings sunshine and flowers to the wildwood around Burrow Cave. Wood anemones, violets and celandines are showing off their colours and wild garlic and bluebells are in bud promising carpets of white and of blue flowers in a week or two. Some of the trees are beginning to unfurl their leaves, especially the small trees that must get their leaves going before the taller trees take all the light.

Emmy and Scraggy have been out all day, mapping a new 'lookout' tree. On their way home, they pass by the hollow cherry where Gabbee and Waggl nested. Emmy has an idea.

"Hey, Scragg, let's go and see if Waggl's about, and maybe the cherry tree will be flowering. I love seeing the cherry blossom."

"Good plan, Em. I 'ope Waggl's at 'ome 'n I 'ope 'e's flyin' by now," replies Scraggy.

During the winter, they had made a few visits to see Waggl, giving him presents of nuts and seeds, and each time they visited they saw that his feathers had grown a little more. Gabbee would open hazelnuts with her strong bill, giving the kernel to Waggl. The last time they visited the parrots, there was no sign of them whatsoever. Where could they have gone?

Coming closer to the cherry tree, Emmy and Scraggy hear the humming of bees. The tree is in full bloom, a fountain of white blossom reaching as high as any of the other big trees. Insects are attracted to the tree by the nectar, that the blossom provides, and while they forage for nectar their hairy bodies pick up pollen grains, which they carry from flower to flower, and from tree to tree, helping to fertilise the flowers and make new seeds.

Emmy and Scraggy climb up inside the hollow trunk of the tree. It is something they have done quite a lot and know how to do. The loose, dusty stuff has mostly fallen, and they don't get so dirty as the first time they did it. This time, Scraggy goes first with Emmy following close behind. When they arrive, they find an empty nest.

"I wonder where they went?" says Emmy, sadly. "They'll still be needing a nest for shelter, won't they?"

"Maybe they's outside, branchin'," says Scraggy.

The mice climb up to the hole in the tree and look out.

"Let's call Waggl!" says Emmy, and together they shout

Waggl's name.

"Waaaaaaaaaaaaggaaaaaaaaaall!"

But there's no reply.

From the nest hole, they admire the branches of the cherry tree covered with flowers; foraging bees fill the air with the sound of their wings, and there is a delicious smell in the air, a perfume soft and sweet.

"Scraggy, I feel like having a bit of a lie-down. Let's have a nap and see if Waggl turns up."

"Mmm. I's feelin' sleepy too, Em."

They climb back down to Waggl's nest and curl up; in no time at all, they are fast asleep.

~

Emmy yawns and stretches, keeping his eyes closed because the sun is shining through the nest hole, directly onto his face. After a bit, he yawns again.

"Scraggy?"

"Em?"

"It's bright, isn't it?"

"Yep, it's so bright I can't open my eyes!"

"Me too, let's open our eyes together . . . one, two, three . . ."

"Yiiiiiikes! Where are we?" they shout in alarm.

Instead of Waggl's nest inside the cherry tree, what they see when they open their eyes makes them gasp. They can see more blue sky than they have ever seen before, and when they look out from Waggl's nest, they see no wildwood, no ground, but the sea!

Climbing out from Waggl's nest to get a better view, they discover that Waggl's nest is not in the cherry tree in woodland, but tucked up underneath a platform, high on the mast of a huge sailing ship. They scramble through the tangle of ropes and planks of wood that support the structure and climb out onto the platform. From here they can see the ocean in all directions as blue as the sky but darker and with greenish patches, and there is no land to be seen at all in any direction.

"Where's our wildwood?" cries Scraggy.

"Oh, my goodness," says Emmy. "Where are we? How did we get here?"

"We're dreamin', Em."

The two mice are on a platform high on the mainmast of a ship. The mast, the platform and the mice are swaying about in a crazy way, as the ship below rolls from side to side with the force of the ocean waves. In ship talk, the platform is called the crow's nest, but our mice don't know that yet. They are worried about how they got here, and how they will get home.

"Pinch me, Scragg, wake me up. Ouch! Not that hard! Oh dear, we're still here."

"If this is a ship, it 'as to be a giant's ship."

"Scragg, this is a human ship, and it's swaying around like a willow in the wind, and I feel sick — Oh-oh, I'm going to fall off!"

"'Old tight, Em, 'ere, grab a rope."

"There are so many ropes! I've never seen so many ropes, and they're huge. We could climb down . . ."

"We don't know what's down there, Em, there might be 'umans, or cats, or worse."

"We can't stay here forever."

Just then, a bird flies past, squawking.

"Gabbeeeee!" yells Scraggy, at the top of his voice. "Em, that was a parrot bird, it must be Gabbee!"

The parrot, which is flying about looking for something to eat, hears the sound 'Gabbee' floating on the wind, and that makes him very curious. He flies around the ship, looking very carefully for signs of anyone who might have called Gabbee's name, but can see no one, until — ah, yes! — there on the crow's nest platform, two strange-looking mice! He flies down to the platform, landing clumsily and noisily.

"Aaaark — uck — uck — ha!"

"'Allo, Gabbee, oh dear, you're not Gabbee, are you?"

"Me not Gabbee — hoo be yoo? Owdyoo know Gabbee name?"

"Please, slow down," says Emmy. "We can't understand when you talk so fast."

"We're mouses 'n my name's Scraggy," says Scraggy.

"Hallo, my name's Emmy, and I'm a mouse."

Emmy always says this when he meets someone new — well, as long as they don't look like they are about to eat him up.

"Ah, meeces," says the parrot. "Allo, allo, welcum abord."

"What's your name, Mr Parrot?" asks Scraggy.

"Parrot name Gobbee!"

"Hallo, Gobbee, we're friends of Gabbee and Waggl, do you know them?" says Emmy.

"My-wife-my-life-my-familleee-vanished-away I'm-all-at-sea."

Emmy and Scraggy cover their ears, because Gobbee is shouting so loud. When Gobbee stops shouting, Emmy tells the story of how they had met Waggl and Gabbee, and of some of their adventures together, and that just before arriving here, he and Scraggy had been asleep in Waggl's empty nest.

"Ah emtee emtee. Waggl 'n Gabbee fly home soon."

"But how did they get there, and how did we get here?" asks Emmy, feeling very confused by all this.

"Mistree mistree timedreem ti —"

"Oh, Gobbee," interrupts Emmy. "What do you mean? And please don't shout so."

Gobbee makes an effort to slow down and be a bit quieter.

"Timedream make porthole, misstree, misstree."

"Gobbee, you talk in riddles."

"Yes, riddl riddl!" shouts Gobbee, forgetting to be quieter.

"Emmy, isn't a porthole like a window in a boat? Is he meanin' it's all a dream?"

"He says it's a mystery, not a dream, Scraggy."

"Mistree mistree yes."

"So how do Gabbee and Waggl get home? And how do we get home?"

"No do no do, you follow, you see."

"Gobbee, we don't understand you . . ."

"Mistree."

"Gobbee, what do we do now? Can you help us?"

"Gobbee help meeces — 'Gobbee fly meeces."

"We isn't flyin'!"

"Meeces fly Gobbee's back."

"What's down there on the ship, Gobbee? Humans?"

"Oomans-ratses-catsez-meeces."

"Oh no!"

"Oh yes! Wotchout, find meeces, Gobbee help you."

Emmy and Scraggy climb on to Gobbee's back, gripping his feathers. They have had some practice with Gabbee, but Gobbee is a bit rougher with his passengers. Gobbee leans over the edge of the crow's nest, stretches his wings, and with a great shriek, launches himself into the wind.

"Aaaaarkaaaaaark!"

"Yikes!" cries Scraggy.

"Oh Nooooo!" cries Emmy, as Gobbee glides and tumbles between the ropes and masts of the swaying ship, until landing on a huge coil of rope on the deck near the bow.

"That was scarier than flying with Gabbee!" exclaims Emmy.

"Gabbee? Fly Gabbee did you? Gobbee want my Gabbee!"

Scraggy explains: "We's climbin' into Waggl's nest by mistake 'n we's makin' friends with Waggl 'n Gabbee, 'n Gabbee's flyin' us 'ome on 'er back."

"Emtee nest? No Waggl?"

"No Waggl," says Emmy. "Waggl and Gabbee have gone away. We don't know where."

"Meeces, hide quick."

"Gobbee, I'm scared, can we call you if we need you?" says Emmy.

"Call Gobbee yes aaaaakukuk."

Gobbee flies off, leaving the anxious mice looking this way and that, trying to see where to hide before being seen by a cat, or a rat, or a human.

"Scragg, let's not panic, but do something quick!"

"Over there, Em — I's seein' an 'ole in that 'atch".

"Let's go!" yells Emmy, and they jump from coil to coil of the giant anchor rope, and scuttle across the deck so fast they hardly touch the boards at all. Just as they disappear through the hole in the hatch, a scruffy-looking sailor comes along; he's on sentry duty and has two cutlasses and two pistols tucked into his belts. He passes by, continuing his patrol round the ship, thinking about what he's going to eat when he gets off duty.

Under the hatch Emmy and Scraggy find themselves on the top step of a steep wooden ladder leading down into the gloom below.

"Emmy, I's feelin' sick from all the rollin' 'n swayin'."

"Yes, Scraggy. We're burrowing mice and there's no ground here! It's no wonder we feel sick. Come on, let's climb down these steps and explore."

They climb down the giant steps to the deck below, discovering that it isn't as dark as they'd thought it might be. There are cages swinging from beams above them, each one with a flame inside making a yellow light. Emmy remembers seeing a little cage a bit like these in Uncle One-Eye's den, but that one was much smaller and the light it made wasn't yellow, it was pale, and there was no flame to be seen.

Adjusting to the gloom, they find themselves in a storeroom; piles of boxes and stacks of barrels are roped down to iron rings anchored to the floor and walls. Everything is very big, because it's human stuff; to the mice, it is truly a world of giants.

They move carefully forward, listening out for danger. Emmy is thinking that they need to find a safe place to hide, and they need to find food and water — and then what? Emmy doesn't like to think about the 'then what'.

"What's that — what's that noise?" says Scraggy, nervously, peering into the shadows.

"Let's have a look," says Emmy, creeping forward. "It's the ship creaking as it moves."

"I's 'earin' whisperin'!" Scraggy whispers.

They listen and wait but hear nothing more than the creaking of ropes. The ship rolls from side to side, lifting and falling with the swell of the sea. The flame-cages swing on their hooks, and the ropes, holding fast the barrels and crates, creak and strain as the ship moves.

"I've just remembered," whispers Emmy. "Uncle One-Eye calls it a lantern."

"What?"

"The light in his den."

The mice move quietly from the shadow of one pile to the shadow of the next, not knowing where to go — except onwards; suddenly they are startled by a shout from above.

"Stand fast, ye scum! Speak the password, or you'll be tastin' the steel of my cutlass, ahhh!"

"Oh, my goodness! Our time has come, Scragg, oh dear me," Emmy coughs to clear his throat, and speaks in as bold a voice as he can muster. "Er . . . We are Emmy and Scraggy, and we don't know what 'password' is."

"Emmy and Scraggy? Ha! Ha! What names! Well now, ye scavenging scum, ye be under arrest!"

"Oh, gooddee!" says Scraggy. "We's badly needin' a rest, 'n some food would be good too, we's not et in ages. Where are you, I can't see you anywhere?"

The owner of the voice jumps down from the top of a barrel, landing with a thump on the deck.

"Ouch!"

It's a rat! He's wearing two belts, a cutlass stuck under one and another cutlass in his paw.

"Ha! You be mowses! You mowses be my prisoners! Come along with me, and no mowsee business, or I'll cut off your tails!"

"Why?" says Emmy. "And what's your name?"

"Why what?"

"Why everything? And what's your name?" Emmy repeats.

"I be Black-Eyed Bart, if you must be knowin', 'n why anything? I 'asn't got a clue."

"Hallo, Black-Eyed Bart, my name's Emmy and I'm a mouse, and this is my cousin Scraggy; we woke up in your world and we don't know how to get home."

"Ha! Ha! A tall story if ever there were! Never believe mowses, I was always told! This way. Quick march!"

Black-Eyed Bart prods them with his cutlass to make them move towards the dark shadows, where no lanterns swing.

"Why don't you talk to us?" Emmy asks.

"Sentryin' don't allow no chit-chat; git on with you, before I skin thee alive!"

They come to a wall of oak timbers and panels. At floor level, in the darkest corner, is a rat-sized hole through the wall.

"Through there — go!"

Emmy goes first, then Scraggy. Halfway, through the hole Emmy feels rough paws grab him, pulling him sideways, and he hears a whispered 'shhhhhhhh!'. Scraggy is pulled sideways too, to the other side, and there is another 'shhhhhhh!' whispered.

The rat, Black-Eyed Bart, follows them through the hole, and when he is halfway through, a voice challenges him.

"Stop there, Bart, or you will surely lose your whiskers!"

Three mice stand close to Bart's head with their cutlasses pushed against his neck.

"Ah, my dear friends, how nice to see you!" says Bart.

"Drop your cutlass, Bart. Where's the other one? Bring it out where we can see it!"

Black-Eyed Bart does as he is told, and the leader of the mice kicks each cutlass out of reach.

"Now come forward, slowly, Bart, slowly."

"I mean you no 'arm, Whip-Tail Jack!" says Bart.

"Bart, let us go on our way now, and we'll be sayin' no more about it, eh? If you be a chasin' after, I'll be tellin'," says Whip-Tail

Jack, knowing that Bart doesn't want his fellow rats to know how easily he's been defeated.

"Alright, alright, anything you say, Jack, only a bit of fun…"

Black-Eyed Bart crawls through the hole, and retreats, picking up his cutlasses and sticking them back into his belts. The three pirate mice back out of the hole, holding Emmy and Scraggy by their arms. They move off swiftly through the shadows, through a doorway where they have to climb over the coaming board, which stops water sloshing through; on they go, through a small hole in the floor onto a beam, through another hole, and another, until Emmy and Scraggy are dizzy and have lost all sense of direction. At last the three pirate mice stop to rest, and to have a good listen for anyone following them.

"Will the rat chase us?" asks Emmy.

"No."

"You were all very brave, thank you for rescuing us."

"'Tiz nothin'."

"My name's Emmy and this is Scraggy, we're cousins."

"Talk later."

The mouse with the name Whip-Tail Jack has been muttering these few words, while the other two remain silent and watchful. They move on, Jack in front, then Emmy and Scraggy, followed by the other two pirate mice. After many more twists and turns, they arrive at another hole leading to a narrow space above the galley ceiling. In fact, it's above a store cupboard at one end of the galley. *This is their burrow!* thinks Emmy.

One of the pirate mice stays on guard andanother fetches food and water, which Emmy and Scraggy eat and drink hungrily. Whip-Tail Jack watches them intently. At last he speaks:

"Be tellin', 'ow's you gettin' 'ere?"

Emmy tells their story, about what had happened since they went to sleep in Waggl's nest, and he tells about where they had come from, and about Gabbee and Waggl, and that he did not know how he and Scraggy had got here to this ship, or to this world, and he says how worried they are about getting back home.

There's a long silence.

"What's in your backpacks?" says Jack, his voice a bit softer than it had been.

"Oh, let me show you," says Emmy. "It's not much, because we weren't planning a long journey when we set out this morning. We were just going to map one more tree and visit Waggl on the way home, and I've told you the rest. Let's see what's in here."

Emmy takes off his backpack, undoes the straps and takes out some empty nutshells, seed pods, a compass and two small tubes, each with a cork in the end. Jack gasps.

"Who's Tooby?" he demands suddenly, his voice very serious.

"My Dad, my Dad! Tooby's my Dad!" sings out Scraggy, so happy to hear the sound of his father's name. "He's back 'ome where we's come from."

Emmy explains that the backpack, bamboo tubes and compass were all given to him by his Uncle One-Eye, who is helping them learn how to make maps, so he can make a map of where they live.

"And he's got one of those things that swing from the beams of this ship that make a yellow light, except his makes a pale light, and it's got no flame in it. He calls it a lantern."

"Aye, lanterns we's callin' 'em."

"Yes, he's got a lantern in his burrow at home and I always thought it was magic. Do you know Uncle One-Eye?"

"We's all knowin' Tooby. He upp'd 'n vanished. We be missin' 'im."

"What happened?" asks Scraggy.

"Fog there was, when Cap'n Tooby went aloft."

"Do you mean he climbed the mast?" asks Emmy.

"Right enough, in fog thick as soup."

"To the platform high up?"

"Aye! The crow's nest we's callin' it, that's right."

"Whip-Tail Jack — that's exactly where we woke up!" Emmy explains, excitedly. "Gobbee said something about a porthole."

"That parrot be crazy, there's no porthole aloft."

"Have you tried going up there when there's a fog?"

"What? 'n vanish meself? Not on your nelly!"

Scraggy looks up, his voice trembles. "I'll do it, when the fog comes! I'll be gettin' 'ome if it's the last thing I do!"

Whip-Tail Jack smiles for the first time. "All in good time, young Scraggy! Now we be knowin' who thee be, 'n be trustin' thee, 'tiz time to meet the crew! This 'ere be Black-Boot Bess, 'n this 'ere be Stump-Leg Stew."

"Hallo, Emmy and Scraggy, welcome aboard," says Bess.

"Hello, Bess and Stew. Are there more of you?" Emmy asks.

"Two more, we be," says Stumpy. "Call me Stumpy. Others'll be sentreein', we do turns like. It'll 'av been Cutlass Kate who spied thee on the parrot's back! She come to tell us, leavin' Sieve-Brain Sally to follow when Bart got thee."

"Thank you all for rescuing us!" cries Emmy.

"Thank you!" says Scraggy.

"We were frightened," admits Emmy. "And we still are frightened of the human giants, we've never seen humans before."

"Never seen humans?" cries Jack. "Where in the world have you been?"

"In our home world, there's no sign of humans, except old buried things, and we don't know of any creatures that have seen humans. Do you think it's a different world? Oh dear! How will we get home?"

"Or could it be a different time?" suggests Black-Boot Bess.

"Ooo that's spooky," says Stumpy, shuddering.

"Never mind yer fancy ideas," snaps Jack. "We 'as work to attend! Get to it!"

Stumpy knows what Whip-Tail Jack means, and he explains to the newcomers.

"What Jack's meanin' is, we 'as our everyday duties to be doin', and now we 'as thee to be mindin' besides. Thee'll 'ave to learn fast, findin' your way's about and deefendin' thyselves. "Scraggy, young feller, you be with Bess; Emmy, with me. Keep closer 'n yer own shadows!"

Emmy puts his things back into the backpack and straps it on. Since his adventure inside the mountain with Star, he takes his backpack with him wherever he goes.

Scraggy gives Emmy a worried look. Emmy smiles.

"See you later, Scraggy; we are in the middle of a mystery, keep your eyes peeled!"

Scraggy and Emmy hug each other as though they might never see each other again.

18

For the next few days the mice are kept busy with the daily patrols and searching for food, but when there is spare time, Scraggy and Emmy are given some training. There is a lot to learn: how to find their way around, what the dangers are, and where safe hideouts might be. Most important is how to use a cutlass to fight off the rats, if they are unlucky enough to bump into them. It's made very clear to Scraggy and Emmy that it's best not to bump into a rat; they are not all so easy to get around as Black-Eyed Bart.

When Scraggy is first given a cutlass, he has no idea what to do with it, and he keeps tripping over and getting the blade stuck in the floorboards. One day, when he is in a training session with Cutlass Kate, she suddenly charges at him with a great shout, and he has to defend himself. At first, he is frightened, but then he feels strength fill his body and he finds himself fighting back. Cutlass Kate says she is pleased, and that he's a good learner; Scraggy feels very proud and wishes that Emmy had been there.

Emmy is slower to get the hang of it and has to learn little by little, but he, too, feels proud of the cutlass and belt that he's been given to wear.

They do the training on one of the storage decks, in a place where the humans hardly ever go. They have a few different escape routes from there, in case they are taken by surprise by humans or rats, or the ship's cat. There's a lot of noise from the deck above where the sailors are yelling and running about, and that helps to cover the noise they make clashing their cutlasses together.

They always have to be very quiet in the Hideout, or burrow, as Emmy would call it, which is above the ceiling of the ship's larder. It might seem to be a silly place to have the Hideout, but it has one great advantage, and that is that the mice don't have to go very far to get the food that they need.

There are several holes through the larder ceiling, tight in the corners where there is no light, and where humans are unlikely to look. There are shelves lining the walls of the larder laden with jars, tins and sacks, and everything is held in place by boards along the front edges of the shelves. The mice climb up and down these shelves quite easily, taking care to leave no trace of their comings and goings, creeping into the larder at night when there are no humans about. The mice are careful to take only a small amount of food at a time, so that the humans won't notice. Much of the human food is disgusting, things like salted fish and bacon, but there are sacks and barrels of grains and seeds, and sometimes dried fruit, which the mice love.

Emmy and Scraggy help with the missions to the larder, and learn the quick ways in and out, and they learn the First Rule. The

First Rule is that whatever happens, you must not give away the Hideout. If you are seen by a human, or are chased by a rat or a cat, you must run away from the Hideout, and make your way back later by the secret trails.

Emmy loves learning to navigate around the ship. He has always had a good sense of direction, and everything he has learned in the wildwood at home helps him now. As the days go by and Emmy and Scraggy learn the basics of ship life, they begin to get used to the constant movement, and to walk more easily and not feel that they are falling over all the time. Stumpy says they are getting their sea legs.

It's always a surprise to them when they come across a porthole, or hatch, that gives them a view of the sea; they could sit and look at the sea for hours, but it would risk being ambushed by the rats. The sea always makes them feel sad too, because it reminds them that their home is unreachable. They couldn't get home even if they were to jump into the sea and swim! The sea is too big, and anyway, they don't know which way to go.

Whenever they get time off, Emmy and Scraggy explore somewhere new on the ship. They like to be together and talk, remembering their loved ones and everything back at home in Burrow Cave. One day they make their way to the Quarterdeck, which is the high bit at the back, or stern, of the ship. There is a safe place where they can relax and peep through a split in an oak board and look out over the whole ship, from stem to stern, or front to back. The ship is big, making the mice feel very small, but even bigger than the ship is the sea, and the ship is rolled by the waves, this way and that, and the masts are always moving against the sky.

On the Quarterdeck in front of them is the big, spoked wheel, or helm, that is used to steer the ship. Ship's officers are standing about shouting orders, and the sailors are running about all over the place, climbing the rigging and carrying out those orders. There's always a lot to see and learn about how the ship is sailed. Emmy likes to watch the navigator measuring the angle of the sun, or at night, studying the stars. He wants to know how the navigator can be sure which way to go just by looking at the sun or the stars. Star would know, Emmy thinks, and Uncle One-Eye too. Thinking of them makes him feel sad, and tears sting his eyes.

"Scragg," he says, a catch in his voice. "I was just thinking of your dad and feeling homesick. I hope we get back one day."

"Me too, Em. This is a good adventure, but there's no land and no wildwood, and I's missin' 'ome."

"'Allo, lads!" says a voice behind them, startling them.

"Oh, Stumpy!" exclaims Emmy. "You made us jump!"

"Ah-ha! I crept up on thee!"

"'Ow's you movin' so quiet with a wooden leg, Stumpy?"

"I's learnin' runnin' on all threes, Scraggy!" says Stumpy, smiling. "Now then, what plots are you two 'atchin'?"

"No plot," says Scraggy. "We's missin' 'ome. I's missin' my Dad. What's you knowin' 'bout 'im?"

"Tooby? We's all missin' 'im. What's not said is, 'e's vanish'd before, sudden like, 'n 'e's back when we least 'xpects it. 'E never says a word 'bout it. 'E's always collectin' special things 'n when last 'e vanish'd, 'e took some of 'em with 'im."

"What sort of special things?" asks Emmy.

"All sorts, like littl' 'eads o' stone, 'n them pipes like yorn."

"I've seen the little heads in his den at Burrow Cave!" cries Emmy. "They're magic! He said something about dreams — ah yes, he said 'it be full o' magic, that there bowl; nothin' like spells nor troublesome things, but dreams that show the way'."

In the silence that follows, Scraggy looks at Emmy curiously.

"You alright, Em? You looks like you's sleep walkin'."

Emmy shakes his head, trying to snap out of his daydream.

"That was strange," he murmurs. "I was back in One-Eye's den for a moment, hearing him speak those words. Ooo, my fur's standing on end! That's really spooky."

"Ah-ha!" Stumpy exclaims. "This be Tooby alright! He has magic, 'n we be waitin' for 'im."

"Stumpy," asks Emmy. "Have you ever seen when he goes — or comes back — how it happens, or where it happens?"

"Nay, lad! 'N me eye be peeled night 'n day, 'n I's seein' nothin'. Even Tooby never did know when or how."

"He didn't know?"

"Reckon not."

With a faraway look in his eyes, Emmy speaks quietly, almost to himself. "'Dreams that show the way', hmm." He looks at Stumpy. "Are there any of Tooby's things on board this ship?"

"Maybe, maybe not; Cap'n Jack is keepin' Tooby's sea-chest back at the Hideout."

"Let's go back and look inside!" cries Scraggy enthusiastically.

"Not if you's valuin' your life, Scraggy. Jack'll skin thee alive!"

"Maybe we can get Jack to talk about it," says Emmy.

"Hey look! There's Gobbee!" Scraggy cries.

Through the split in the oak board, they watch as Gobbee flies about the Quarterdeck getting yelled at by humans when he gets in their way. But the humans don't try to hurt him; it seems they quite like him being around. Gobbee flies towards the bow, and the mice lose sight of him amongst the rigging.

Emmy turns to Stumpy. "Is there any way we could talk to Gobbee without being seen, or heard, by humans? Is there anywhere we could do that, Stumpy? Maybe Gobbee knows more about the 'porthole' than he's told us."

"There be the Fantail."

"What's *that*?" asks Scraggy.

"That'll be aft; the Fantail be where the over-'ang be, 'n the rudder 'n all. Let's 'ave a look. C'mon, follow!"

Stumpy sets off with the two young mice close behind, going under the floor of the Poop. He knows the gaps in the timbers and holes in the beams where they can squeeze through. At last they see daylight coming through a hole in the stern of the ship; a heavy rope runs through this hole, and the rope is moving, first one way and then the other way.

"T'is from the 'elm to the rudder, you see. There be two steerin' ropes, one each side o' the ship. When the 'elm is turned, the ropes is pullin' the rudder this way or that."

There is plenty of room to squeeze past the rope, and out onto a huge oak beam that holds the top end of the rudder. The wood is old and has been damaged over the years; there are nooks and crannies perfect for the mice to rest in, where they don't feel too much in danger of falling into the sea. Above them is the over-hang of the Fantail, where the Captain's cabin is. This is the first time that Emmy and Scraggy have been so close to the open water, and the sight of it amazes them. In fact, it's scary.

They watch the wake of the ship for a good long time.

"Gobbee can land on this 'ere beam," says Stumpy.

"How do we call him?" asks Emmy.

"We 'as a code," says Stumpy. "Any old squeak, as 'igh as you can, too 'igh for 'umans to be 'earin'. Let's 'ave a go."

They all three make high-pitched squeaks, but Stumpy is not satisfied with their efforts, and so they do it again, and again.

"That'll be alright, now you's knowin'. Gobbee would come if 'e 'eard us, 'n 'e ain't, so you'll 'ave to be tryin' another time."

"Stumpy, was there another parrot?" asks Emmy.

"Aye! She upp'd 'n vanish'd one day, 'n Gobbee's been lookin' for 'er ever since, flyin' everywhere lookin', lookin'."

"She turned up in our world, Stumpy," says Emmy. "She nested in a hollow cherry tree with a baby, called Waggl. She's called Gabbee. Waggl had no feathers, because he was too young, but it was autumn in our world and he got cold. During the winter

Gabbee and Waggl disappeared; we don't know where they went. We went to their nest to see if they'd come back yet, but they hadn't. We were tired, and we had a little nap, and when we woke up we found ourselves in your world! The cherry tree and the crows nest must be the 'porthole', as Gobbee calls it."

"Hmm," says Stumpy. "Strange things happen! And stranger things happen at sea!"

"You've got no ideas about what happened?"

"Nope."

"Oh." Emmy feels disappointed.

"Let's go 'n ask Whip-Tail Jack if we can look in my Dad's sea-chest!" says Scraggy.

"Good plan, lad. C'mon!" says Stumpy, and he leads the way back through the labyrinth of secret trails, while Emmy and Scraggy try hard to remember the way, so that they will be able to return to the Fantail another time.

~

"Where's you all been for so long?" growls Whip-Tail Jack.

Stump-Leg Stew, Emmy and Scraggy have returned to the Hideout only to find they are in trouble already.

"I show'd 'em the Fantail to call the parrot," says Stumpy.

"We'd finished our jobs, Jack," says Emmy.

Sieve-Brain Sally clears her throat before speaking.

"You missed your turn on lookout, and Jack's not happy."

"I'm sorry, I never knew," says Scraggy.

"Sorry, Jack," says Emmy.

"It'll be down to me, Cap'n. 'Twas my idea," admits Stumpy.

"Alright, alright, enough!" says Jack, impatiently.

Emmy is thinking this is probably the worst moment to ask Jack if they can look inside Tooby's sea-chest, but he has a feeling it's got to be now — or never.

"Captain Jack, may we look in Tooby's sea-chest, please?"

"Over my dead body!" Jack shouts. "I did swear by my life to guard that chest for Tooby, and that's what I'll do."

"But 'e's my Dad!" pleads Scraggy. "Let me see my Dad's things, please, Jack."

Jack turns away, unrelenting. Emmy takes a deep breath.

"Scraggy and I are newcomers on this ship, Captain Jack. We didn't ask to come here, and we're grateful to you for helping us and being so generous.

"We have fresh eyes. We can see that the humans are

sleepwalking as though they are enchanted. There is a deep magic that has all of you trapped in a dream. We don't want to fall under the spell. We need to do something, and finding out what happened to Tooby is a good way to start."

Jack still has his back turned. After an awkward silence, he heaves a deep sigh.

"We's been 'ere a long time, our lives given to seekin' freedom, but we's forgettin' what freedom is. I know these humans are trapped in a dream, as you put it; they sail this ship forever in search of — something — they never find. We have our routines, there's no end to it."

Jack's shoulders slump down, defeated.

"How did you get here?" asks Emmy, his voice gentle.

"I's not rememberin'."

"Please, Jack, we are still free, please let us help you."

"You's just wantin' to get 'ome."

"Yes, we want to get home, and we want you to come too, if you will."

"You mean that?"

"Yes! All of you."

Jack turns to face them.

"I'm not against thee, children of Tooby, how could I be?" says Jack, his voice softer now, and beginning to sound interested. "How do we find out what happened to Tooby?"

"It'll be a riddle," says Emmy. "Everything to do with One-Eye'd Tooby is a riddle. But we have the sea-chest, and whatever Tooby has left in there will tell us what to do, I feel sure of it."

"Alright, open it."

Jack drags the sea-chest to the centre of the room from the corner where it normally lives. It's a simple box, with a domed lid hinged at the back. It has black lines painted on, pretending to be iron bands, and there is a lock painted on too, but really there is no lock at all.

"Scraggy, you should be the one to look inside," says Jack, lifting the lid.

"Thanks, Jack!"

Scraggy looks inside, reaches in and lifts out an object wrapped in cloth. "It's a map tube, Em!"

Emmy watches intently as Scraggy removes the cloth.

"Scragg, don't open the tube yet, put it on the floor, on its cloth. Let's get everything out before we open them, just so we know what there is in there."

"Are you expecting a surprise, Emmy?" says Sally.

"Yes!"

Scraggy takes another, much larger, bundle out of the chest and carefully unwraps it. It's a map tube, but this one is short and fat, whereas the first one had been long and thin. The next bundle is like the first, then comes a collection of small things that turn out to be little heads, just like the ones that Emmy has seen before in One-Eye's den. Emmy remembers One-Eye speaking of the magic of the bowl of little heads, saying about 'dreams that show the way'.

Scraggy has unwrapped everything, placing each thing carefully on the floor on the cloth that had wrapped it. He sweeps his paw around in the sea-chest to check for anything else, finding some seashells. He lifts them out, putting them on the floor.

"What's in the big thing?" Stumpy asks.

"You open it, Jack," says Emmy.

Jack hesitates; he picks up the big tube and slowly unbends his body until he is standing up as straight and tall as he is able. He feels calm now, his unease and irritation quite gone. As he eases the plug from the end of the tube, a pale light shines out from the opening; he tilts the tube a little and the light pours out gathering itself into an Orb, which floats in the air. It is spherical, but not like a ball, because it doesn't have a surface.

The mice gasp in astonishment, and in that inrush of breath, something new enters their lives.

"We must call Bess and Kate," says Jack softly.

"I'll go," says Stumpy.

The Orb is beautiful to look upon, and the mice feel peaceful. Stumpy returns with Bess and Kate and they, too, gasp and are astonished. They gaze at the Orb for a long time, speechless.

At last, Sally breaks the silence.

"I have never before seen anything more beautiful," she whispers. "What is it?"

"How does it come to be here, in this box?" asks Kate.

"That Tooby is a mysterious one!" says Bess.

Jack is silent.

"Jack?" says Emmy.

He says nothing.

"Jack? You know something, don't you?"

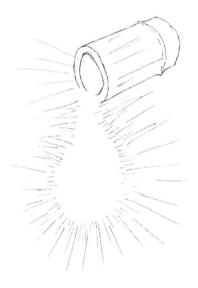

Jack shifts his body awkwardly, clearing his throat. "Huwa. Erm, Tooby was tellin' me some . . . it's from the Island o' Mist. The humans is sailin' over the ocean searchin', 'n they reckons they'll be comin' across the fog 'bout every six moons. They's sailin' straight for the fog, 'n into the fog they's goin', 'n if the Island o' Mist be showin' itself they's anchorin' in the bay.

"They's goin' ashore in the longboat, takin' barrels 'n crates for sweet water 'n food, 'n they's off into the wilds to 'unt animals 'n search for treasure, which they's never findin'. When all's done, they returns to the ship with the barrels 'n crates, weighin' anchor 'n sailin' away to be searchin' ocean for six moons, or however long it be."

Jack's voice grows in strength and confidence as he talks, as though the remembering is bringing him out of a dream.

"When Tooby was first 'ere, 'e was bent upon goin' to the Island o' Mist. We's watchin' as the ship she slips into the fog 'n the island shows 'erself; humans row to the shore in the longboat, they's goin' back 'n forth time 'n again, gettin' all the water 'n fruit 'n meat back to the ship. Tooby took it into his 'ead one night, when the longboat was made fast to the side of the ship, that 'e would stow away 'n get to the island. 'E climbed down 'n 'id 'iself somehow 'n got rowed to the island, 'n 'e never come back.

"The humans does their searchin' for treasure 'n returns to the ship, weighs anchor 'n we sails away, leavin' poor Tooby on the island. We was 'eartbroken.

"Many moons on, we sees the fog 'n the ship she sails into it, 'n after a night or two the island looms out of the mist. One night, when the longboat returns, who should climb out when all the humans is out o' sight, but Tooby.

"'E 'ad 'is back-pack stuffed so full 'e could hardly carry it, 'n when we got 'im back to the Hideaway, it wouldn't fit through the 'oles so we's 'avin' to take things out 'n carry 'em in one be one. That's when I's first seein' them tubes. Tooby asks us to search for a sea-chest. We never finds nothin', but Stumpy, 'e made one, 'n Tooby put all 'is things in there.

"'E's tellin' me, 'n me alone, 'bout the tubes, 'n 'e showed me the light. Pour out, it did, 'n made a ball what 'e called an Orb, 'n pour itself back it did, 'n 'e made me swear by me life to protect it, if 'e ever went away.

"'E didn't know 'e was goin' away but go 'e did. We 'ad a set-to with the rats 'n we lost Red-Belly Ron, who was cut to pieces, bless 'im, 'n they's chasin' Tooby up the riggin' 'n there was lightnin', 'n 'e vanish'd sudden."

Jack sighs. "It were many moons after, six, maybe more, before Tooby turns up again with one eye missin'. 'E tells us nothin', not one thing, 'bout what 'ad 'appened to 'im, or where 'e'd been. 'E likes bein' 'ere, that's plain to see. 'E vanish'd again, turnin' up many moons after . . . and so it went.

"That's 'bout all I can be sayin' 'xcept 'e 'ad 'is back-pack on when 'e first vanished, 'n there would 'ave been some things in it, but I's not knowin' what."

"Map tubes and little heads!" cries Emmy. "And — oh yes! His lantern! He must've had another Orb, but smaller, and he put it in the lantern."

"You mean 'e vanish'd from 'ere 'n turns up in your world?"

"Yes, Jack, in his den at Burrow Cave. The light is still there now! The light is the key to the 'porthole', as Gobbee calls it."

"'Portal', it'll be called," says Jack. "Tooby's tellin' me this."

"Portal? What's that?" asks Sieve-Brain Sally.

"It's an 'uman word, he's sayin', Tooby that is, meanin' gateway, or some such."

"Like a burrow?" suggests Scraggy.

"Maybe so."

"But how does he disappear?" says Emmy.

"We's not knowin'," says Jack.

"Let's see what's inside the other tubes," suggests Emmy.

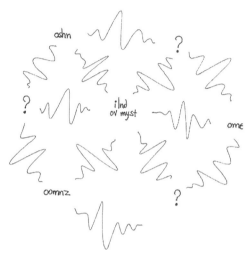

Scraggy opens one; it's empty. He opens another, and inside is a rolled-up birch bark parchment. Is it a map or sea chart? It's just a lot of wiggly lines with some words here and there, such as 'ilnd' and 'oshn'. It's very mysterious. Scraggy opens another tube, and light pours out, forming into a small Orb.

"Ah!" cries Emmy. "This must be about the same size as the one Tooby carried through the portal and put into his lantern back in our home world. So, when he left the Island of Mist, he was carrying one big light ball and two little ones. And maybe more that we don't know about." As Emmy gazes at the Orb, an idea pops into his head — he must go to the Island of Mist.

"Scraggy and I should go to the Island," he announces.

"Oh no, not you as well!" moans Jack. "We don't want you disappearin' too."

"It'll be alright, Jack, at least I hope it will. How long has it been since this ship was last at the island?"

"We's not knowin'. There's no time keepin', not like that; time doesn't keep, it drifts away with the wake o' the ship. She's called 'The *Wreckless*'."

"Who?' asks Scraggy.

"The ship," Jack replies.

"Alright, the island will just come, I know it," says Emmy.

"D'you really want me comin' with you, Em? Maybe better if I's stayin' 'ere with the Orb."

"Hmm, that could be the best idea, Scraggy," Emmy replies thoughtfully. "One-Eye will be looking for us, and Flimsy will do her seeing. If you're close to the Orb, they're more likely to see you. Keep everything in the sea-chest, and open it every day; count the days, mark down each day that passes. We must open the tube and look at the light every day to remind us that this world is an enchanted world. It's an in-between world, and we don't want to get stuck here."

"Maybe all worlds are dream worlds," says Jack. "I'll be comin', Emmy, I want to be 'elpin' Tooby, 'n be seein' 'im again."

"Thanks, Jack, yes, let's go together."

"Stumpy?" says Jack sternly. "You'll be Cap'n when we's gone. Keep this rabble in good order, 'n guard Tooby's sea-chest with your very lives!"

"Aye-aye, Cap'n!" they all chorus.

When it is time to put everything away in the sea-chest, Jack picks up a light tube.

"Feast yer eyes on this!" he cries, and everyone watches in amazement as an Orb pours itself back into the tube he is holding.

"Just look at that!" exclaims Emmy.

The large and small Orbs return to their tubes; Scraggy wraps the tubes again, putting them carefully back in the sea-chest. The charts, little heads and the seashells are all safely put away too; the chest is closed and left standing in the middle of the Hideout where they can easily get to it.

Everything goes on as before, except that the mice are all wide awake now and looking forward to the fog, and the Island of Mist. They are all aware that the world they are in is not quite real, and now that they have woken from a dream, they do not want to become enchanted again.

They keep a tally of the days by putting one seed each day into a shallow knothole in the floorboards. It works for a while, but it's a bore, because the grains are awkward to count and anyway Black-Boot Bess and Sieve-Brain Sally have a habit of eating them. Scraggy remembers having a lesson in numbers with Scribbla, and how to tally with making marks.

"You's makin' a mark like this," he explains. "'I', for each thing you's wantin' to count, so, we's countin' one for each day. When four days 'as gone the tally's lookin' like this: 'IIII', 'n next day's lookin' like this: 'HHH', meanin' five. When you's gettin' to 'HHH III', that's eight 'n 'HHH HHH' is two fives, wot's ten."

"Good plan, Scraggy! Well remembered," says Emmy.

They all agree that this is a good idea, and Emmy makes the first mark with his penknife in a big oak beam in the wall.

The days pass by, and life goes on much as before. The humans do all the things that sailors do, always looking for land, always looking out for the fog.

They see storms in the distance from time to time; they see a whale breaching, and one day an albatross appears, flying with the ship for a few days before vanishing again. One morning the sun doesn't rise; the sky is heavy with storm clouds, and the wind picks up, gaining strength as the day goes on.

The *Wreckless* begins to heave, dangerously, as the wind gets fiercer and the sea swell rises; the sailors reduce sail to slow the ship. Before long, all sails have been furled except a scrap for steerage, but this scrap is soon torn to shreds by the fierce wind. The ship is driven before the wind in the mountainous seas.

Emmy and Cutlass Kate are on sentry duty in the cargo hold, where the barrels and crates are roped down to iron rings on the floor. The ship pitches and rolls alarmingly, the wind screaming and howling as waves crash over the decks, the seawater leaking through the cracks in the timbers. It's crazy staying on duty; they should get back to the safety of the Hideout, but without Jack's permission, they dare not.

They hear a loud bang from somewhere above them, and a moment later the top of a broken mast crashes through the deck, smashing through into the cargo hold. In comes the wind like a furious beast, sucking and pulling, searching everywhere; anything that is not fixed down disappears at great speed through the torn deck, and up into the black storm clouds above. Splinters of wood are sucked up into the sky and, as they watch, Emmy and Kate see a rope snap under the strain, and the freed barrels wriggling for a moment before leaping up and out of the ship like cannon balls.

"Hold on! Hold on!" cries Cutlass Kate.

The two mice hold on for dear life to ropes that haven't yet broken. Kate manages to wrap her tail around her rope, but Emmy can't do it, because the rope is too tight against a barrel. The wind howls, tugging at his body, and his feet lose their grip. His body is pulled upside down, he holds on with all his might, but then he loses his grip, and is sucked, shrieking, into the sky.

"Emmy!" screams Kate, but her voice is drowned out by the wind. It takes all her strength to hold on, and even though she is very determined, she begins to weaken, thinking, *How long will this wind last? I can't hold on much longer.*

At last, the noise begins to die down as the whirlwind moves slowly away from the ship.

"Emmy, where are you?" she shouts at the top of her voice, but she knows that he won't hear her. "Emmy?"

The centre of the storm may have passed by, but the sea is still huge, and the ship continues to pitch and roll like a mad thing. Kate can let go of her grip at last, one hand at a time, slowly and carefully, because her hands are numb and cramped. At last she loosens herself up enough to be able to walk, and she stumbles her way back to the Hideout, falling many times because of the movement of the ship. At last she arrives to find all the mice there, and at the sight of them she bursts into tears.

"The whirlwind — the wind has sucked Emmy into the sky!"

"Emmy, nooooooooo," screams Scraggy, falling to the floor, moaning and banging his fists on the hard, oak boards. He is so upset, he forgets to balance against the rolling ship, and he rolls about like a dead thing until Jack grabs him, holding him tight.

"Son o' Tooby, do not despair. Keep your 'eart light, lad, Emmy 'as been taken by the wind, but we don't know what it means, or if he lives or dies. Keep him in your 'eart, 'e needs you."

Jack is different; the spell of enchantment is broken.

"Scraggy, we'll go to the Island o' Mist, you 'n me, 'n look for sign of Emmy, 'n your father, One-Eyed Tooby."

But Scraggy is inconsolable; he sobs and sobs. All the mice are shocked and tired, wanting the storm to finish, but it drags on for another day and a night before abating. At last the wind drops and the sea begins to settle down, and in the coming days the human sailors set about repairing the ship. There is damage all over the ship, and the humans are everywhere, sawing and chiselling and hammering. It goes on and on, for two moons or more. The mice lie low most of the time, sneaking into the pantry for food when everything is quiet in the dead of night. But they don't go out and about much because there are humans everywhere.

As soon as the masts and the rigging are sufficiently repaired, sail is set and the *Wreckless* is under way once again, continuing the search for land in an ocean without land.

The mice open the sea-chest every day, opening the big light tube to release the Orb. They bask in the light, feeling refreshed and restored. Scraggy cuts a mark into the beam every day, carrying on from where Emmy had started. *Oh Emmy, I's missin' you,* he thinks, every time he cuts the beam. The tally has got to 81. That's 16 x H̶H̶ plus one more. Nine days later, on day 90, the *Wreckless* enters the fog.

~

The ship makes slow headway through the fog, or so it seems, judging by how little wind there is in the sails, and by the sluggish slap of water against the hull. But in truth it is impossible to judge the passing of time because the fog is as dark as night. It might be two days that pass, it might be one, or it might be five.

Whip-Tail Jack and Scraggy have made their way through the darkness to the Quarterdeck, where they can look out through a split in the boards. From this vantage point it is normally possible to see the whole length of the ship, but at the moment they can see nothing, because the fog is like a thick, dark soup.

They wait for a long time just in case anything should happen. They hear the human sailors talking and grumbling, shouting and cursing, as they stumble about in the dark trying to sail the ship; even the lanterns are no use in such thick fog.

Just as the mice are thinking of going back to the Hideout, a shout from above can be heard. The sailor on crow's nest duty yells something, and the sailors on deck cry out, cheering.

"The lookout must 'ave spied somethin'," says Jack.

"Maybe the fog is burning off," says Scraggy. "Let's wait a bit and see what happens."

Slowly the fog brightens; a hazy light in the swirling fog above the ship tells of sunlight beginning to come through. A while later, after the fog has thinned, they at last catch a glimpse of the sea; before long the mice can see land —it is the Island of Mist! They see a sandy beach, and rocky cliffs topped with woodland that slopes steeply up, disappearing into clouds. The *Wreckless* stays in deep water, but as close as possible to the beach; sailors busy themselves furling the sails, dropping anchor and securing the ship.

The two mice watch as a longboat is lowered, with ropes and pulleys, into the sea. Sailors climb over the side of the ship and down scramble nets to the longboat. Barrels, chests and guns are lowered down until the longboat is loaded and ready for the sailors to row to shore; there, the cargo is unloaded onto the beach. Two sailors remain with the cargo while a third sailor rows back to the ship for another load.

The sailors on the beach stack the cargo at the foot of the cliffs; after the final load the longboat is hauled ashore and made secure so that it won't drift away when the tide comes in. Ready, now, to go hunting, the three sailors pick up their guns, a barrel and a crate, and set off up the nearby river. The humans have landed on the Island of Mist.

Jack and Scraggy return to the Hideout to report to the others what they have seen. They eat and rest, and later, when the sun begins to set, the mice go to the Quarterdeck lookout to see what can be seen. Daylight is fading, but they see the sailors returning. The longboat is made fast to the side of the ship, and its cargo is hauled up and stacked on the deck.

On deck, there is great excitement among the crew as they look hungrily at the crates and barrels the hunters have filled during their day in the jungle. The sailors will eat fresh vegetables and meat tonight, with fresh water to wash it all down; things they have not tasted for so long, they are impatient to get them open. More lanterns are lit and crates are hoisted down to the hold, all except one, which is opened and the contents carried to the galley. The activity on deck dies down as the sailors go below.

"Scraggy," says Jack. "This very night we'll be stowaways on that longboat 'n be goin' to the island when the sailors goes again. We knows they's goin' back, as they's 'avin' things still there to fetch. We can't be sure when that'll be so we needs to get aboard

'n 'ide ourselves. Get yourself ready, lad, bring your backpack
'n anythin' 'andy. Stumpy, it'll be the same as before when we's
plannin' this with Emmy, you'll be Cap'n while I'm gone; guard the
sea-chest with your very lives 'n be prepared for adventures. Plan
for leavin' the ship at any time, so be ready with everythin' close to
'and. Now then, let's be gettin' back 'n ready ourselves."

~

Later that night, accompanied by Cutlass Kate and Sieve-Brain
Sally who are armed to the teeth, Jack and Scraggy make their way
out onto the deck. They climb onto the gunwale of the ship and
look down at the longboat and the scramble net that's hanging down
the side of the ship. It looks a long way down. The ship is at anchor
and not moving much, but the longboat rises and falls on the swell;
they will have to leap into it from the scramble net.

"Jack, be careful, and look after young Scraggy. We wish you
good adventures!" whispers Sally.

"Aye, Sally, thank ye. Look out for us 'till we's 'id, 'n scarper
quick. Look out for each other, you all!"

"Bye, Jack! Bye, Scraggy!" says Kate. "Come back soon!"

"Bye, Kate. Bye, Sally! I'sll be missin' you," says Scraggy.

"Let's do it," says Jack, and with that, he and Scraggy climb
down the scramble net. When they reach the bottom, and after
watching the movement of the longboat to time their jump, they leap
across, finding themselves rolling about in the bottom, on slatted
timber with water sloshing about underneath. It doesn't look at
all like a good place to hide under there. At the stern of the boat,
under the seat, there are storage spaces and there is a good-sized gap
between the back of the storage box and the hull of the boat. The
mice, with their backpacks on, wedge themselves in as comfortably
as possible. They doze, but it is still dark when they are woken by
the sailors returning to row to the Island of Mist.

These humans are giants to the mice, clumsy and noisy, and
very smelly; they seem to be unable to do anything without a fierce
argument, involving lots of cursing. Somehow these clumsy giants
manage to row to the shore and to pull the longboat up onto the
beach. They carry the anchor further up the beach until the rope is
tight, and then stamp it into the sand. They busy themselves around
the barrels and crates stored at the foot of the cliff, and as dawn
breaks in the eastern sky they set off up the river into the interior of
the island.

When things have been quiet for a long time, Jack whispers:

"Scraggy, I'll climb up 'n see where 'umans is."

And so he does, soon calling to Scraggy:

"Come up, Scragg, they's gone."

"Let's do some tight-rope walkin', Jack!" says Scraggy, climbing up onto the gunwale of the longboat, and onto the anchor rope. They run along the rope all the way to the anchor; the last bit to the cliff they do on the dry sand, which is loose and difficult to travel on, so they go very fast, skittering along the surface.

"We 'as to get away from 'ere," says Jack, panting for breath. "Let's get climbin'!"

The cliff rocks are weathered and rough, and easy to climb. Soon they reach a ledge where they can sit safely and look back over the bay towards the ship. The sun is up now, and the sea is blue; the *Wreckless* rides peacefully at anchor, as though everything is completely normal. As the mice relax after the effort of the climb, they begin to think about what to do next.

"Where's we at, Jack? What're we doin' 'ere?"

"You's knowin' as well as I, Scraggy."

"I's missin' Emmy."

"Ah! I know, lad, be 'oldin' 'im in your 'eart."

They sit quietly for some time before speaking again.

"I likes bein' on solid ground," says Scraggy. "It's funny, feels like the ground's movin' about."

"Ha-ha! We's needin' our 'land-legs' now! I 'asn't been on land since I were a nipper."

"Where shall we go now?" Scraggy wonders.

"Follow our noses."

"Hmm, I's smellin' all sorts I's never been smellin' before."

"Come on, let's 'ave a look up there!" cries Jack, leaping up.

They climb to the top of the cliff and enter the trees. The woodland floor is a tangle of plant stems and roots, dead leaves and twigs, made all the more tangled by creepers and vines, which curl round everything. There are animal trails, which the mice follow when they lead uphill.

"I's never seen so many creepy-crawlies," says Scraggy. "'N birds I's never 'eard before!"

The trail winds uphill, as it must, because the island is a single mountain. Maybe it was a volcano once upon a time, but now it is green with jungle.

"Look at these plants!" says Scraggy. "They's like light tubes."

"You's right, Scraggy, 'tis bamboo! This may be where Tooby made them tubes."

Rounding a corner, they come to a small clearing. It would

have been a big space for a mouse, but the space is filled with the body of a very big creature. Scraggy thinks of Waggl, when he was a baby with no feathers, only this creature is bigger and does have feathers, well, fluffy feathers at least. Thinking of Waggl reminds Scraggy how Emmy greets strangers.

"'Allo, my name's Scraggy, 'n I's a mowse," he says.

"Hallo, mouses," replies the creature, its voice slow and sad. "How nice to meet you. My name is Pudge and I'm a Dodo. Where in the world have you two come from?"

"We's come from a ship, p'raps you's seen it," says Jack. "I's Jack 'n I's 'appy to meet you, Pudge."

"Hallo, Jack. Oh yes, I know about the ship," says Pudge. "The humans come with their guns and shoot us creatures and carry us off to their ship. Some of us are kept alive in their horrible boxes so that they can kill us later when they are hungry. It's really too irritating."

"Oh, Pudge, that's horrible!" cries Scraggy.

"We are all dead already, so it makes no difference."

"What's you meanin', 'dead already'?" exclaims Jack.

"We are extinct," says Pudge, in a matter-of-fact sort of voice.

"What does 'stinct' mean?" asks Scraggy.

"'Xtinct's meanin' there be no more left alive in all the world," says Jack.

"But you's 'ere! 'Ow can you be 'xtinct?" cries Scraggy.

"We are not in the world, young Scraggy," says Pudge. "I see that you haven't been here for very long. Everything on this island is extinct, even the volcano on which we stand."

The Dodo stands up, shaking its body and ruffling its feathers. Scraggy notices the little wings, like a baby bird.

"Ah! You've noticed my wings, young mouse. As you will have guessed, I cannot fly, and this is the truth. My kind used to live on beautiful islands where there were no creatures hunting us, so we didn't bother to fly; over many generations our wings became useless. When the humans arrived, they killed us all off in no time at all, because we couldn't escape them."

"Pudge, is you meanin' all the creatures 'ere 'as been 'xtincted by 'umans?" asks Jack, horrified.

"That is a most perspicacious enquiry, I can see that you are a thoughtful mouse. No, it is not true that all the beings here were made extinct by the deeds of humans. All the creatures and growing things alive in the real world are few, compared with all those that have ever lived and are now extinct. Life is a wave . . . the great wave . . ."

"Yes! We call it the great wave too!" says Scraggy excitedly.

Pudge turns slowly to look at Scraggy.

"The great wave, yes, and the creatures living are the ones that happen to be at the very top of the wave, in a manner of speaking, and without the depths of the wave there would be no wave at all."

"Why's you 'ere then, Pudge?" asks Jack.

"Ah! Your sharp questions again. Dreams seem to need no reason for being. However, now that you are here, I can safely say that we have been waiting for you."

"Us? Why us?" says Scraggy.

"Oh, how tiresome. It is necessary, otherwise the dream would not continue."

"Whose dream?" asks Scraggy. "Is Scraggy bein' dreamed?"

"It is the invisible ones dreaming the dream," explains Pudge. "And yes, you too are being dreamed, Scraggy, even though you are alive."

"It's all a bit complicated," says Scraggy.

"Pudge, if you's waitin' for us, what is it we 'as to be doin'?" asks Jack.

"What happens is — what happens. You do what you do."

"Oh dear, I's more confused than ever," moans Scraggy.

"Don't worry, just follow your feet, like always. I wish you good fortune, and may your journey be long."

"We thank you, Pudge, we 'as to be goin' 'n bid thee farewell," says Jack, pulling Scraggy to his feet and setting off along the trail once more.

"Goodbye, mouses!" Pudge calls out after them. "Come back to see me!"

"Hey, Jack, what's the 'urry?" asks Scraggy, after they have climbed further up the hill.

"We's fallin' again, I's feelin' it. I's feelin' the spell creepin' over us. We 'as to keep movin'."

"But I's likin' Pudge."

"Aye! But you might never 'ave woken up if we 'adn't moved. Keep alert, Scraggy, let's move!"

They travel inland and uphill for a night and a day. Whenever they get tired they find dry places to sleep, in little crevices in the rocks, or in a hollow tree. The mountain is gradually getting steeper and there are many outcrops of rock that are old and weathered.

While travelling they come across strange creatures and plants that they have never seen before. Sometimes they stop to chat, such as with the parrots and the lizards, but they are wary now not to spend too long in the company of these creatures, because of the enchantment.

"Jack," says Scraggy. "'Ow's we findin' the Crystal Cave?"

"I don't know. We 'as to trust it'll be findin' us, 'n put one foot before t'other."

"Now you's talkin' riddles like Pudge! Look there, Jack, there's some more o' that bamboo grass. Is this where Tooby sat 'n made the tubes?"

"'App'n 'tis."

"I's carryin' a light tube, p'raps it'll show us the way."

"What's you meanin', Scraggy?"

"We lets the light out, 'n follow it 'ome!"

"Ahh! Good plan!"

"Now?"

"Er — it's soon to be dark, Scraggy, we's not wantin' 'umans seein' the Orb 'n bein' curious, 'n followin'. We'll wait 'till mornin', 'n find a cave to sleep."

Climbing a little further up the mountainside, they find a crack in the rocks big enough for them to enter, and inside there is room for them to curl up and sleep. Scraggy is excited to think that they might soon find the Crystal Cave, and it's hard to get to sleep; he listens to the sounds of the night, thinking how different they are to the sounds at home, at Burrow Cave. He imagines Burrow Cave, and he sees in his mind's eye all his beloved family gathered and listening to a story being told by One-Eye. Scraggy smiles as he drifts off into sleep.

~

When they wake, it is still not quite light outside, so they talk while eating some of the grain that they brought from the ship. When it's light enough they go outside. Jack takes the light tube from Scraggy's backpack, handing it to him. "You should be doin' it, Scraggy, be thinkin' of Emmy 'n your Dad."

"What if it doesn't work, Jack? What if it makes a portal 'n we's disappearin'?"

"I's been thinkin' on it. I's rememberin' Pudge sayin' 'bout invisible ones dreamin' the dream — the light will take us where we needs to be goin'."

Scraggy opens the light tube; as ever, the light streams out, forming into an Orb that floats in the air, hardly visible in the bright sunlight except as a pale patch. It moves slowly, and the mice follow; the Orb speeds up and slows down, giving time for them to climb over, or round, whatever obstacles there are in the way, and so to keep up. The mice follow the Orb until Scraggy is so tired that he simply has to stop.

"I's needin' rest, Jack, you follow the light 'n I'll catch up."

"No, we's stayin' together. The light'll wait for us."

"How do you know?"

"Just look."

The Orb is motionless, nearly invisible. The mice feel safe just where they are, and soon they are fast asleep.

~

"Ready, Scragg? Let's be movin'," says Jack, awake again.

Off they go once more following the Orb, ever further up the mountainside, until, at last, it stops moving. When the mice catch up, the Orb moves towards the rocky mountainside and abruptly disappears. The mice scramble over to find a hidden opening in the rock. It is very small, and they have to take off their backpacks to squeeze through, pulling the packs after them.

After a short distance the tunnel widens out a little.

"Let's leave our backpacks 'ere," suggests Scraggy. "Looks like more squeezy tunnel comin' up."

They drop the packs against the wall and follow the Orb, as it moves further into the heart of the mountain. They follow along the twisty tunnel for so long that they begin to feel that they must be getting close to the middle of the world by now. They come to a stream and walk along beside it until they reach the end of the tunnel, where the stream disappears into the ground; deep in the water they can see a glow. The Orb gently sinks into the water, moving towards the glow.

Jack and Scraggy look at each other and laugh.

"Looks like we's in for a wettin', Scraggy!" cries Jack.

Filling their lungs with air, they plunge into the pool and swim towards the glow through a narrow underwater tunnel, helped on their way by the flow of water. Surfacing at last, spluttering and gasping for air, they find themselves in a light-filled cave.

The ceiling is not much above Jack's head — he could just touch it if he were to reach up; the cave is about three times wider from side to side and more or less round, and so, as you can imagine, it's not a very big cave. In the middle is a sort of rocky rim forming a round pool which is full to the brim with pale light just like the Orb they have been following. The cave sparkles with light reflecting from crystals embedded in the rock; some crystals have fallen to the floor and lie sparkling at their feet.

Jack and Scraggy are speechless. Their worries and fears fall away as a delicious warmth arises in their breasts. They watch the Orb, which has been so faithful a guide, move slowly towards the pool of light and merge with it, returning at last to where it belongs.

The two mice sit down, back to back, leaning against the rim of the light pool. They are feeling light-headed, and although they don't say anything, they suspect they are slipping into enchantment. Unable to resist, and not wanting to resist, they fall asleep smiling happily.

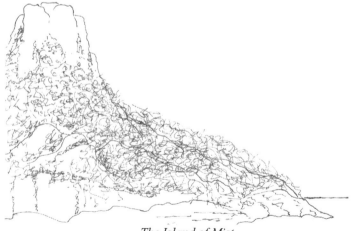

The Island of Mist

Chapter Two

More Little Humans

Emmy learns a lot when a new story arrives, and in recent days there have been two new stories: 'Silk and Sad' and 'Ocean'. He has learned a lot about what happened to his family and friends, and this helps him to remember, but he also learns about things that he did not know before. One thing that he didn't know about, before the story of 'Silk and Sad', was Flimsy's 'seeing' — the seeing that happened when she was in Uncle One-Eye's den, and she spoke for the first time after being so ill for the whole winter. She spoke of the Island of Mist, and she saw a ship, and she saw a mouse being sucked into the sky by a whirlwind, but she couldn't see if it was Uncle One-Eye or not.

He didn't know what happened to Scraggy after the typhoon, when Emmy himself was sucked into the sky. Now he knows that Scraggy and Whip-Tail Jack managed to get to the Island of Mist, and to the Crystal Cave; now he knows that they fell asleep there and may never wake up. He must find his way home and rescue them.

Pip is relaxing after all that reading. LuLu is on the sofa, and Larky and Billy are on cushions on the floor. Emmy waits for them to wake up.

"Pip, thank you for reading the story," says LuLu, yawning, the first to wake. "It must be very upsetting for you, Emmy, hearing about all that has happened."

"We's gettin' 'Wot 'Appnd', littl bi littl," says Emmy, sounding a little mournful. "I's needin' to be kno-in, LuLu."

"I wish I could meet Cutlass Kate!" cries Larky.

"I'm thinking about Flimsy," says Pip, remembering 'Silk and Sad'. "And Beechnut."

"Oh! I love Flimsy, I wish we could see her," says Larky.

"I feel for her the same way you do, Larky," says LuLu. "I'm feeling for you too, Emmy; remembering things about your home world must be very painful for you. Emmy, are you alright?"

"I's 'urtin', LuLu, you's rite, n I's missin' Beechnut, n Flimsy, n Scraggs, n all evry one."

"Stupid wool!" snarls Billy, thinking of 'Silk and Sad', and angry at everything that happened just to get some wool. "What's it about wool, so you 'as to be riskin' evryfin' like that? You's not even needin' it."

"We's makin' fingz we's needin', Billee, like Ping Ling's shawl wotz 'elpin' save Flimsy, n rope wot saves Mowzl n Star inside mountin, n pouchiz wot we's needin' now. N be merembrin', Billee, mouses iz bein' et bi owlz n weaslziz, n all sorts of 'untaz. It's way ov great wave."

"Stupid," says Billy, grumpily. He just can't see the point.

"Mowzl's right, Billy," LuLu says gently. "But I do understand your anger. It doesn't make any sense, does it? But it's happened, and we can find wisdom in it, like Flimsy, if we try."

"I'll try," says Billy, reluctantly. "But what I's really wantin' is wild talk — I wants to make a pouch, Emmy."

"And I do too!" cries Larky.

"Emmy iz very 'appy you's wantin' pouchiz. Me, Pippee, n LuLu'z 'elpin' you, but we's all lernin'. First fing iz yor bowl ov fingz wot'z a luv battree for powerin' yor pouchiz."

"Pip's read us your stories about 'Wot 'Appnd', Emmy," says Larky. "We know you've said the bowl of things is like a battery. I've got some things to put in my bowl, I've got pressed flowers and a peacock feather, and some little pine cones, a tiny shell . . ."

"Perfik, Larky; it's fingz you's feelin' in yor 'eart."

"I 'as a tenner conker, 'n me knife, 'n stones, 'n shells, 'n a fox's skull, 'n a compass," says Billy.

"Good, Billee, good. You's both feelin' wot to be doin'."

Emmy talks about what they can do next, saying that they each need to find a bowl that they like, go through all their things and feel about them — really, deeply feel — that's like thinking about things, only feeling about them, and remembering them in your heart. Do you want to put it in your bowl, or not? Fill your bowl with things that live in your heart. It doesn't have to be big things.

"You's fittin' big luv in littl place," says Emmy. "N be keepin' bowl ov fingz close wen you's sleepin'. Now, me's finkin you's 'ad all betta git 'ome, 'coz you's late n I's not wantin' for you to be gettin' a tellin' off."

Billy and Larky get ready to go, thanking Pip for looking after them and for reading them the story of 'Ocean', and thanking Emmy for telling the story of 'Silk and Sad' yesterday; they give LuLu big hugs, and they're ready to go.

"Come and find me anytime," says Pip. "I might be at work, but I am sure you will be able to find me."

"What do you do, Mr Pip?" asks Larky.

"I'm a gardener, so you'll find me in a garden somewhere!"

"Pleez be takin' choklit from mi bowl ov fingz," says Emmy. "N be puttin' it in yor bowl ov fingz. You can be eatin' choklit n keepin' rappa."

"Thanks, Emmy! Bye!" cries Larky, as she and Billy set off home, chattering excitedly.

"Emmy," says Pip, after a few quiet minutes have passed. "Do you think that Flimsy and Dreamer are able to 'see' where you are right now?"

"I's nevva kno-in' till now Flimsy woz seein' Island ov Mist, n tyfoon. I's finkin' they's nevva seein' 'uman world, but they's 'elpin' Purl n One-Eye to be sendin' parsl frew portl."

"What is the portal, Emmy?"

"I's not kno-in', 'xcept it's fog."

"Where is the portal?"

"Every where n no where. I's not kno-in'."

"Who was it Flimsy saw — being sucked up by the wind?"

"You's kno-in' in yor merembrin', Pippee, coz you's rit all 'bout typhoon. You's kno-in it woz me, Mowzl Emmy."

"Emmy," says LuLu, wanting to bring the conversation back to the present. "We'll have to show the children how to gather wool, and how to spin the wool and crochet the pouches — and we haven't done it ourselves yet! It'll be a lot of learning."

"They's findin' them selvz bi doin' it, LuLu, n they'sll be 'avin' quiet 'earts 'coz they's really 'avin' to be wishin' for it."

"Emmy, Pip, I'm tired; I need to be with Muffin, and to sleep."

"Of course, LuLu. My love to Muffin, I hope you rest well."

"Bi, LuLu, n fankz. I'sll be stayin' wiv Pippee."

"You're very welcome, Emmy. Good night!"

When LuLu has gone, Pip turns to Emmy. "Time for a bit of a lie-down, Emmy!" he says.

"I's needin' some choklit foomz, Pippee, if you izn't mindin'."

"No problem. I'll put some taste bombs in the bowl of things," says Pip, carrying Emmy to the bowl.

"Fankz. Nite-nite." Emmy jumps into the bowl, snuggling into a bundle of wool threads.

"Goodnight, Emmy."

Pip gazes at Emmy, wondering how this little creature can hold so much in his heart. *Humans have so much to learn from creatures,* he thinks. *It's like we've missed the point of being alive.*

~

Larky wakes up the next morning after a deep sleep. Memories from the last few days tumble in her mind, and she smiles, her eyes sparkling. She remembers meeting Rattltap, and then LuLu, who was tiny like a flower fairy, and Priklstik and Emmy! She remembers listening to Mr Pip reading the first chapters of 'Wot

'Appnd', and now she feels excitement welling up inside: she knows — she just knows — that this is the beginning of something special.

She thinks about Billy, about how moody and difficult he is. It's not surprising that he's moody. Billy's Mum died when he was only five years old. His Dad is a sailor, well, a merchant seaman, and he's away most of the time and hasn't been home for a long time; Larky remembers him as a dark, mysterious man, and she's a bit afraid of him. Billy lives with his Nan and Grandpa. Billy's Nan dotes on Billy. His Grandpa, Frank, spends a lot of time staring into space, talking with people that aren't there; he's always smiling.

Larky thinks about her own family: quite ordinary really, she supposes, and special too at the same time. Her mum, she's called Donna, works from home so she can be around for the children. She takes in sewing work, making repairs and alterations to clothes, and she gets orders for curtains and cushions; sometimes she's asked to make dresses. She's a bright and lively person, but every once in a while, Larky sees her mother's face looking sad.

Larky's Dad, Bernie, is a builder and carpenter and is usually cheerful, in that 'boots on' sort of way that people who do his sort of work generally have. He's always up early and doing things, before setting off for work. Coming home after a day's work, he often has a puzzled look on his face, which lasts until he's had a glass of beer and his supper; then he's all smiles again, trying to help with homework.

Like her Dad, Larky gets up early; she likes it especially when it hasn't got light yet, so she can write her diary by candlelight and then go downstairs, and outside, without putting any lights on. In the little garden at the back of the house, her Dad has built a small shelter; there are plants growing over it and there's a bench, just big enough for two people to sit on. Larky likes to sit there, perhaps with a friend after school, or at weekends, but she especially loves it when it's early morning and she is alone.

In the very early morning the shadows look mysterious and unfamiliar. Larky could be frightened but she isn't—she's just tingly. She watches the shadows change, as the light grows stronger, and bit by bit she recognises the familiar things. There's a flowerpot, and there's Mum's watering can, and — oh! — *that* shadow moved! It's a robin, sitting on the watering can spout with its head cocked to one side, its beady eye looking straight at her. Larky thinks about the way she knew it was a robin the first instant her eye saw a movement. She wonders about how there is 'robin-ness' in even the littlest movement the bird makes. She remembers Emmy talking about 'isness', and now she can really feel the robin's isness!

The robin trills a little song, flying closer to her, the wings making a soft sound that brushes her ear like snowflakes. The robin is whispering now, the tiny sounds tickling Larky's hearing; she can almost hear the bird speak. "Hallo, robin," she whispers. "I want to be able to talk the wild talk with you. I bet you are just saying that you are hungry, and that you'd like something to eat."

The robin stares at her, and Larky is sure that she hears, or feels, the robin saying: 'No, that's not what I said.'

But then the robin flies off, leaving Larky wondering — maybe understanding the wild talk is about feeling, not hearing and speaking. Larky thinks about her two best friends, Stomper and Penny. She could talk to Penny about the robin, but not Stomper. Stomper and Penny are as different as chalk and cheese, except these days cheese tastes like chalk, well, sometimes. But it's not the taste, it's the sound of the words, isn't it? The way the sounds shape your mouth when you speak them. Or is it the other way around? Larky tries it, out loud.

"Chork," she says, her mouth making an 'O' shape.

"Cheese," her face is almost round, her mouth grinning like the Cheshire Cat.

"Charlotte?" calls Larky's mother, from the back door of the house.

"Hallo, Mum, I'm in the arbour," Larky replies.

"Alright, dear, I thought I heard you talking."

"Yes, I said 'hallo' to robin."

"Breakfast in five minutes."

"Thanks, Mum, I'll come in soon."

Larky's mother, Donna, smiles as she closes the door, happy that Charlotte loves Nature. But she has noticed that Charlotte is spending more time alone these days, and it's a bit worrying. Donna wonders why she is worrying: it's probably just a phase that will change soon enough.

Larky is still thinking about her friends, Stomper and Penny. They are so different from one another that Larky can't imagine being with them both at the same time. Larky likes to be with people one at a time. When there are a lot of people together, they get all tricky and competitive and try to get one up on each other and all that. None of that feels real to Larky. It doesn't feel truthful. Because of this, she likes to be alone unless she can be with a friend.

Billy is a good friend, but he's usually cross and doesn't want to talk much. Larky doesn't mind that, because with Billy she gets away from the noise of the town, and they walk for miles and spend time in the woods. She likes that they don't talk much.

Larky thinks about her sister, Sarah. Sarah is 12, she's started at big school and already she's different; she doesn't spend time with Larky any more. They used to play together lots, and get up to all sorts of mischief, but not any more. Sarah has got serious about how she looks, spending time working on her face and her clothes.

"Charlotte!"

"Coming, Mum."

Larky goes indoors for breakfast. She's cold and hungry, glad to have a hot bowl of porridge, followed by toast and a boiled egg. Sitting next to her, Sarah picks at her food and doesn't say anything.

"Mummy, would you teach me to crochet?" asks Larky.

"Of course, dear. We did try once, do you remember? But you lost interest."

"Well, I'm interested again now, Mum."

"I'll find some yarn and the crochet hooks; maybe we could have a go this afternoon."

"Great! I want to spin wool too, Mum, could we do that too?"

"Not all in one day, steady on!"

"What would I need for spinning wool, Mum?"

"Tools you mean? Well, a spinning wheel, or a drop-spindle, I'll ask in the shop. Maybe Bernie could make a drop-spindle."

Donna looks at Sarah, and her uneaten food.

"Come on, dear, you should eat a bit, it'll be cold outside."

"I'm not going to be outside."

"You'll be walking to school."

"I'll wrap up warm."

Bernie comes in; he's been up for a while, pottering about and sorting tools for work.

"I'm off to work now — can I give you two a lift? I'm going your way this morning."

Bernie drives a van and the girls like to ride in the cab.

"Yes, please, Dad, I'm ready," says Larky.

"Come on then, get your coats and bags."

Sarah moves slowly and without enthusiasm; she's reluctant to go at all, but would rather not walk, so she gets herself ready.

Donna watches Sarah and is worried. Donna is a very positive person, but like all parents, she worries for her children. Something isn't right. Maybe Sarah doesn't like the new school. Maybe she's being bullied and doesn't want to talk about it. Perhaps it's teenage changes already happening, and she needs to be left alone. Oh, it can be very hard being a parent.

She makes sure that they have their packed lunches, homework and everything, and she waves them goodbye at the door.

"See you later!"

"Bye, Mum!" calls Larky.

Bernie winks at Donna, blowing her a kiss.

~

Billy wakes from a deep sleep, and memories of the last few days tumble into his head. He smiles when he remembers the look on Larky's face, when she first saw LuLu purling in her little pouch. It makes him laugh out loud now, after all his fears and worries that Larky would never believe him.

Billy's thoughts jump to the story of the wool-gathering, and of Beechnut's death and Flimsy's illness. He remembers the anger that sprang up inside him while he was listening to the story; it's the unfairness, the meaninglessness of it. But in the last few days he has had different feelings happening, unfamiliar feelings, deeper and slower than the racing anger, and he thinks of Emmy. *This little mouse is changing my life,* he thinks.

Remembering the story of 'Ocean', a shiver runs up his spine; the stories about Emmy's home world, and the ocean world, are so strange that Billy worries about Emmy. *I just wants purlin' 'n wild talk!* he thinks, trying to forget the stories and his worries.

"Billy, are you up yet?" calls Nan, Billy's Granny.

"Comin'!" yells Billy. He's usually up earlier than this, but yesterday had been a big day, a tiring day, but the best day ever!

He pulls on some clothes and runs noisily down the stairs.

"Are you alright, Billy lad? You look like a scarecrow! Look here, you've got your shirt buttons done up wrong, and your hair looks like you've been dragged through a hedge backwards — ah-ha! — there we are, you'll do. Will you have some breakfast?"

"Yes please, Nan, I could eat a small country."

"You'll have to make do with porridge, lad, and toast."

"Whatever you've got, Nan, you know me. How's Grandpa?"

"Frank's alright, I fed him his porridge and he's talking to someone I can't see, but he seems happy enough."

"Good-oh. Nan, can you teach me krotchettin'?"

"You must mean crocheting, yes, dear, I could teach you how to do that. Do you want to make a hat for winter?"

"A little 'un, maybe. What 'bowt an egg-cosy for starters?"

"Good idea, I'll see what wool I can find."

"Thanks for lookin' after me, Nan," says Billy, unexpectedly.

"Why, Billy! You are my grandson! No need to thank me."

"You's been ever so good to me since Mum died. Life ain't fair, is it, Nan?"

"I know it doesn't look fair, Billy, but remember, you can only see a bit of the road; you can't see what's not yours to see."

"Hmm. But I's always gettin' angry, Nan."

"Billy, love, it's natural that you should feel angry, don't blame yourself for that. Let it be and ask your Mum for help."

"Ask me Mum? She's dead, Nan!"

"She will never be dead in your heart, lad. Just talk to her."

Billy suddenly gets what Emmy means by 'bowl ov fingz'. "Nan, 'ave you got anythin' of Mum's what's really Mum?"

"There are some photos, Billy, and some little bits of jewellery. Oh, and I've got some letters she wrote to me when you were born."

"Nan, could I 'ave some little things of Mum's to 'ave near me?"

"Of course, Billy, I'll look some out for you today."

Nan is surprised by Billy's questions, and his renewed interest in things. He hasn't talked about his mother like this ever before. And Billy isn't done yet!

"Nan, 'ave we got a big bowl what's not used, 'cos I's needin' one?"

"There's a big bowl that I used to use for bread-making; you can have that if you like, it's cracked, but not too badly. Whatever for, Billy?"

"Just to 'ave special things in, Nan."

Nan rummages in one of the cupboards, finding the bowl under crockery, baking trays, and other odds and ends.

"There you are, lad."

"Thanks!" Billy finishes his breakfast and, putting his last piece of toast between his teeth, he picks up the bowl with both hands and carries it upstairs to his room. When he's eaten his toast and had a good look at the bowl, he yells downstairs: "Thanks, Nan, it's perfect."

He looks at his things scattered about: things on the floor, under the bed, in the cupboard, on top of the cupboard, even behind it. Things are everywhere. *Why's I keepin' all this stuff?* he thinks, deciding to start sorting it all out right now, putting special things in the bowl and making a pile of stuff to throw out. Nan might take some to the jumble sale, if she thinks it might be useful to someone.

"Billy! Time for school!" calls Nan.

"Right, Nan," replies Billy. Leaving everything as it is, he skips downstairs with a lighter heart. Now he knows what to do.

"Nan, I's sortin' all me stuff 'n me room's a mess. I'll get on with it when I's back. See you later!"

"Bye, love."

"Bye, Nan; bye, Grandpa!"

Slam.

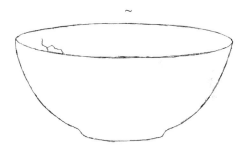

At school, the children are kept inside at morning break, because of rain. Mr Weatherstone sits in on Billy's class to make sure the noise doesn't get too much, and to keep an eye on things. Billy sits at his desk trying to write a list; he chews on a pencil and frowns, looking up at the cracks in the ceiling. He's planning what to put in his bowl of things.

Billy's list goes something like this: sumfin' of mum's from nan like jewlery 'n fota 'n letta / my fings, like me best conka 'n me best marbl 'n pikcha ov dad 'n ship in a bottl from dad / 'n ded beetl inna matchbox . . .

"Hallo, Billy, would you like to meet Nosey?"

Billy's face has a 'faraway' look, that changes to a 'leave me alone' look, which changes to a 'who's Nosey?' sort of a look. When he realises that it's Penny talking to him, he relaxes and turns towards her with a smile.

"Penny, I was dreamin'."

"Off with the fairies, like Dungl said?"

"Don't you start."

"Sorry, only a tease."

"Who's Nosey?"

"Here, look."

Penny is wearing a jacket with side pockets that have little flaps covering them. She carefully lifts a flap, holding the pocket open with her fingers. A whiskery nose emerges, sniffing the air, then a face with big beady eyes appears, and then a head with big ears. Nosey is a wood mouse.

"'Allo, Nosey, I's Billy 'n I's an 'uman, I wish we's talkin' with each other."

"You can, Billy," says Penny. "You can learn to if you really want."

"You's always said you's talkin' with creatures, Penny, but you's kiddin', ain't ya?"

"No, Billy, I'm not kidding, but it's not talk, it's not words like

we speak them. It's something else."

Billy looks into Penny's eyes. Penny is a quiet person, keeping herself to herself. Somehow, she gets left alone and is not teased as much as the other quiet children. Billy sees that Penny's dark brown eyes are gentle and truthful, and he doesn't see any fear there at all.

"He's a wood mouse," says Penny, simply.

Nosey has climbed into Billy's hand and is washing his face. Billy thinks of Emmy. Emmy says he is a wood mouse too.

"Penny, let's talk later, if it ain't rainin' at break."

Penny smiles, puts Nosey in her pocket and returns to her desk.

Watching her go, Billy notices Bottl nearby, half sitting, half leaning on a desk, his arms folded and a smirk on his face. He just looks at Billy, smirking. Billy tries to ignore him, but he can't concentrate. He can feel Bottl's eyes boring into him, and anger begins to boil up inside him. He feels hot, and suddenly he can bear it no longer and he jumps up, turning to face Bottl.

At that moment, the bell rings and Mr Weatherstone calls out:

"Lesson time, children; please sit down at your desks."

Billy and Bottl are glaring at each other.

"Sit down!" calls Mr Weatherstone firmly.

Bottl turns away, going to his desk three rows behind Billy's. Billy can feel those horrible eyes boring holes into his back.

Glancing sideways across the classroom, Billy catches Penny's eye, and she looks at him with a steady, calm look. With a little smile, she looks away. Billy suddenly feels ashamed of his anger.

Mrs Weeble comes in to teach, and Mr Weatherstone returns to his own class.

~

When the bell goes for lunch, Billy realises that he hasn't been listening to a word. Somehow, he got away with being in a daydream from beginning to end of the class. He doesn't even know if homework has been set.

The rain has stopped, and the sky is grey with hurrying clouds; it's not very cold, but Billy puts on his coat anyway. He goes outside hoping to meet up with Penny again. The playground is tarmacked with lines painted on it for games; there's a tree in one corner where the tarmac has cracked and pushed up, because of the tree roots growing bigger. Billy likes to be close to the tree because it is the only visible living thing in the playground — apart from the children. He sees that Dungl and Bottl are already there, by the tree, so he turns away and goes towards the bike shed instead.

"Hallo, Billy, did you want to talk?"

"'Allo, Penny, yeah, but there's Dungl 'n Bottl."

"Why do they upset you?"

"Dunno, I's just gettin' angry."

"What do you want to talk about?"

"Creatures, Penny, talkin' with creatures."

"Animals, you mean?"

"Yeah, animals 'n birds 'n insects 'n everythin'. Somethin's 'appened."

"What, Billy?"

"Larky 'n me 'as been talkin' with creatures in the woods. Will you come with us when we goes again?"

"Yes, I'd love to. When?"

Billy glances over his shoulder before saying anything, and sees Dungl and Bottl just behind him, close enough to have been listening to what he and Penny have been saying. He spins around, glaring at Dungl.

"Why's you followin' me?" he says, angrily.

"'Cos you're very entertainin' when you're talkin' to fairies! Ha-ha!" says Dungl, and he and Bottl fall about laughing. Billy gets cross.

"Billy!" cries Penny. "They don't understand, don't let them wind you up."

Dungl squares up to Billy.

"You're a fruitcake, Billy, just like your Granddad, torkin' to fairies down in the woods. Why don't you have proper friends?"

"He's a nutter alright, he spends too much time by `is self. says Bottl.

All this attracts attention; other children are gathering round, and Stomper is one of them. She yells at Dungl and Bottl.

"Why don't you two leave him alone? What's the matter with you? Why are you always picking on someone?"

Dungl snarls at her. "He's weird, that's what, 'n that Penny, she's weird 'n all, with 'er stinkin' mouse."

"Come on, Penny, let's see the mouse then!" taunts Bottl, as he moves towards Penny, reaching towards her coat pocket.

Billy steps in between them, blocking Bottl's way.

"Leave 'er alone!"

"Get out my way, you little bag o' beans."

Billy stands his ground; Bottl shoves into him, grabbing for Penny. Billy's anger boils over and he grabs Bottl's arm, twisting it into a half-nelson arm lock.

"Ow! You're 'urtin' me!" yells Bottl.

Dungl steps forward and hits Billy hard on the shoulder with his fist. Billy turns on him, letting go of Bottl, and with fury in his eyes he strikes Dungl in the face with his fist. Dungl falls to the ground. He doesn't move. Suddenly the playground is silent.

The duty teacher, Mrs Weeble, who has been watching with

growing alarm, comes running. She kneels down to examine Dungl.

"He's breathing, thank goodness. Susan, please run to the School Office and ask them to call an ambulance, and get someone to bring a blanket and pillow, quickly now!"

Susan, one of the children, runs off while Mrs Weeble carefully moves Dungl's body into the recovery position. When she is satisfied, she stands up and looks around at the children. Bottl had started to edge away as soon as Dungl went down.

"Brian! You are not to go anywhere!" says Mrs Weeble sharply, using Bottl's proper name. "I want you and Billy, and any witnesses, in the Head's office now! Who saw what happened?"

Penny and Stomper put their hands up. "Miss," they chorus.

"Very well, off you go, the four of you. Tell Mrs Proctor what happened here."

The four children walk across the playground with all eyes upon them.

"You miserable creep," says Stomper, under her breath, flashing her eyes at Bottl.

"Silence!" shouts Mrs Weeble.

When someone from the office arrives in the playground to take over from Mrs Weeble, she marches at top speed to the Head's office. She finds the children standing outside the door, waiting.

"Well, knock then!" she says impatiently.

"We knocked, Miss, and Mrs Proctor said 'Wait!'." says Penny, patiently.

Mrs Weeble knocks.

"Come!"

Mrs Weeble opens the door. "A fight in the playground, Mrs Proctor. May I bring four children to see you?"

"Yes, come in."

They troop in. Mrs Weeble describes what happened, confirming that David is being taken care of and an ambulance has been called. Mrs Proctor is quiet, looking at Billy and Brian.

"What have you got to say for yourself, Billy?"

"Please, Mrs Proctor, I's sorry I 'it 'im, I's 'avin' sudden anger."

"Why were you so angry, Billy?"

"Things they's sayin' — and they's goin' to bully Penny."

"Penny?"

"Mrs Proctor, Miss, Dungl and Bottl are always teasing Billy, and sometimes they go too far."

"What was said that made Billy so angry?"

"It was something like 'he's weird and off with the fairies like his Granddad'."

"Is that true, Brian?"

"Yes, Miss, but I's never sayin' it," says Bottl.

Mrs Proctor asks each of them if they have anything else to say. Stomper says she thinks they were winding Billy up deliberately.

"Alright, I have heard enough. You three return to your classes, Billy, stay here — and Mrs Weeble, could you stay too, if you have time?"

Penny gives Billy an encouraging look as she leaves the Head's office. When the three have gone, Mrs Proctor re-arranges the papers on her desk, her face serious.

"Billy, I'm sending you home. Don't come to school again until you hear from me."

"Is I 'xpelled?"

"No, Billy."

"I's sorry I 'it 'im, Miss."

"I believe you are, Billy. Mrs Weeble and I have been aware for some time of those boys' bullying behaviour. We have also been aware of how angry you are, Billy, and we would like to help you if you will let us."

"What 'elp is there, Miss? It's only people what makes me angry. I's alright in the woods."

"Billy, I think it would be good if you had someone to talk to who isn't family, or friend, or school - someone who understands what it's like to lose your mother when you are five."

The room is very quiet; Billy looks at the floor and his face reddens. The only people he wants to talk to are Emmy, and Pip, and LuLu, and Larky, and Penny . . . His life has changed, and Dungl is threatening all that. But he can't explain all this to Mrs Proctor. Billy thinks of Emmy; what would Emmy say? He would say something like: "Be calmin' down, Billee, be lettin' troof 'appn' in yor 'eart."

Billy takes a deep breath. "Thank you, Miss, I'd be 'appy for 'elp 'cos it's 'ard on me Nan."

Mrs Proctor glances at Mrs Weeble. This is a breakthrough.

"Billy, sit down please and wait while I write a letter to your grandparents. Mrs Weeble, thank you for your help, you can return to your class now."

Mrs Weeble goes out, closing the door behind her. Mrs Proctor begins her letter to Billy's grandparents.

"Thing is, Miss . . ."

"Yes, Billy?"

"Me Grandpa *is* off with the fairies, 'e's always starin' into space, 'n talkin' to people what ain't there."

"Does it hurt you when you are teased about him?"

"Yes, Miss," says Billy, standing up again.

"Billy, I know it is hard to bear teasing like that, and bullying, but I think you know that you're teased because you're different, or some children see you as different. Perhaps they see you as having something that they don't have, and they feel jealous. You're a bit of a loner, Billy, aren't you? And that can make others feel that you don't need them, and they don't like to feel left out."

"Alright, Miss."

"Alright? What do you mean by that?"

"I's seein' what you's sayin', Miss, 'n it's truth. I 'as anger comin' 'n it's stupid."

"Billy, it's not stupid, there is nothing wrong with anger, it's just that there is a time and a place for everything, and your anger is running your life; that's not good for you, or anyone else."

Mrs Proctor licks the envelope to seal it, putting it down flat on the desk and sliding her hand over to press the seal into place.

"Here's my letter to your Nan. I have not said much, just that I've asked you not to come to school tomorrow so that she knows you are not playing truant."

"Thank you, Miss."

"Off you go now."

Billy leaves Mrs Proctor's office and goes to collect his coat and bag. The coat pegs are on the wall in the corridor outside his classroom, so he doesn't have to go in. He manages to get away from the school without seeing anyone.

He walks straight home and tells his Nan about what's happened, giving her the letter from Mrs Proctor. He goes up to his room to change his clothes and seeing all his things spread out all over the place, he remembers the plans that he had been making. It's a pity not to get on with it straight away, but right now he must get outside. The plans will have to wait. He must get to the woods. Maybe there will be someone he can talk to in the woods.

Nan has read the letter from Mrs Proctor and now she watches Billy pull his boots on. "Are you alright, Billy?"

"I's alright, Nan, thanks — just needin' a wild walk."

"Well, you take care, dear."

"Course, Nan, see you later!"

Billy walks hard and fast, thinking about everything that's happened; he feels the anger still in him, and he walks all the harder to work it out of his body. The rhythm of walking gradually soothes him, and he calms down, beginning to notice the world around him once again. He had been looking blindly at the ground as he walked, but now he sees the muddy path clearly; he is aware of the smell of earth and leaf mould, the calls of birds and clouds moving in the sky. The natural world floods his senses, and he heaves a great sigh of relief; tears well up and he sobs his heart out, right there, miles from anywhere, in the woods. A great weight has been lifted, and even though he is crying, he is smiling too.

It's raining again now, and Billy decides to go to the bivouac, even though that's exactly where Bottl would look first if he came after him. When Billy arrives at the bivvy, he finds that it has been torn to pieces and scattered, and wind has blown torn plastic into the bushes. Anger surges inside him, and the familiar hot rage, but then, to his surprise, the wave of anger fades. Instead of feeling that he has lost something by the bivvy being destroyed, he feels that something new is happening; he is thinking of Emmy, of Pip and LuLu, Larky and Penny, and how his life is brand new.

He looks around for a plastic bag that's not torn too much, and he sets about picking up all the plastic rubbish that's blown everywhere, stuffing it into the bag, piece by piece. He comes across another big plastic bag that isn't too badly torn and uses his penknife to cut holes in it — one hole for his head and one for each arm. He pulls it over his head like a T-shirt. Finding a smaller bag, he rolls the edges up and wears it as a hat.

When all the rubbish has been collected up, including the bits of string and baler twine, Billy has a last look at the ruined bivvy. He thinks of the good times spent here, on his own, or with Larky, and he thinks of the day that he met Emmy here — only a week or two ago — and how his life has changed; it's time to move on.

"Thanks, bivvy!" he says out loud, and walks away, carrying the big bag of rubbish. He wanders around the woods, rain streaming over him; he loves the feeling of being dissolved by the rain into the earthy body of the woods. With a light heart, he heads for home.

By the time he reaches the edge of town he is very wet, in spite of the plastic bags he's wearing. He's about to turn up the road to his Nan's place, when he hears a call.

"Billy! Billy, wait for us!" calls Larky, as she and Penny come running. "We've been looking for you, Billy. Hey! Look at you! You look like a scarecrow! What's in that huge bag?"

"The bivvy's wrecked, Larks, this is all rubbish 'n plastic what was scattered all over."

"Oh, no! How did it get wrecked?"

"I can guess, Larks."

"You mean — Bottl?"

"Must 'ave been."

"He's in trouble for bunking off school after seeing Mrs Proctor."

"Billy," says Penny, "Dungl is alright, no injury except he'll have a black eye. How are you?"

"Alright thanks, Penny. I's been thinkin' of you two, 'n the mouse, 'n Pip 'n LuLu, 'n I's alright again."

"Who's the mouse, and Pip and LuLu?"

"They're our new friends!" says Larky.

"I's been wantin' to tell you, Penny," says Billy.

"Billy, let's visit Pip now and get out of the rain!"

"Nice idea, Larks, but 'e'll be workin'."

"It's raining, so he might be home — I bet he is!"

"May I come too?" asks Penny.

"Course, Pen. Let's be careful 'n be goin' by 'lotments."

They walk by way of the allotments, looking back to see if they are followed. Penny asks who would follow them, so Larky tells her about Dungl and Bottl spying on them, and she tells Penny a little bit about Pip and LuLu. But before she can get going with her story, they arrive at Pip's house and knock on the door. Pip pokes his head out into the rain.

"Is it Christmas already?" he says. "Or Guy Fawkes? You look like a guy, or a scarecrow; it's Billy, isn't it? And Larky, and who is this? Come in, come in, out of the rain."

"'Allo, Mr Pip, this is Penny who's talkin' with creatures."

"Hallo, Penny, it's lovely to meet you. Come in all of you, kick off those wet shoes, please, and let me have your coats; I'll hang them somewhere to dry."

Billy peels off his plastic bag 'coat' and 'hat', and stuffs them into the rubbish bag.

"What's all that, Billy?" asks Pip.

"Rubbish from the woods."

"Ah! We'll leave it outside, shall we?"

Pip makes hot chocolate drinks to warm them up, while they get settled around the kitchen table.

"I don't have much milk, so it's half milk and half water."

Soon they are sipping their drinks, feeling warmer.

"So, Penny, tell me about talking with animals," says Pip.

"It's not really talking, Mr Pip, it just comes into my head."

"What? Like a picture?"

"Not really. It's hard to explain. You know when you've had a dream and you wake up knowing exactly what you dreamed, but when you try to think about it in words, you just can't describe it?"

"Ah yes! I know that feeling very well."

"Well, it's simply like that. I know exactly what an animal is telling me, but it isn't in words."

"Penny, that explanation is about as useful as a chocolate hammer — I'm sorry — I don't mean to be rude. It's just that I never seem to understand these things."

"I's been thinkin'," says Billy. "I's beginnin' to get it, I's not 'earin' creatures, but I's feelin' 'em."

"That's right, Billy," Penny agrees. "You have to be quiet inside."

"That reminds me of Emmy," says Pip. "He's always telling me to stop thinking and to be empty. As if that's possible!"

"Mr Pip," says Larky. "Would you tell us that story again, please, the first one when you see Scraggy and Mowzl fishing in their home world? Penny hasn't heard it, and it would be a good start for her to know what's been going on."

"Good idea, Larky! Remind me, please, what stories have we had so far?"

"Mr Pip, you told us that you are writing 'Wot 'Appnd' for Emmy and you told us the first one, which is 'Typhoon', and the second one, ''Allo', and you said we couldn't have the third story because it might make us ill, and so you read us the next few stories. Then Emmy and LuLu arrived, and Emmy told the story of 'Silk and Sad', about Beechnut dying and Flimsy getting very ill. Oh! I nearly forgot, you read us 'Ocean' too."

"Thanks, I remember now; you have an excellent memory, Larky. I agree we should start from the beginning, because Penny is here, and she should hear the whole story — well, if you would like to, Penny."

"Yes, please, Mr Pip!" says Penny.

"Thanks, Mr Pip!" says Billy.

"Let's move to the front room," says Pip, and he leads the way through. While the children get settled, he tends to the wood-burner, putting in another log and riddling the grate.

"It's been such a cold few weeks lately, I've needed the wood-burner every day, and it's not really autumn yet."

"It's lovely, Mr Pip, I love watching the flames," says Larky.

Pip fetches the orange ring binder from the bookshelf, sits on the sofa and opens the ring binder on his knee.

"Hmph!" says Pip, clearing his throat. "The Adventures of Horatio Mowzl, Chapter One, 'Typhoon'." He pauses for a few moments and begins to read.

The children listen to the sound of Pip's voice and watch the flames in the wood-burner, which begin to grow stronger as the log burns. Pip interrupts his reading to close down the damper on the wood-burner, and the flames become soft and lazy. Watching the sleepy flames is mesmerising, and as Pip reads once more, the children are lulled into story-sleep.

When Pip reaches the end of the first story, 'Typhoon', he pauses, and the room is quiet. After a few minutes, he continues with the story called ''Allo!', and when that is finished he pauses again. This time the children wake up, finding themselves once again in Pip's front room, gazing at the flames dancing slowly in the wood-burner.

Penny is the first to speak.

"Wow! Did all that really happen, Mr Pip? Is that really how Mowzl came to the human world? And you pulled him through the fog? I can't believe you really saw Pearl, and Mowzl and Scraggy fishing."

"Yes, Penny; it was so real I got quite discombobulated and haven't been feeling well ever since. And yes, that is how Mowzl came to the human world, and things have been very strange ever since he arrived."

"Who's this Bob you 'ated?" asks Billy.

"'Discombobulated', it means feeling confused, or out of sorts, jangled, or something like that."

"How did you two meet Mowzl?" Penny asks Billy and Larky. "And why do you call him Emmy?"

"Ah!" says Pip. "Mowzl is given his new name, 'Emmy', in a later story."

"Billy met Emmy first, I mean Mowzl," explains Larky. "Mowzl was in his pouch floating about in the woods. I met him when Billy took me to the woods, 'cos I wouldn't believe him when he told me about Mowzl. I couldn't believe my eyes when I saw him and LuLu, they were floating in mid-air in their pouches, and while they were there we could understand the wild talk, and we talked with Rattltap and Priklstik."

"Who are they?" cries Penny.

"Rattltap is a woodpecker, and Priklstik is a hedgehog."

"Emmy 'as magic," says Billy. "'N 'e said we'll be talkin' with creatures if we's really wantin' to."

"I really want to meet them, Mr Pip, do you think I can?" asks Penny.

"Of course! Why don't you all call Emmy while I read the next chapter?"

"What do you mean, 'call Emmy'?" asks Penny.

"Ha!" exclaims Billy. "Emmy's tellin' me to call 'im wiv my 'eart, 'n when I's sayin' 'ow does I do that, he just says 'yous'll be kno-in'."

"Well, now's your chance to practise," says Pip.

"Mr Pip?" asks Penny. "Did you write the stories you just read to us?"

"Well now, that's a good question, Penny. Mowzl, who's now called Emmy, tells me that it's my job to write 'Wot 'Appnd'. What actually happens is that I wake up in the mornings to find pages written and scattered all over the floor! The first time it happened I was quite shocked, but I've got used to it now. All I have to do is pick them up and put them in the right order, which is easy because they've got page numbers."

"You must be asleep when you write it, Mr Pip," suggests Larky.

"Maybe you go into a trance," says Penny. "There's something called 'automatic writing' or something like that, isn't there?"

"I really don't know, Penny, it's all a bit strange."

"And, Mr Pip?"

"Yes, Penny?"

"Exactly who is telling the story? The way it's told, the storyteller isn't you, or Mowzl or LuLu. Who is it?"

"Good question! Who's the narrator? I've never really thought that one through, we'll have to ask Emmy about it. Isn't it called writing in the third person?"

"Who's the third person?" says Penny, laughing.

"Alright," says Pip. "Shall we read some more?"

"Yeah!" says Billy.

Billy is not really interested in who's telling the story, or writing it or whatever, he just wants to get on with it and he wants to hear chapter three.

"Let's read chapter three, 'Time Capsules'," says Pip.

"*Alright!*" cries Billy, excitedly.

"I thought you couldn't tell us that yet," says Larky.

"I think it's time you heard it, Larky," replies Pip. "A lot has happened in a very short time, and I think you're ready."

Pip checks the wood-burner, deciding not to put another log on just yet. He sits quietly, waiting while the room becomes still. He imagines Emmy, sitting in his Gypshun Boat on the windowsill, waiting for the little chick-hens of his thoughts to settle down and go to sleep.

Pip reads the story about himself and Emmy going to the seaside where they walked the cliff tops, and how they found a sheltered nook for a rest and a picnic, and how they talked about Emmy's world. They talked about ancient human 'Time Capsules', and how the scholar mice had learned to understand that humans had made too many holes in the life-skin, and the great wave had swept humans away.

While Pip is reading this, the children drift into story-sleep, and the fire in the wood-burner dies down, becoming a red glow of embers. Pip finishes reading; he sits quietly for a while before getting up to put another log in the wood-burner.

Penny is the first to speak:

"Thank you, Mr Pip. Do you really believe Mowzl? Do you really believe that humans will be extincted?"

"I don't know what to believe, Penny, I reckon that's why I got ill. You see, I know that humans are destroying the ecosystems of the planet, and it hurts me deeply to see it happening. I see it all the time, everywhere, and the scale of the destruction has been getting greater for my whole life, which is quite a long time now. But there's always good people doing all sorts of good things, and science is inventing wonderful solutions to problems. But in my heart, I know that humans have chosen a path that I cannot accept, and I seek a different way. Maybe that's why Emmy came to me.

"I have been watching what is happening for many years, and I see that humans are now in the service of machines, and no longer hear the wisdom of deep Nature; humans no longer make their own choices and decisions, they do what the machines need them to do, and the humans believe that the evolution of machines is progress.

"Emmy says that his home world is the same as our own world, but it is eight thousand years in the future. He says that there are no humans in his home world, as far as any of his family knows, or the wild creatures that he knows. But Emmy is not bringing us sadness and despair, he is bringing us something new."

For a while nobody speaks. Pip worries he's said too much.

"I really want to meet Emmy," Penny says, sighing.

"'Ow come Emmy's world's in the future?" asks Billy. "'Ow did he get 'ere?"

"We don't know, Billy, that's why Emmy needs 'Wot 'Appnd' to get written down!" says Pip. "He doesn't know how he got here, or how he's going to get home!"

"Listen! I can hear singing!" cries Larky.

They listen, hearing a faint 'Laa La', which gets slowly louder until it is quite clear.

"Laa La Laa La Laaa Laaa . . ."

"That's Emmy coming," says Pip. "He's felt your call."

Emmy doesn't come in through the door, or through the window. He's purling, and he arrives in the middle of the room, appearing suddenly with a 'pop'.

"'Allo! I's very 'appy to be seein' 'uman cubz wiv Pippee."

"Hallo, Emmy!" cries Larky.

Emmy floats in his pouch towards Penny, coming close and looking into her eyes. No words are spoken. After a while, Emmy speaks.

"Pennee's xplaynd wotz 'appnd n I's tellin' 'er some fingz. Pennee's good wiv unwurdz."

"You two ain't said nothin' to each other!" protests Billy.

"The wild talk doesn't have to be words, Billy, as you know yourself," says Penny.

"Why do we have to use words then?" asks Larky.

"'Coz you's learnin' wiv 'elp ov a littl majik," explains Emmy. "N you's 'avin' to be merembrin' wot 'umans 'as forgot."

"Emmy," says Pip. "We've just been reading 'Typhoon', ''Allo' and 'Time Capsules', and we've got lots of questions; Penny, what was it that you asked me?"

"Emmy, I asked Mr Pip if he really believes that human beings get extincted. Do we?"

"Ha! Pennee, you's 'avin' good kwestchn. Ooman beins iz really ooman doin's, 'coz they's nevva simplee bein' theyz always doin'. Pennee, I's not kno-in' 'bout wot 'appns. I's been 'ere in ooman world four wintaz, n I's learnin' from creachaz 'bout wotz 'appnin'. Creechaz *iz* wild web, n they's sayin oomans iz 'urtin' wild fingz, n makin' too mennee 'oles, n wild web's tearin'."

"What do you mean 'too many holes'?" asks Penny.

"Wild nature iz all livin' fingz wotz needin' each n evry uvva to make wildniss 'ealthy. Oomans n masheenz iz all evry where, n wildniss iz bein' broke n dedded."

"I 'ates 'umans," growls Billy angrily.

"Billee, oomans iz very clevva, but they's not 'avin' 'wareniss ov wild web, n theyz needin' to be wakin' up. Billee, you's wakin' up, n you's needin' to be learnin' from creachaz n tellin' oomans."

"But what happens, Emmy?" cries Penny, her voice pleading. "It's our whole world we are talking about, and you say you're from the future, so you must know what happens!"

Emmy is quiet for a few moments. He looks at Penny, and says, gently:

"Pennee, I's feelin' 'ow big you's 'urtin' n I's sorry you 'as to be 'urtin'. Itz 'coz it 'urtz iz why oomans stayz unwareful. Mi world iz yor world in foocha but I's not kno-in' wot appnz'."

"How far into the future?"

"Eight fowsand, one 'undrid n twennee eight wintaz."

"Why exactly that?" says Pip.

"I's nevva kno-in'."

"Well? What happens to us humans?" cries Penny.

"Time Capsules wot oomans berrid tells ov terribl fingz. They's nevva tellin' wot 'appnz afta. I's nevva seed an ooman in mi 'ome world, Pennee, n weez nevva kno-in' wot great wave iz bringin'."

"But what can we do? What can we do?" Penny sobs, as Larky puts an arm round her to comfort her.

"Mennee oomans iz 'urtin' n poorly sorted, n they's nevva kno-in' why. Oomans iz seein' masheenz gettin' clevra n oomans iz doin' wot masheenz iz needin'. Oomans iz seein' wild web dyin' before they's very eyz."

"How do you know all this about humans, Emmy?" asks Pip.

"Emmy's learnin' from creechaz wen 'e's purlin'."

"I'm goin' to learn from creatures too, 'n do somethin'!" says Billy, defiantly.

"Hooray!" cries Larky. "Yes, Billy, let's all do that!"

"Oomans iz ready," says Emmy.

"But ready for what?" asks Pip.

"Oomans iz not kno-in' wot, p'raps itz you all wotz findin' out. You'sll be feelin' 'ow creechaz iz feelin', n be seein' wild web wiv yor 'earts."

"Emmy," says Billy. "Can we all 'ave pouches, like you 'n LuLu?"

"Billee, you's all to be 'avin' pouchiz, wot you's makin' your selvz. We'sll all be gaverin' wool togevva."

"It's Saturday tomorrow!" says Larky excitedly. "Could we go wool gathering tomorrow? I asked my Mum if she would teach me to crochet, and she said yes."

"Yeah! Let's go tomorrow!" says Billy.

Penny says she would like to go too, and tomorrow is fine, and Pip agrees too.

"I's very 'appy you's all 'xcited. Letz all be 'ere at Pippee's tomorro, wiv LuLu. Now Emmy's goin'. Bi!"

"Goodbye, Emmy!" says Pip, and before anyone else has a chance to say anything, Emmy disappears with a pop.

"'Ow weird is that!" says Billy. "Awesome."

"Alright now, gang," says Pip. "It's getting late for your bed times I expect, you should all be home by now, I'm sure. If you can get your families to agree, come back here tomorrow at 10 o'clock, with a backpack, food and water."

They all three happily agree and get themselves ready to go home. At the door Pip says:

"Billy, you can leave that bag of rubbish here, I'll put it out for the rubbish collection next week."

"Thanks, Mr Pip."

"Thank you, Mr Pip," say Larky and Penny at the same moment, and they laugh.

"Bye!" says Pip. "See you tomorrow. Thank the mouse, not me."

~

The three children walk together, chattering excitedly. Penny is still feeling shocked and upset, but she does have the feeling now that together they can do something. She needs to ask about Emmy.

"Did we just talk with a toy mouse floating in mid-air, or am I asleep and dreaming?"

"You're not dreaming, Penny, Emmy's real," says Larky. "I'm so glad you've met him."

"Me too," agrees Penny. "So Dungl was telling the truth when he said he'd seen you two talking with fairies!"

"Don't rub it in," says Billy. "Hey, see ya tomorrow, I's goin' down 'ere."

"Bye, Billy," says Larky.

"See you tomorrow, and thanks, Billy," says Penny.

"It ain't my doin', I's glad you's with us, Penn." So saying, Billy turns down a side street towards his Nan's place.

Larky and Penny have to go their separate ways as well, but they stop walking, reluctant to split up.

"Are you alright, Penny?" says Larky. "I could see how upset you were by what Emmy said."

"I'm still upset; I'm not surprised that Pip got ill, it makes me feel sick too. I suppose we all just think everything will be alright. What surprises me is that Emmy doesn't know what happens, even though he's from the future. He's not saying we get extincted, he's saying that it's a mystery. Well, that's how I'm seeing it."

"Like Billy said," says Larky, "we have to do something, don't we?"

"Yes, we do. I don't understand what it is yet, but I'm glad I'm with you all. I'm looking forward to tomorrow!"

"Me too. See you, Penny."

"Bye, Larky!"

~

As Larky approaches her family's home, she can see lights on and her mum working at the big table in the kitchen. There's somebody there with her; Larky peers through the window.

I don't believe it! she thinks, *It's LuLu! How did she get here?*

Larky uses her latchkey to open the front door, and as she hangs up her coat and kicks off her shoes, she calls to Donna. "Hallo, Mum, I'm home. Sorry I'm late."

"Hallo, dear, come and meet my new friend."

Larky enters the kitchen.

"This is . . ." begins Donna.

"Larky!" cries LuLu in surprise, not meaning to interrupt.

"LuLu! How did you get here?" asks Larky.

"Do you two know each other already? Wonders will never cease," says Donna.

"I met Donna in the fabric shop," explains LuLu. "Donna overheard me asking the shopkeeper for advice about spinning wool, and I asked if she sold drop-spindles."

"That's right," says Donna. "I could hardly believe it, because you and I had been talking about spindles only this morning, Charlotte! Anyway, Mrs Fuller, the shopkeeper, made a joke about spinning a yarn, but she didn't know where to get a drop-spindle. So, I said to LuLu — I didn't know LuLu's name then — that I could ask my husband to make spindles for you both!"

"And then Donna invited me home for a cuppa and a chat, and here we are!" says LuLu.

"Mummy," cries Larky. "I've just come from Pip's place — he's LuLu's friend — and there's a plan to go wool gathering tomorrow! Can I go, Mum? Please can I go? And, LuLu, can you come too?"

"Yes," says LuLu. "What time?"

"10 o'clock at Pip's."

"Well, I'll see how Muffin is in the morning. Who's coming?" asks LuLu.

"Um, Mr Pip, Billy, me and Penny, and Emmy of course."

"So, you . . ."

"Who are all these people?" interrupts Donna, an astonished look on her face. She suddenly feels uneasy; this stranger knows more about her daughter than she does herself.

"It's alright, Mummy, these are new friends I've only just met and I haven't had a chance to tell you, but now we can catch up!"

LuLu is beginning to feel uncomfortable and decides to leave.

"I should leave you to your family evening," she says, standing up. "Donna, thank you, it's very good to meet you."

"Please don't go yet! Oh, Mummy, can't LuLu stay longer?"

"Er, yes, of course, if you would like to, LuLu, you would be most welcome. Charlotte, you look wet, dear, you'd better go and wash while I get tea ready."

"Thanks, Mum!" says Larky as she goes upstairs.

"Let me help, Donna, what can I do?" offers LuLu.

"Would you fold those fabrics, please, and get the table ready? Bernie will be home soon, so that's five places."

"Five?"

"Oh! I haven't had a chance to say, there's Sarah too, Charlotte's sister. Sarah is twelveteen."

"Ah!" says LuLu.

"I'm just going to do a vegetable stir-fry and rice, is that alright?" asks Donna.

"Perfect."

"Do you mind chilli?"

"The more the better."

"Good, we all like chilli."

Donna washes, peels and chops the vegetables.

"Donna . . ." begins LuLu.

"It's alright, I was a bit upset just now because I felt that my new friend had been stolen from me by my own daughter . . ."

"There's no danger of that, Donna."

"I know that really. I'm always surprised by how vulnerable I can feel, all of a sudden. It always takes me by the blind side."

"Thank you for talking about it, Donna, It's all too easy to avoid feelings like that, and pretend that they're not happening."

They hear the front door opening, and voices; it's Bernie and Sarah. Donna explains:

"Bernie has just collected Sarah from her music lesson on his way home. Hallo, Bernie, hallo, Sarah, come and meet my new friend."

Sarah enters the kitchen, followed by Bernie, who is looking work-worn and grubby. Sarah glances at LuLu, and looks away, and then her eyes sneak another look, sideways, at the way LuLu is dressed, and a spark of interest lights up her face.

"LuLu, this is Bernie, and Sarah."

"Hallo, I'm glad to meet you," says LuLu.

"Hallo, LuLu," says Bernie. "Hope you're staying for tea — I need a wash, so I'll be a little while."

"Do you want some tea love?" says Donna.

"Thought you'd never ask!"

Bernie goes upstairs with a mug of tea in his hand. Sarah dumps her school bag on the table and listens to LuLu explaining how she and Donna had met, and that they both work with material.

"Is that your coat on the peg?" asks Sarah. "Very posh."

"Sarah, LuLu made it," says Donna.

"Wow," says Sarah quietly, looking at LuLu with something like admiration.

"How was your music lesson?" asks Donna, giving the sizzling vegetables a stir.

"Boring, as usual."

"Don't you enjoy it any more, love?"

"Not really."

"What do you play?" asks LuLu.

"Piano, 'xcept we haven't got one."

"Can you read music?"

"Simple things, yes."

"Sarah, dear," says Donna. "Please unpack your school bag and get ready for tea."

"Yes, Mum."

When Sarah has gone upstairs, LuLu finishes setting the table and filling glasses with water. Donna's cooking fills the air with delicious smells and chilli heat that LuLu can feel in her throat. When the rice is cooked and rested, Donna dishes up.

She yells up the stairs. "Ready!"

Soon they are all eating, gasping a bit with the chilli, and Donna talks about meeting LuLu at the fabric shop.

"Well, Mrs Fuller said, and she knows a thing or two about wool, that we will have trouble finding a drop-spindle for spinning wool, unless we send away to a specialist supplier . . ."

Bernie looks up from his food.

"A spindle? Isn't that like a wooden rod and a disc of wood?"

"That's right, Bernie, and it's got a little hook in one end to thread the yarn through," says Donna, winking at LuLu. "I've seen a picture somewhere."

"I'll make you one!" says Bernie, always enjoying a challenge.

"Could you really make one?" asks LuLu.

"It'll have to be a bit simple, as I don't have a lathe to make the disc. I'll have to saw out a round and use sandpaper to make it smooth."

"That sounds perfect."

"Daddy, would you make me one as well, please?" asks Larky.

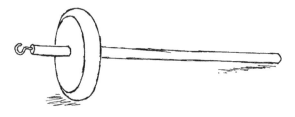

"It's as easy to make two as it is to make one; yes, Larky."

"Oh thanks, Dad!"

"Why don't you just buy the wool at the fabric shop?" suggests Sarah, in a bored sort of voice.

"LuLu and me want to learn how to spin wool, that's all," says Larky.

"That's 'LuLu and I', dear," says Donna.

Larky frowns and goes on. "And we are going to gather wool tomorrow morning. Do you want to come, Sarah?"

"Not on your life."

"Where will you look for wool?" asks Bernie, scraping the last traces of juice from his plate with a knife, and licking the knife.

"Daddy! Don't lick your knife!"

"Oh dear, yes, you're right, Larks. I think a good place for wool would be on the hill above Tillings Wood. They've got sheep up there and wool gets caught on the barbed wire and in the thorn bushes. I walk up there sometimes, Cloud Common they call it."

"Good idea, Dad, thanks."

"Well, you will be careful, won't you?"

"Yes, Dad, LuLu will look after me."

"Charlotte?" says Donna.

"Yes, Mum?"

"May I come with you tomorrow? It's not often that we go out together."

"Erm . . . it's not really up to me, Mum, we'd better ask LuLu."

"I'm sure it's fine," says LuLu. "So long as you are happy with mud, and surprises!"

"What sort of surprises?" asks Donna.

"The surprising sort!" says LuLu, giving nothing away.

"Ooo! Exciting!"

Bernie looks hungrily at Sarah's plate. She hasn't eaten much.

"Are you going to eat that, Sarah, or shall I help you out?"

"I'm not really hungry, Dad, you can have it." Sarah pushes her plate towards Bernie.

"Sarah, you've not been eating much recently, are you alright?" asks Donna.

"Yes, Mum, just not very hungry."

"Waste not, want not," says Bernie. "Thank you, Sarah!" He tucks in to Sarah's supper. "I'll make the spindles tomorrow," he says between mouthfuls. "While you're out."

"Thanks, Dad," says Larky.

After they have finished eating, LuLu does the washing up while Larky and Sarah do the drying and putting things away.

"Are you happy about your Mum coming tomorrow?" LuLu asks Larky.

"Why shouldn't she be?" says Sarah.

"Sort of," says Larky. "But what about Emmy?"

"Who's Emmy?" Sarah demands.

"A new friend, you can meet him if you come too."

"I'm not traipsing through mud all day, you must be joking."

"Suit yourself," Larky says, feeling hurt by the way Sarah is with her these days; it's not how they used to talk together.

"Well I must go now," says LuLu. "I'll just say goodbye to Donna and Bernie."

With the goodbyes said, LuLu puts on her coat, and Donna shows her out.

"It's been good to meet you, LuLu, see you tomorrow."

"Yes, Donna, I am glad you're coming. 10 o'clock, Larky knows where. And thanks again for tea!"

"You're welcome, bye!"

"Bye!"

~

It rains most of the night, and it's a very damp world that our wool gatherers walk through in the morning on their way to Pip's place. At 10 o'clock, Pip is outside his house ready to go. As people arrive, he checks that they have got everything they need.

"Hallo, Mr Pip!" calls Penny, as she and Billy appear.

"Hallo, Penny, hallo, Billy. I see you're ready for the mud!

Have you got food and water?"

"Yeah, we 'ave, Mr Pip," says Billy, "'n a bag for wool."

"Is Emmy here?" asks Penny.

Pip shakes his head. "No, he'll meet us there."

"O — wa!" says Penny in disappointment.

"'Ere's the others!" chirps Billy, happily.

Donna and Larky met up with LuLu at the corner of the road and arrive together at Pip's. LuLu introduces Donna to Pip and Penny. Donna knows Billy already, as he's been round for tea a few times.

"Have you got food and water? And will you be warm enough?" asks Pip.

"Stop fussing, Mr Pip!" teases Larky. "Let's go! But where's Emmy?"

"Emmy's going to meet us there," says Pip, again. "Come on, let's be off."

"Where's 'there'?" asks Larky.

"Tillings Wood, I suppose."

"Dad says Cloud Common would be a good place to find wool," says Larky.

"Good! We'll go there."

Pip leads the way down the road and along the path, familiar to Larky and Billy, that will lead out of town towards Tillings Wood. Donna walks with Pip asking him about Emmy and what the wool gathering is for. Pip says that he will have to let Emmy explain.

The children walk together, chattering away, soon getting a long way ahead. At the top of Tillings Wood, they find a place to stop where they can rest and wait for the others to catch up. LuLu arrives first, and she sits next to Penny.

"How are you, Penny? There has been a lot to take in with all the stories recently."

"I'm alright, LuLu, I was upset yesterday, because of the talk about humans dying out, but now I'm feeling good about doing something even though I don't know what it is yet."

"That's good, I'm glad. How about you, Larky? Are you still feeling alright about your Mum coming today?"

"I'm fine, LuLu, thanks. We've been talking about that, and Billy and Penny agree it's really good that Mum's here."

Somewhere in the wood, a green woodpecker calls.

"Yaffle! That'll mean rain's comin'," says Billy.

"That's a safe bet, Billy!" says Penny, laughing. "It's rained every day for weeks!"

Pip and Donna arrive, puffing a bit because of the slope they've just climbed. Glad to sit down, Pip opens his backpack.

"I'm thirsty already, and peckish," he says. "Time for a little something. Hmm. I seem to remember reading that somewhere."

Billy cocks his head, listening. "Can you 'ear singin'?"

They listen carefully, and soon hear Emmy's familiar song.

"Laa la laa la laaa laaa."

"It's Emmy!" cries Larky. "Where is he?"

Emmy is purling, and he appears in mid-air in the midst of them all. At first, he is a faint blur in the air growing more definite until, with a 'pop', he arrives.

"Hallo, Emmy!" chorus Larky, Billy and Penny together.

Donna stares at Emmy with a frown on her face. In her hand is an apple that she was about to bite into, but now she is motionless, her mouth open, staring at Emmy.

"Emmy," says Pip. "Please meet Donna, Larky's Mum. Donna very much wants to come with us today."

Emmy purls towards her. "'Allo, Donna, I's very 'appy to be meetin' you. Mi name iz Emmy n I's a mouse n I's comin' from uvva world where I's a real mouse."

As he speaks, he moves close to her, looking deep into her eyes. He doesn't say any more, and with the help of the magic that the pouch brings, Donna feels the unwords. Tears stream down her face; she smiles. Larky moves to sit next to her, putting an arm around her, hugging her.

"Oh, Mummy, I'm so glad you're here."

At this moment Rattltap arrives, swooping down to cling to the trunk of the nearest tree.

"Tchak! Good morning, Mowzl Emmy, and good morning, human cubs and elders. I see that there are two here to whom I have not yet been introduced; may I say hallo, I am Rattltap, and I am a woodpecker — as you can see — and I am at your service."

"Hallo, Rattltap, this is my Mum, Donna, and this is my friend, Penny," says Larky.

"Hallo, Rattltap," says Penny. "How come we understand what you are saying?"

"Ah!" says Rattltap. "For this you can thank the flying mouse, Mowzl Emmy, whose magic makes possible the wild talk with words. There are no humans still living who can feel the unwords."

"'Xcept Penny!" says Billy.

"Then all is not lost. I am very happy to meet you, Penny."

"I'm very happy to meet you, too, Rattltap," she replies.

"H-hallo, Rattltap," says Donna, her voice wobbly. "I can't believe we're talking, I can't believe anything I'm seeing or hearing! Will I wake up in a minute?"

"You're awake now, Donna, welcome to the wild talk. Emmy called me so that you could hear the wild talk. And now, my mission fulfilled, I must bid you farewell and return to my beloved Tattlrap. Goodbye, one and all! Tchak!" And away he flies.

There's a long, easy silence.

"Wot'z in yor 'eart, Donna?" says Emmy.

"Wonder, and warmth."

"I's verry 'appi. You'sll be orite, Donna."

Emmy purls higher. "Let's be gavrin' wool!" he exclaims.

"Come on, gang!" says Pip, stuffing things in the backpack.

They set off again, with Emmy leading the way up the hill above Tillings Wood towards Cloud Common. The footpath goes from field to field, sometimes with a stile to climb over, sometimes a gate. It's not until they reach the top of the hill that the fencing ends and the sheep are free to roam the Common. Here, old hawthorn and blackthorn bushes make prickly thickets; the sheep like to push through the bushes, the thorns combing their fleeces. In so doing, they leave strands of wool snagged on the thorns.

"Pleez be gavrin' wool, n be merembrin' why we's 'ere," says Emmy. "You's needin' sheepziz wool, but we's not needin' spidaz sylk."

"It's fiddly getting the wool away from the thorns," says Penny.

"Mind you ain't scratchin' your 'ands," warns Billy.

"Erm . . . Emmy," says Donna. "Emmy, you said: 'remember why we are here' — what did you mean? Why are we here?"

"You's 'ere to gavva sheepziz wool for makin' pouchiz for purlin'."

"Oh dear, I don't understand."

"Mummy," says Larky. "We want to make wool pouches like Emmy's, so that we can be purling like he is. Then we can learn the wild talk."

"What do you mean, 'purling'?"

"You's not 'avin' to wurree, Donna, you'sll be seein' troof ov wotz 'appnin' littl bi littl."

"I don't understand yet either, Donna," says Penny. "So, don't feel you are the only one."

"Donna, it's a lot to take in," says LuLu. "It's been hard for all of us to keep up. We've had stories to help us understand what it's all about and I'm sure Pip would read 'Wot 'Appnd' to you, wouldn't you, Pip?"

"Yes, I would, Donna, anytime," says Pip. "And more stories for you too, Penny."

"Thank you, yes, it's all got a bit overwhelming," says Donna. "I had no idea, Charlotte, no wonder you seem different recently."

"I'm alright, Mum, and now you know!" says Larky.

They walk and talk, finding little bits of fleece here and there on thorns and thistles as they slowly move across Cloud Common.

Stopping for a rest, Pip sits on the ground using a plastic bag from his pack to keep his bum dry.

"How are we doing wool-wise?" he asks. "I seem to have quite a lot already, but I don't know how much we need."

"If we are going to make a — pouch, or whatever you call it," says Donna, "big enough for each of us, we'll need lots and lots more than we've got now."

"Mummy, no!" cries Larky. "We'll make the pouches the same size as Emmy's."

"Oh, what? Now I *really* don't understand."

Emmy had drifted away when he saw the wool gatherers doing well, but now he returns, hearing the last bit of the conversation.

"You'sll 'ave 'nough wool wen you's been ova Clowd Common n bak. I's 'avin' to be leavin', n I'sll see you innabit. Pleez be merembrin' Beechnut."

"Emmy, are you alright?" asks LuLu, concerned for him.

"I's 'urtin' in mi 'eart 'coz I's feelin' Beechnut n Flimsy bein' close, like they's 'ere, so I's feelin' 'appy n sad. Oh-oh! I's bein' pulled. Bi!"

Pop. Emmy disappears.

"Blimey!" says Billy, breaking the silence.

"Who are Beechnut and Flimsy?" asks Donna.

"That's quite a story, Donna," says Pip. "It begins with a team of five mice, in Emmy's home world, setting off to go wool gathering, just as we are doing now, and what happens is . . ."

Pip tells the story of 'Silk and Sad', mainly for Donna and Penny who haven't heard it before, but also for anyone else who wants to listen. They pack up the picnic and continue across Cloud Common, collecting wool. Mist closes in, becoming a fine rain, and soon it feels a lot colder. Donna, Penny and Larky are in tears when Pip tells of Beechnut being taken by the owl. LuLu is sad too, and she cries in her heart for Flimsy, who became so ill that she touched the edge of life, returning with the gift of seeing. LuLu thinks of Muffin with a sudden pang of anxiety; *I must get home as soon as I can*, she thinks.

The wool gatherers are exhausted by the time they'd crossed Cloud Common and re-entered Tillings Wood. It is as much as they can do to carry their backpacks which are now full of wet wool, and they agree that they need to go home as quickly as they can. They plan to meet again next weekend at Donna's place to begin working with the wool, and in the meantime, the wool should be washed and dried, ready to use.

They trudge through Tillings Wood in fading light, the rain getting heavier. By the time they part company to go their separate ways, they have in their hearts a strong feeling for Flimsy on the march to Tumble Cave through the wind and rain, after the owl had taken Beechnut.

~

LuLu walks home, tears streaming down her face. The mystery of death is close, so close that she feels the touch. Does this mean it's Muffin's time to let go of the world, and to go with the great wave? *Can I get home in time?* she thinks.

With a heavy heart, she rushes home wishing she hadn't been out all day but had stayed with Muffin instead. When she arrives home, Muffin is waiting for her, sitting calmly on her haunches with her front paws tucked under. She looks at LuLu with a welcoming 'hallo' look and starts purring.

Perhaps I'm wrong, thinks LuLu. *It's not your time yet, is it, my love? How will I know?* But even as this thought happens, she realises it's just wishful thinking; it *is* Muffin's time. Muffin has settled on a cushion under the stairs, a place she has liked to be in recent days. LuLu sits on the floor next to her, stroking her, feeling the vibration of the purring through her hand and into her body.

She thinks of Beechnut and Flimsy, and of the great wave and how she had felt up at Cloud Common walking home through the rain. The great wave is not a wave of water, it is a wave of life: it is a wave of joy, of wonder, of love, of sadness and of grief, and right now, it is a wave of tears.

With her fingers combing through Muffin's soft fur, LuLu can feel the wildness of this magnificent creature; she feels Muffin's animal nearness, which has been such a blessing for so many years. Muffin's trust fills her heart with joy.

LuLu feels herself being carried by the great wave, and for a time she cannot be sure if it is Muffin that is dying, or herself — or both of them. When she becomes aware again of sitting on the hard floor with her hand on Muffin's motionless and silent body, she at once feels the terrible absence that, from now on, will always be with her. Her fingers comb through the wild fur, absorbing the memory of that special softness. She stays there for a long time;

she stays there for all the ages that it takes for the wave of tears to stream forth.

When at last she comes to, she prepares another cushion, with layers of white tissue paper; she tenderly lifts Muffin's body and lays her in a circle on the tissue paper. Taking roses from the vase on the kitchen table, she separates the petals to lay them one by one over, and around, Muffin's body. She places a lighted candle on a stool nearby.

Muffin looks peaceful; she could be asleep, except that she isn't here any more. Wrapped in a blanket, LuLu sits close by wishing that her own spirit might fly to wherever Muffin's spirit has gone.

~

After the wool gathering, Pip hurries home through the rain. Glad to be indoors, he peels off wet clothes and hangs them up to drip; he washes the mud off his boots knowing it's much easier to do while they are still wet. The rain had soaked through his clothes and now he's feeling cold, so he has a hot bath to warm up.

"That's much better!" he says out loud when he's done. "Now then, what to do with all that wool?"

The wool is wet and muddy, with twigs and sheep poo, grass and burrs tangled in it. Filling the sink with cold water, he tugs the wool from the backpack in handfuls, mushing it into the water. When all the wool is in the water, he mushes it lots more with his hands flat and fingers spread, pulling out the biggest bits of twig, grass, and sheep poo. Satisfied, he leaves the wool in the water to soak. After wiping the inside of the backpack to get most of the wet out, he hangs it up so air can get inside to dry it.

Time for a cup of tea, he thinks to himself, as he walks towards the kettle — but he doesn't get to the kettle. A funny feeling comes over him; he stops moving, standing as though rooted to the spot, feeling a shudder running through his body.

Pop!

Emmy arrives, purling a few inches in front of Pip's eyes.

"Ah, Pippee, I's seein' you's feelin' great wave."

"Hallo, Emmy, is that what I'm feeling? It feels a bit too prickly to be a wave."

"Pippee, you's 'avin to breave a deep bref 'coz Muffin's time 'as come."

"You mean Muffin is dying? Quick, let's get to LuLu's! She'll be needing us!"

"We's not goin' to LuLu's, 'coz LuLu's needin' loneniss."

"What do you mean, Em? She might need help, she might need company."

"She's 'avin' all 'elp she's needin' from 'er luv ov Muffin, n from great wave. We'sll be leavin' 'er 'till she's ready."

"I understand, I would want to be alone too, now I come to think of it . . . Poor LuLu," says Pip, sadly. "Do you know, Em? When we were on Cloud Common, after you'd gone, and we walked back in the rain gathering wool, I'm sure that Beechnut and Flimsy were with us — just invisible. Is that why Muffin is going now, at this particular time?"

"You's rite, Pippee, it's a mystree. Great wave iz close n touchin' evry one n LuLu's kno-in' in 'er 'eart Muffin's time 'as come."

"What should we do now, Emmy? What can we do for LuLu?"

"LuLu's callin' wen she's ready."

"I don't know what to do with myself. Ah! I know, I'll wash the wool!"

"Perfik, 'xaklee wot wool'z wontin', n I's 'avin a li down, bi."

Emmy disappears at once, with a pop.

"Emmy, are you here, or at LuLu's?" calls Pip as he turns to go back to washing the wool, but Emmy doesn't reply. Pip walks through to the front room where he keeps his bowl of things — and there's the mouse, asleep, curled up like a dormouse, snuggled into a tuft of wool-ends that LuLu gave him, what he calls his 'fredz'.

Pip returns to washing the wool. He thinks about LuLu and Muffin, about how much he will miss Muffin; he can imagine the sound of her purring and his heart remembers with a pang of love.

~

The next morning Emmy wakes Pip early.

"LuLu's needin' you, Pippee!"

"O . . . what? LuLu? Muffin?"

"Pleez be wakin' up."

"Alright, I'm awake."

Pip splashes his face with cold water and cleans his teeth as he always does to wake himself up.

"Emmy, what's happening?"

"We's goin' to LuLu."

"I'm ready, let's go."

LuLu is pleased to see them; she smiles for a moment, but she doesn't speak. She leads them through to where Muffin is lying on the tissue paper with rose petals, and the candle nearby.

"Oh, she's so beautiful," Pip whispers. "Oh, Muffin! May I touch her?"

LuLu nods. Pip strokes the familiar soft fur, feeling Muffin's unfamiliar, cold and stiff body underneath the fur. Muffin is not there any more. Tears spring to his eyes.

"Where's Em?" asks LuLu.

"Oh, here," murmurs Pip, taking Emmy from his pocket and holding his hand out towards LuLu. "Sorry, Em."

"LuLu, mi 'eart iz full wiv Muffin n you."

"Thanks, Em." LuLu tries to find her voice. "I . . . er . . . can we bury her now, please? I'm ready. Emmy, I need you." She tucks him into the folds of her shawl.

"I'll dig her grave," says Pip, standing up, wiping tears from his eyes. He gives LuLu a hug. "She's gone, LuLu, there's a big space now . . ."

"A lion-sized absence . . ." whispers LuLu.

Pip goes out into the back garden to fetch tools for digging from the shed. LuLu told him weeks ago where she wants Muffin to be buried: a place where she will be able to sit close by.

He digs a deep hole, deep enough to ensure that Muffin's body will not be dug up by foxes or dogs. He piles up all the earth into a heap next to the grave. When the hole is dug, he tidies up as well as he can, covering the bottom of the grave with sprigs of fresh rosemary, cut from bushes growing in the garden. Ready now, he calls LuLu.

She comes with more rose petals, sprinkling them into the grave while Pip carries Muffin on the cushion. LuLu carefully lifts Muffin's body, with the tissue paper, and lowers her into the grave; she carefully arranges her body while sprinkling her with more rose petals. When she is satisfied, she folds more tissue paper gently over Muffin, tucking the edges down. After sprinkling a few more petals, LuLu is silent for a long time; at last, she heaves a deep sigh and speaks.

"Oh, Muffin, thank you for the joy that you have brought me and for your loyal companionship; thank you for your wildness, and for your trust in me. You are a lion and will purr in my heart for as long as my heart lives."

LuLu is quiet for some time before taking a handful of earth and scattering it gently onto the tissue paper covering Muffin. The earth patters down onto the paper with a sound that will echo forever in her memory.

"Please put the earth back now, Pip," she whispers.

Pip slowly spades the earth back into the grave. There isn't

room for all of it because it's loosened and takes up more space; he wonders what to do. Before he can say anything, LuLu steps on the grave and, with great sobs, she treads the earth down and goes on treading as Pip spades in more earth.

At last it is finished; Pip places a flat stone to mark and protect the grave, and LuLu lays two roses there.

"Thank you, Pip. I need to be alone now."

Pip returns home, glad that Emmy is staying with LuLu.

~

In the evening of the day of Muffin's burial, sunlight finds a way through the cloud, shining onto the roses lying on her grave. LuLu remains close to her all day, getting very cold and tired. She watches the evening sun sink down, and she goes indoors at last, shivering with cold, to lie on the sofa under a blanket.

"I miss you, Muffin," she cries out, her heart aching.

Emmy is quiet, feeling for LuLu, holding her in his heart.

LuLu dozes, dreaming of woodland and a low sun lighting up a grassy field just visible through trees. Standing in the shade of the trees, silhouetted against the brightly lit field beyond, stands a deer. Drawn to the deer, LuLu realises that she is purling; she is Emmy-sized in her pouch and floating in mid-air, moving through the woods toward the deer.

Purling is as natural to LuLu as breathing; she watches in wonderment as she moves closer to the deer. She feels released from the physical weight of her body, and purls just by the will of her heart.

Her pouch slows to a stop and the deer regards her with great interest. "Hallo. What sort of a creature are you?"

"Hallo, my name is LuLu and I'm a human," says LuLu.

"Hmm. My name is Willow and I am a deer. LuLu, if you're human, how is it that you are so small? I think you are an elf."

"No, I'm not an elf, although I might like to be; I am human, and it is the magic of this pouch which allows me to be so small and to float in mid-air like a flower fairy."

"Come closer, little human. I am feeling great sadness in your heart. Will you tell me?"

"My heart is flooded with tears because Muffin has died. Muffin, a little lion, a cat with a lion's heart, has shared her wildness and her creature love with me for twenty years, and now I miss her so very much, and feel her absence as a pain in my heart."

"This is not your first touching death, is it, LuLu?"

"No, Willow, death doesn't happen only at the end of life, death happens all the way through, in many different ways, giving meaning."

"And this can hurt?"

"Yes, this hurts," says LuLu.

"You are brave, you are like a deer. And because of this I will speak to you. When one that we love returns to the great wave, their body gives life to others, and their isness lives on in our hearts, as a flame leaping free within darkness. Our sadness is our longing to follow."

"When Muffin was dying," says LuLu, "I felt that I merged with her, got mixed up with her somehow, and it was me leaving."

Willow replies, "And then you heard, or felt, something saying 'No, it is not your time'."

"Yes, you're right, Willow, and I felt disappointed."

"Of course, because you are a spirit, and that is the source of all; until it is time, we are stardust growing isness."

"Growing isness!" exclaims LuLu.

"Yes. You may think of your Muffin coming in to your life already with her isness. Well, it's true up to a point, but she grew her isness in how she lived, and in how you enriched her life, and how she enriched your life. Isness grows like a flower, like any being." Willow pauses, allowing the space of silence for a moment.

"The great wave is all the isnesses that have ever been — and ever will be."

"Willow, do you fear dying?"

"I do not fear dying, LuLu, it is a returning; but I do fear, because I am a creature. I fear danger, and being hunted; I fear pain and loss, and I fear fear itself, but that is not my isness."

"Willow, thank you for talking with me and for your wisdom. I am reminded of someone saying, 'you will learn to welcome your sadness because this feeling bears witness to your love'."

"It is strange for me to hear a human say such things."

LuLu tells Willow about Emmy, and about the children who want to learn the wild talk. Willow is encouraged to hear about the children and offers her help when the time comes. They talk together for some time before LuLu realises that it is time to go.

"Willow, my pouch is pulling me away — goodbye!"
"Goodbye, LuLu, we shall meet again, I have no doubt."
And LuLu, in her pouch, fades away, disappearing with a pop.

~

Emmy watches over LuLu; she sleeps through the night and all the next day. He knows she is purling, and he is glad. LuLu has taken to purling as though she has known it always, so he is not worried; Pippee, on the other hand, is a worry, because he isn't ready to purl yet - he isn't strong enough.

Emmy climbs onto the windowsill to see what's happening outside. He can see the stone marking Muffin's grave, and the last of the sun shining on the roses; he watches the coming and going of birds and insects, busy in the sunlit evening.

The last few days, since the wool gathering and Muffin's death,

Emmy has been in a very strange mood. It is to do with feeling Beechnut and Flimsy so strongly, and the touch of the great wave. This touch has started something new.

~

Pip invites LuLu and Emmy to his place for a catch-up; he's been missing them. It's a blustery wet day, so he gets a fire going in the wood-burner to make things warm and welcoming for LuLu. Well, for everybody of course, but Pip knows that LuLu appreciates being kept warm, because she gets cold so easily. *She's like Flimsy,* he thinks. *LuLu's got Pearlness and Flimsyness!*

When LuLu arrives, she's looking pale and far away. She sits down. Emmy climbs from her pocket onto the arm of the sofa.

"'Allo, Pippee, iz you orite?"

"Hallo, yes, I'm alright; are you, Em? Are you, LuLu?"

"I'm alright," says LuLu quietly. "I've needed to, well, just be with Muffin." LuLu looks at the fire, taking some deep breaths before continuing.

"I've been purling a lot and find that it's good for me to be with wild creatures. I'm missing Muffin's wildness. I know she is — was — a house cat, but she had wildness all the same, and I miss that so much. It has been wonderful to be with creatures."

"Oh, LuLu, I wish I was purling too," says Pip.

"You's not to be 'urryin', Pippee."

"I know, Em, but I do hope it's soon! LuLu, tell me a little of what's happened."

"After we buried Muffin, I just sat for ages. I must've gone to sleep and at first, I didn't realise I was purling, it seemed like a dream, but then I was in the woods with a deer. Her name is Willow and she talked with me about death, and about the great wave — she said some lovely things."

"Like what, LuLu?"

"She said: 'the nature of the great wave is softness, and all that is hard in the world of things becomes soft, and this is the isness of being'."

"LuLu, you's good wiv creechaz n you's like a deer. You's tremblin' n soft like Willo iz."

"Emmy, Willow also said: 'touch me, feel this body trembling, alert and tense, ready to spring; but my isness is softness, and when my body leaps I am water and willow'."

"Ooo, that's beautiful," says Pip.

"It's so strange," LuLu continues, "to be hearing wild creatures talking about the great wave and the wild web — just like you do, Emmy!"

"I's 'opin' you's likin' it, LuLu."

"I am, and the purling and talking with creatures has helped me cope with the first days without Muffin."

"I's very 'appy you's talkin' wiv creechaz, LuLu."

They watch the lazy flames in the wood-burner.

"I must find the courage to go home," says LuLu. "It will be so lonely without Muffin."

"LuLu, I's comin' wiv you, n weezl 'ave Muffin in our 'eartz."

"Thank you, Emmy."

Chapter Three

Heartstrings

The weekend comes at last; Pip, LuLu and Emmy are on their way
to Donna's to join in with the wool-spinning. Pip carries the wool
that he and LuLu gathered last weekend. It's a cool day, and LuLu
wears a brown shawl; she tucks Emmy into the folds of her shawl,
so he can peep out above her coat.

Since Pip read the story of 'Ocean', things have been very
quiet. Emmy stayed with LuLu, needing to talk things over with
her: they talked about the ship and the typhoon, and what happened
to Scraggy; they talked about Muffin's death, and Beechnut's death
and Flimsy's illness.

LuLu has spent a lot of time sitting close to Muffin's grave,
feeling her closeness and remembering her isness. LuLu has been
purling too; she loves the relief of having no weight, and being able
to feel the unwords, and she loves to be close to wild creatures.

Pip has spent the last few days doing his gardening work and
trying to understand what's going on.

"Emmy," says Pip, as they walk towards Larky's place, "I keep
thinking about the 'Ocean' story. I'm worried about what it means."

Emmy's voice emerges from somewhere in the folds of LuLu's
shawl. "Pippee, I's wurrid too but I's 'appy we's findin' out 'Wot
'Appnd', littl bi littl."

"Whatever might have happened after the typhoon," says LuLu,
"you're here now, Emmy, thank goodness."

"Look, there's Penny — hallo, Penny!" Pip calls.

"Hallo! Emmy, thank you for your story the other day, I can't
stop thinking about it. Do you know what it means?"

"I's not kno-in', Pennee."

"I want to know what happened after," says Penny. "Whatever
happened to you, Emmy, and to Whip-Tail Jack and Scraggy?"

"We'sll be 'avin' more storeez, Pennee."

"Here we are!" says Pip, knocking on the door. Larky let's
them in, her hazel eyes alight with excitement.

"Hallo! Come in. Everyone's here so we can start!"

She introduces Bernie to Pip and Emmy. Donna has told Bernie
about Emmy, but even so, seeing the toy mouse for the first time and
hearing him speak is a surprise.

"'Allo, Bernee, I's 'appy to be seein' you."

LuLu takes Emmy from the folds of her shawl, handing him to

Bernie who is amazed to be holding him.

"Bernee, fankz for makin' spindlz. Pleez put me in littl bowl."

"You're welcome, Emmy, I'm glad I could do something to help. Do you mean this little bowl on the table?" says Bernie.

"Yip, fankz."

Bernie puts Emmy carefully into the bowl, and then he calls out to everyone to come and get a spindle. He pulls a cardboard box out from under the table, holds it under his arm and hands out spindles.

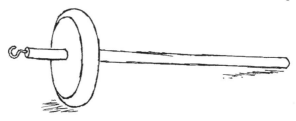

"I hope I've made enough!"

When Bernie understood that lots of people would be coming to learn to spin, he made lots of spindles, but he didn't know how many to make.

"They were quicker to make than I thought. They're a bit rough but should do the job."

"Thanks, Bernie," says LuLu.

"Yes, thanks, Bernie," says Pip.

"I've done a bit of research," says Donna. "And what we have to do first is to 'card' the raw wool. Has everyone washed their wool?"

"Yes."

"Yes."

"What's 'card'?" asks Billy.

"It's like fluffing it up," says Donna. "Or 'teasing' it, so it gets fluffy and easier to spin. 'Teasing' used to be done using the seed heads of teasels! But I thought we could make do with these old combs and hairbrushes."

Donna demonstrates, and with two hairbrushes worked against each other, she teases up some wool into a fluffiness. She combs the wool out of the brushes and has a fluffy mass of wool that looks a bit like grey candyfloss.

"You've been practising, Donna!" says Pip.

"When you've done that — and we can take turns with the combs and brushes — it's time to begin spinning. I'm going to try showing you . . ."

Donna holds some fluffed-up wool in her left hand and hooks the hook of the spindle into the fluffy wool, snagging just enough woolly hairs for the hook to get a grip. Letting the spindle hang in the air she spins it, clockwise (seen from above), with the fingers of her right hand. As it spins and winds up the wool, she uses the fingers of her right hand to stretch the fluffed wool out into a thread ready for it to be twisted. The spindle slows down and she spins it up again, continuing to stretch the fluff into a thread. The thread gets longer and longer, and eventually she has to stand up, so the spindle doesn't touch the floor.

"Mummy, that's brilliant!" says Larky. "Can I have a go?"

"In a minute! It's a bit lumpy, but practice is all," says Donna. "And now there's a length of thread, called the 'leader', which I'm going to take off the hook and tie onto the bottom part of the spindle — like so — and wind up some of the thread — like so — pass the thread through the hook — like so — and carry on spinning!"

"You make it look easy," says Bernie. "I bet you've been up all night practising!"

"Well, I've done some, it's true. I really want to help everyone get started. Right! Off you go!"

The day is spent happily, and noisily, talking and carding, spinning and laughing, grumbling and teasing. Even Pip turns out to be quite good at it after a lot of bad starts. Eventually they stop for tea and sandwiches.

"Emmy, do you need a little something?" asks LuLu.

"Fankz, LuLu, I's not needin' choklit foomz, 'coz mi 'eart growz big wiv 'appiniss, seein' wot you's all doin', n I's wantin' to say fankz to you's all."

"Emmy, we're loving it! We thank you!" says Penny.

"Yeah!" yells Billy from across the room.

The spinning goes better than anyone had expected. It's true that the threads are too thick and lumpy, but that doesn't matter, because they will all get better at it with practice. They learn that the better the carding, the easier it is to spin a fine thread, so everyone works at their carding.

They do so well that the spindles are soon filled up with thread. Donna shows how to make a ball of wool, winding the thread around her fingers to start the ball, and then winding around the ball — while the spindle wanders about on the floor — first one way and then cross ways, until the spindle is nearly empty, but not quite. Then she breaks the thread, and the spindle can be used to do more spinning.

Donna had made a ball of wool earlier while she was practising;

now she has two balls of wool and wants to show everyone how to ply two threads together.

Putting the two balls of wool on the floor, she ties the ends together onto the bottom part of an empty spindle. The two threads together are hooked through the hook and then the spindle is spun the other way, that is, anti-clockwise (seen from above). The spinning plies the two threads together and the plied thread is then wound onto the bottom part of the spindle.

"This 'two-ply' yarn is what we use to make a plait," says Donna. "By plaiting three strands of two-ply yarn together, we make the 'heartstring', and we'll use this to crochet the pouches!"

"Donna, you're amazing! You've learned all this in a week!" exclaims Penny.

"Donna," says LuLu, "it's only a week since you met Emmy for the first time; you've really taken him to your heart. Thank you for all your hard work and good teaching."

Donna is silent for a moment, gathering her feelings.

"I was so moved when we listened to Emmy's 'Ocean' story," she says. "The humans on the ship — the *Wreckless* — like robots just following a routine, driven by habit, every day doing everything all over again, chasing . . . what? Treasure? What is it they want? I cried when I realised that I've allowed my life to get like that, it's nobody's fault but my own. Emmy has woken me up from a kind of sleep walk. Thank you, Emmy, my life will never be the same again."

Donna looks at the floor, bashful, suddenly self-conscious about her 'newness'.

"Mummy," says Larky, going over to hug her.

"Well, I don't know what this wool thing is all about," says Bernie, "but I'm very happy that you're all here and are such good friends."

Donna recovers herself.

"Right, everyone, let's spend the rest of the day carding , and then you can take your wool home ready to spin. Let's meet again soon to begin crocheting. We could meet here again if you like, how about next weekend?"

"Sunday's good," says Bernie.

"Yes, Sunday," chorus several voices.

"Right! See you then!" says Donna.

"Would somebody tell me what all this wool business is leading to?" asks Bernie.

"Bernee, you's rite to be askin' 'coz we's all forgettin'. Wool iz for pouchiz wotz for purlin', n purlin's for wild talk."

"Emmy," says LuLu. "That's very concise, but I don't think Bernie will know what you mean."

"I'll explain!" says Donna. "Bernie, I told you that I'd seen Emmy 'purling', didn't I?"

"Well, y-e-s."

"We can all do that if we make our own pouches from wool we've gathered and spun with our own hands. When we can do 'purling', we'll be able to understand the wild talk with creatures."

"Sounds good to me!" says Bernie. "You can count me in."

"But you must have a 'bowl of things' to power your pouch," says Pip.

"I knows 'bout them!" says Billy. "You's needin' somethin' to be puttin' special things in, like a bowl, 'n sort out all your things 'n put what you loves best in your bowl. Keep it close 'n keep your pouch in it when it's made."

"It's all very strange, but I don't mind having a go," says Bernie.

"Hooray! Dad's coming too," sings Larky.

"Coming? Where?"

"Oh, just to the woods."

"Ah!"

They work with the wool all day, talking and laughing and getting excited about what purling will be like; they are all looking forward to purling and being with creatures, and their excitement is mixed with a little bit of fear. Someone asks Emmy a question about purling, and he replies simply that purling will happen when they are ready. He doesn't say any more than that.

Whenever Emmy needs a nap, he snuggles into his pouch in the bowl of things. It might be his bowl, or it might be LuLu's or Pip's, it doesn't matter. If his pouch isn't there, he curls up in a bundle of wool threads. Within moments of going to sleep, he will be purling.

He can never tell where purling will take him — except when he is being called by someone. It might be in Tillings Wood or in the open fields, in the town or by the sea, or even high in the sky. He meets creatures when he's purling and talks with them, learning about their lives and the wild web.

Emmy is thinking about Dungl; he knows that Dungl is not dangerous, he's not a threat, he's lost and angry like Billy. Emmy goes to sleep asking the great wave for help.

He finds himself purling above fields, and looking down, he sees Dungl standing on the wreck of an old car whacking what remains of the glass in the windows with a stick. Hovering above, just out of reach of the stick, Emmy watches. Dungl doesn't notice him because he is working so hard at smashing up the old car. It's hot work and after a while he stops for a rest.

"I's very 'appy seein' you killin' masheen, 'coz I's nevva 'avin' big luv ov masheenz."

Dungl looks around in all directions, except upwards, trying to see where this strange voice is coming from. Even though he'd spied on Billy and Larky and seen the mouse purling, he hadn't heard the mouse's voice properly.

"Who's there? Where are ya?"

"You's lookin' all evry way but nevva mi way, I's up 'ere."

The boy looks upwards — and gasps!

"I's seein' fairies 'n all!"

"Iz you Dungl?"

"Who's askin'?"

"Mi name's Emmy n I's a mouse from uvva world. I's only toy mouse in ooman world but I's a real mouse bak 'ome."

Careful to stay just out of reach, Emmy moves as close as he can to Dungl's face. They are quiet, looking at each other.

"Be comin' wiv Emmy," he says, purling slowly up and away. Dungl shrugs and jumps down from the car to follow the mouse.

"Must be gettin' soft or summat," he mutters. "But I's 'avin' a feelin'."

The place where Dungl has been smashing up the abandoned car is at the end of a track where there's a gate to a field. The sheep grazing in the field take no notice of Emmy as he purls towards the trees growing on the other side, but they move away as Dungl climbs over the gate to follow.

Emmy goes on into the woods, waiting while Dungl scrambles over the fence; he is silently calling Rattltap with his heart. They come to a clearing in the woods.

"Pleez be sittin'," says Emmy. Dungl sits on a fallen branch. They are quiet; Dungl fidgets, feeling uneasy.

With a loud 'tchak' and the sound of wingbeats, Rattltap flies down from the treetops to cling to the bark of the nearest tree.

"Good morning, Mowzl Emmy. I see that you are with another human cub, would you please introduce us?"

"'Allo, Rattltap, please be meetin' Dungl."

"Greetings, Dungl, welcome to the wild talk. You are a lucky human to have met up with the flying mouse."

Dungl is surprised and puzzled. Perhaps it's because there are no other humans there making him feel angry, perhaps it's to do with the magic that the mouse brings, but whatever it is, Dungl is interested in spite of himself.

If there were other humans there, Dungl would have sneered and snorted and he would have broken the spell because that's what he's used to doing, but not this time. This time he's interested.

"Dungl, I's needin' your 'elp. Rattltap, pleez be 'xplaynin'," says Emmy.

Rattltap clears his throat with a 'tchack' or two.

"Wild creatures are not happy with what humans are doing to the wild web. What humans are doing is tearing the wild web, and it has become so badly injured that something has to be done. The problem is that humans have closed their hearts and no longer listen to the wild talk, and so they can no longer hear us, or understand us, even if they want to. Please help us by learning the wild talk."

"'Ow come I's gettin' it now?" asks Dungl, finding his voice.

"That's because of the magic that Mowzl Emmy brings. If the mouse were not here, you would not understand anything I'm saying. But you can learn, if you want to."

"'Ow does I learn it? 'n what then?"

"Be tellin' wot'z in yor 'eart, Dungl," says Emmy.

"What's it matter?"

"Dungl, pleez be tellin' Emmy wot'z in yor 'eart."

"What's it to you? It's none of your business!"

Silence. Rattltap shinters up and down the tree trunk, making a soft churring sound under his breath. Dungl feels the sound like something tickling the inside of his head.

"Dungl, pleez be tellin' wot'z in yor 'eart," says Emmy again.

Dungl is feeling defensive and cross; he can feel the anger rising up inside, but there are other feelings coming up too that he would normally cover up. He feels confused and all the feelings boil up; suddenly he shouts it all out.

"Why can't you leave me alone? I 'ates everyone, I 'ate 'em 'n I 'ates you! Leave me alone!" Dungl shrinks down, his anger spilling out of him as tears pour down his face. "I 'ates bein' me," he says quietly.

"Dungl, you's bein' truly brave."

Emmy comes close to Dungl now, right up close; and looks deep into his eyes.

"All of wot'z wild iz livin' in yor 'eart, n iz real n troof. Growd up oomans iz tellin' you uvvawize n yor 'eart iz in darkniss. I's needin' you to be livin' in yor 'eart, Dungl, livin' wild troof."

Dungl is quiet, his shoulders hunched; he stares at the ground. Rattltap flies from his tree trunk to settle on the fallen branch next to him. Dungl has never seen a wild bird so close before and he sneaks a look at the beautiful pattern of colours in the feathers, and at the wild aliveness of Rattltap's eyes and movements.

"From this day onwards," says Rattltap. "Think not about the anger that has lived in your heart for so long but think about all the things that bring the light and wild truth to your heart. Think about that acorn just there on the ground among the leaves; you have been staring at that acorn and your tears have fallen upon the acorn. Take this acorn with you now and plant it in two places: first, plant it in a place where it will be able to grow and not be interfered with so that

it can become a mighty oak and live for a thousand winters; second, plant the acorn in your heart and feel that mighty oak growing in the very middle of your being."

Rattltap pauses for a moment, before continuing.

"This acorn is your key to the wild web."

With these words, Rattltap jumps down to the ground, picks up the acorn in his bill and flies back to the broken branch; he hops onto Dungl's knee, dropping the acorn into his hand.

"Until we meet again, goodbye, young human cub," says Rattltap, and off he flies.

Dungl is stunned. Emmy breaks the silence.

"Dungl, you's very brave."

Dungl watches Emmy fade away and disappear. He remains sitting on the fallen branch for a long time, his mind a blank. Tears stream down his face and his heart aches. Suddenly he is awake! He knows exactly where to plant the acorn! Up he jumps, setting off at a run to plant his acorn — in two places at once.

~

Larky and Billy have been over to Penny's and all three are now walking to Stomper's place. The shortest way takes them along a road with trees growing beside the pavements and the houses are set back from the road. They are big houses, with gates and gardens and everything.

"Hey! Isn't that Pip's car?" says Larky, pointing at a car parked in a gateway.

"I don't know what kind of car he has," says Penny.

"You're right, Larks," says Billy. "Let's go 'n' find 'im."

"He did say we could visit him at work," says Larky, squeezing between the car and the stone gate pillar.

The children find themselves in a very tidy front garden.

"Blimey," says Billy. "I wish we 'ad a garden like this."

"I don't see Pip," says Penny.

"P'raps 'e's visitin'," says Billy.

"Let's have a look round the back," suggests Larky.

"Or knock on the door?" adds Penny.

Just then Pip appears, coming round the side of the house.

"Hallo! What a surprise! It's good to see you all; come and have a look at the garden."

"We've been looking, Mr Pip, it's brilliant!" says Larky.

"You haven't seen anything yet! Come and see."

Pip grabs a rake from the back of the car and leads them round the house to the back garden. The children gasp. They see a big tree in the background with neat, formal lawns in the foreground, and paved paths and herbaceous borders. Everything is in its right place looking very proper.

"Oooo, I wish I lived here!" cries Larky.

"Are the owners here, Mr Pip, will they mind?" asks Penny.

"No, Penny, they work in the City most of the week and come here for weekends, but not this weekend."

"Are you their gardener?"

"Well, no, funnily enough. What I'm doing is cutting that hedge over there. I'm doing that because the hedge belongs to the neighbour, and I do gardening for him, Tom Wylder."

"We could play snooker on 'ere!" cries Billy, eyeing the grass.

"Yes," says Pip. "The lawn is perfect, isn't it? There's just lawn grass, and no weeds and no moss."

The edges of the lawn are crisply trimmed, and the bordering flower beds are laid out with exotic plants, big ones at the back and smaller in front.

"Wow, it looks like it should be open to the public!" says Penny. "Mr Pip, those hedge clippings look untidy, can we help you to clear them up?"

"Yes please! Here's a rake, Billy, if you could make a start; Penny and Larky, here's a canvas bag to put the clippings in. We'll carry it out to empty it when it's full and come back for the rest."

"Where do you empty it?" asks Penny.

"Next door, you'll see in a minute," says Pip.

"Ha! That sounds like Emmy!" Larky laughs. "He's always saying 'you'll be seein'.'"

"Hmm, I wonder what he's up to today," says Pip. "Thanks for your help, I'm just going to take the tools we don't need any more back to the car, I'll be back in a minute."

The children take it in turns to rake and pick up clippings.

When Pip comes back they've almost finished and he inspects their work admiringly.

"Thank you! You've done a great job clearing up. We need to do just a little bit more because this garden is so squeaky clean. Let me show you how I do it." He sets about raking the last few leaves and when he's done there's a small pile of leaves.

"We got most of it, Mr Pip," says Billy.

"Yes, you did! Thanks, fantastic. I'm not criticising you, just showing you how I do the last bit. You've stuffed the bag well, and we've got everything in one load. I have to cut this hedge several times a year because the people who live here are very particular, as you can see. Come on! Let's go and see next door!"

Pip gathers together the corner handles of the big bag and hauls it towards the road.

"Bring the rake, please, Billy!" he calls.

"That looks heavy, can we help?" offers Penny.

"Thanks, Penny, but it's a bit awkward for two people to walk with. I'll just drag it along, it'll be fine."

Pip had moved his car earlier when he put the tools back, and now he drags the bag through the gate and along the pavement, into the gateway of the house next door.

"Please would you shut the gate for me," he says, as they leave the first garden.

Pip stops for a rest in the front garden next door. The children look around in wonder; this garden is quite different from the first garden — it's a jungle. There are bushes and trees, and patches of rough grass with wild flowers, and the house itself is overgrown with creepers and climbing plants.

"Come on, let's go around the back," says Pip, dragging the bag of hedge clippings along a path of flagstones set into the grass, like stepping stones.

At the back of the house is a small patch of lawn leading to bigger patches of long, rough grass; there are bushes and trees with grassy paths going off between them.

"It's like being in the woods!" says Larky. "How can it be so different from next door's garden?"

"The man who lives here is a wildlife photographer," explains Pip. "He's away a lot, filming. Years ago, I did a job for him and he asked me to look after his garden permanently; I said that I like to make gardens for wild plants and animals to thrive in, and he said great, do it! That was twenty years ago or more, and you can see for yourselves how things have turned out."

"Mr Pip, can we 'ave a look around?" asks Billy.

"You bet. I'm going to take this bag of stuff to the compost heap, you go and explore."

The children run off along the grassy paths, disappearing among the bushes. Pip drags the canvas bag full of hedge clippings to the back of the garden where the compost heaps are shaded by trees. The heaps are contained with old pallets placed on edge and tied to posts. Pip heaves the bag up onto one of these piles, rolling it upside down to empty it out. The children suddenly reappear, running and breathless.

"It's wonderful, Mr Pip! It's so alive, I love it!" says Penny.

"I'm glad, Penny, I'm really glad you like it."

"Is you burnin' that stuff? I loves a bonfire," says Billy.

"Sorry to disappoint you, Billy, but no, I don't need to burn anything as Nature does that herself, and much better. These heaps are like very slow fires; the plant material rots down, and the heaps can get quite warm. This heap is the 'compost heap', and is for leaves, soft prunings, and kitchen waste. It rots down quite quickly. I'm spreading out the new clippings and treading them down. Sometimes I sprinkle some soil over the top to add the soil bacteria and fungi that rot it all down; invertebrates — you know, creepy crawlies — help a lot by chewing it all up as it decays.

"The other heaps are what I call 'bug heaps', and these are for the woody prunings that rot down very slowly. I put heavy stones or logs on top to squash the heaps down. These heaps are really good for invertebrates to hide away in and for hedgehogs to hibernate in. Grass snakes too, and slow-worms.

"I haven't burned anything in this garden, or taken anything away, in twenty years. That's one reason it feels so good here, everything belongs here and things that die go back into the soil."

"What if a tree's fallin' or dyin' or summat?" asks Billy.

"You may have noticed piles of logs here and there, left to rot and feed the invertebrates and fungi. Mr Wylder, the photographer, has a wood-stove a bit like mine, and he burns some of the logs on that. But we leave as much dead wood as we can in the garden — as long as it's not likely to fall on someone's head."

"Mr Pip," asks Penny. "How can this garden feel so different from the one next door?"

"Well, Penny, that's a good question. I don't know the answer except to say what Emmy might say: in this garden, the wild web is healthy and not too torn. Next door the wild web has been cut, mown and poisoned, until there is nearly nothing left. Nearly all the plants growing next door are cultivated varieties and exotics, which means that they come from faraway countries and don't belong here — ecologically, I mean.

"You see, many people see nature as untidy and frightening; some people like to make things tidy and orderly, and in so doing they destroy the homes of the plants and creatures that would naturally be living here. When the wild web is destroyed, the place feels lifeless, even though it might look like an exhibition garden.

"Mr Wylder wants his garden to be home to as many living things as possible: plants, animals, insects, birds, fungi, everything!" Pip pauses, looking around at the children. "I'm boring you, I think."

"Not exactly," says Penny. "It's good to understand a bit more about what Emmy means when he says that humans are making holes in the wild web."

"And you two?" Pip asks Larky and Billy.

"Yeah, Penny's right, we's needin' to know what Emmy's on about," says Billy.

"Sometimes I just stop listening 'cos I'm listening to the birds," says Larky.

Pip knows that the children are on the edge of boredom, but he decides to go on talking anyway. "Just now I said about things not belonging — what do you think 'belong' means when we are talking about the wild web?"

"I know," says Larky. "Things that would be living here if no one meddled with it!"

"Exactly right, Larky, good for you," says Pip. "Let me give you an example. There's a young oak tree over there, well, it's probably sixty years old or so, but that's quite young because it could live for five hundred years and more. Now, that oak tree provides food and shelter to many more species of insect, moss and lichen than there are days in the year. How many is that?"

"Three hundred and sixty-five!" chorus the children.

"Yes, good. Now then — next door, did you notice the big tree in the middle of the lawn?"

"Yea," says Billy. "That's an oak 'n all, ain't it?"

"Right, it is an oak but it's a different species, called Turkey Oak, that grows naturally in eastern Mediterranean countries. It grows well here, but the number of creatures and mosses and lichens and fungi that it supports is . . . guess what?"

"I've no idea," says Penny, shrugging.

"Well neither do I," says Pip. "But if you look closely you will not find much. You won't find lots of species of caterpillar eating the leaves, you won't find the bark thick with moss and lichen, and you won't see birds foraging in the canopy because there aren't any insects there to eat. Why do you think that is?"

"Maybe the tree is poisonous," suggests Penny.

"Good, Penny, that's part of the answer. Any more ideas?"

"Well, why?" says Billy impatiently.

"In countries where that kind of tree naturally grows, there are many insects and plants and creatures that have evolved alongside it, and are able to live in and on it. That's what the wild web is: each place has its own 'ecology'."

"Mr Pip, if all these things are eating the oak tree in Mr Wylder's garden, why doesn't it get ill and die?" asks Larky.

"It might look ill if anything ate too many leaves but when things are healthy there's a balance; lots of caterpillars means lots of birds feeding on them and there aren't too many birds because they are eaten by sparrow hawks and other predators."

"Ugghh, that's horrible," says Larky.

"As Emmy would say, it's the wild web and the way of the great wave."

"But what about next door?" asks Penny.

"Next door there are not many species, and none of them, or very few of them, 'belong'. There is no wild web," says Pip.

"So, what's the problem?" asks Billy, fed up with all the talk.

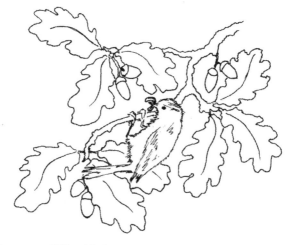

"I'm sorry, Billy, I'll shut up now, but I just want to say that the problem is that there are now so many humans doing things like next door that nature is disappearing, the wild web is disappearing… hey, I've got an idea! Let's go for a drive! I want to show you something."

"Can we pick up Stomper on the way?" asks Larky "We were on our way to her place when we saw your car."

"Yes, let's do it. You'll have to show me the way."

Pip finishes tidying up in Mr Wylder's garden, and they set off for Stomper's place. She's pleased to see them, but she hasn't met Pip before, so she's a bit shy to start with.

Her mum, Linda, invites everyone in, offering lemonade and biscuits all round.

"Thanks, Linda! We're really thirsty!" says Larky.

"You're welcome," says Linda.

Linda makes tea for Pip and herself, and they carry their mugs into the garden, leaving the children to themselves at the kitchen table. Pip tells Linda about how the children have been helping him with gardening, and explains that a friend, Emmy, introduced him to Billy and Larky. Since then he's met Larky's Mum and Dad, and Penny too.

"I want to take them for a drive to show them some fields up on the hill," says Pip.

"Show them some fields? Whatever for?" says Linda, surprised.

"Well, it's a long story, but it's about wildlife and ecology."

"Oh, what's that?" says Linda.

"You're welcome to come and find out, if you would like to."

Linda looks uncertain.

"You might feel better about Stomper coming with us if you come too," says Pip.

"Stom... I mean Jackie is welcome to go with you anyway, I'm not worried. I would like to come, but how long will you be?"

"Not long."

"Alright then, I'll come."

"Good!" says Pip. "Come on, you lot! We're off!"

Pip has to re-arrange the tools in the back of his car so that he can put the seats down to make enough room. Linda gets into the front passenger seat.

"Mum! Are you coming too?" asks Stomper.

"Yes, Jackie."

"Good-oh."

Pip drives out of town and up into the hills. He parks in a gateway to a field where they look over a field of young wheat.

"Let's climb over — climb the hinge end!" says Pip. "Keep to the edge of the field so we don't trample the crop. Alright, I'm going to risk giving you a little lesson in ecology."

"What's ecology?" asks Stomper, as she pulls on the jumper she'd grabbed at home. Her curly red hair pops out all frizzed up.

"Well, ecology is about how wild nature works; it's about food chains, food webs and homes for living creatures and plants." Pip pauses to see if anyone says they are bored or anything, but nobody says anything, so he carries on.

"This field is planted with wheat, you can just see where the stems are beginning to bulge as the flower head grows inside; wheat is a type of grass. Do you see how clean the crop is? The ground underneath the wheat is bare of weeds right to the edge of the field. You can see the edge of the grass by the hedge, it's yellow from the weed killer that was used to stop the weeds from spoiling the crop.

"I want you to listen and look with all your might, and then tell me what you hear and see."

They are silent, listening and looking.

"Mr Pip, 'ow long is I lookin' and listenin'?" asks Billy.

"As long as it takes to know what I'm getting at."

"I's gettin' it already," says Billy.

"I thought you might, Billy. Tell us."

"Well, Mr Pip, there ain't nothin' to 'ear nor see 'cos there's nothin' 'ere 'xcept that plane over 'ead 'n cars makin' a racket."

"Right, Billy, well observed. There are no insects in this field. There's no weeds; it's just one cultivated variety of wheat, there's not a natural plant in sight except the hedge, which was cut to within an inch of its life last winter and is only now beginning to grow again.

"There are no birds because there's no food or habitat for them. This field is about sixty acres, and the surrounding fields are a similar size. Most of the land up here is like this. It's a perfect crop, efficiently grown, but the wild web has been destroyed. Even though this field looks green and healthy, it's really an extinct habitat. This is an ecological desert."

"What's the wild web?" asks Linda. She doesn't know what Pip is talking about but tries to show an interest.

"Imagine, Linda, before humans ploughed this land, before humans had cut down the trees to make pasture for their grazing animals, back then this land supported a wildwood of many thousands of species of plant, animal and insect, lichen and moss, fern and fungus. Everything you can imagine. If you could stand in that ancient woodland and close your eyes, you would hear the soundscape of the natural habitat for this bit of the Earth's surface, and you would feel the isness of the habitat.

"The wildwood developed after the ice retreated following the last ice age and changed as climate changed. The health of that primeval wildwood is what the wild web means. There were humans then, it's true, but they were few in numbers, and they were not yet cutting down the trees on a big scale.

"So, what's you sayin', Mr Pip?" says Billy, sighing.

"Well, imagine what we see here happening all over the world, and happening more and more because there are ever more humans, humans needing more food and homes, needing more land — imagine how this tears holes in the wild web. Imagine how the wild web is being torn, all over the world! This is how I understand what Emmy is telling us. His message is that we have to give land back to nature. We must learn to farm without destroying nature. Well, that's how I see it anyway."

Everyone is silent, looking at Pip.

"I'm sorry," says Pip. "I shouldn't rant like that, it must be very boring. Stupid of me. I get carried away, because I've seen so much wild nature disappear, just in my own lifetime."

"No, Mr Pip," cries Stomper. "Not stupid at all. I haven't got the foggiest what all those words mean, but I'm hearing what you're saying and yeah, I'm right there with you!"

"Me 'n all, Mr Pip," says Billy. "Whatever you's sayin'."

"We all are," says Penny. "You know how upset we've all been recently with the stories. Mr Pip, you have just made it easier to see. We know what to do, we just have to figure out how to do it."

"Thank you, all," says Pip, relieved. "I thought for a moment I'd gone too far talking too much."

"What should we do, Mr Pip?" asks Larky.

"We do as Emmy suggests; we make our pouches, we learn the wild talk, we learn from creatures about the wild web, and it's from learning about the wild web that we'll know what we have to do."

"I don't have a clue what you're on about," says Linda.

"Mr Pip, can we have stories for Linda and Stomper? Then they'll get it!"

"Good idea, Larky. Why not all come around to my place some afternoon after school, or two afternoons perhaps, and we'll read 'Wot 'Appnd'? I hope you'll come, Linda, and you too, Stomper Jack!"

"Hey! I like that!" says Stomper. "Stomper Jack!"

Pip drives back to town, dropping everyone off at Stomper's place. He leaves them there, driving on alone. He has a worry nagging at him. *I wonder where all this is going?* he thinks but has no answer. It's a question for Emmy, but Pip can imagine what he would say:

"Pippee, we's nevva kno-in' wot great wave iz bringin'."

~

Dungl is quiet and thoughtful after his encounter with the mouse and the woodpecker. By Wednesday he can't remember how long it's been since he met them, but it was only last Sunday.

Bottl is always talking at him and egging him on to do stuff, but he feels confused and irritated. At lunch break Bottl finds Dungl under the tree in the playground.

"'Ere, Dungl, that Billy's up to summat. Look at 'im, thick as thieves with them girls 'e is. Let's go 'n 'ave a laugh."

"Forget it, I ain't doin' it," says Dungl.

"Gone soft 'ave ya? What's up?"

"I've got stuff to think about."

"Come on, you'll 'urt your 'ead!"

"Just drop it, Bottl," says Dungl, fiercely. "Just leave it."

"Ooo. Temper, temper. 'As some girlie got to ya?"

Dungl turns away from Bottl. He can't talk to *him* about how he's feeling. Dungl realises that the only person he might be able to talk to is Billy.

Bottl watches Dungl staring over the fence into the distance. *He's lovesick for sure, I wonder who it is?* Bottl thinks, walking off across the playground. *I'll 'ave to keep a close eye on 'im.*

~

"I'm going out for a bit, Mum," says Dungl, after tea.

"Alright, David, don't be late back, please."

"Alright."

When Dungl has gone, his mother gazes thoughtfully at the closed door; she's been worried about him since he came home from school with a black eye. Whatever it is she's feeling, she can't quite put her finger on it.

Dungl walks without a plan, wandering aimlessly about. He decides that he's got to pluck up the courage to do what he's got to do, like getting into cold water. Thinking about how cold it's going to be isn't going to help. Just have to jump. But no, this is going to be harder than that.

"I'm going to visit Billy," he says out loud, turning his steps towards the street where Billy lives, walking fast, determined, with no more hesitation in him at all. He arrives at Billy's house and, with his heart in his mouth, knocks on the door.

"Hallo, dear," says Nan, answering the door. "I expect you are looking for Billy."

"That's right, missus," says Dungl.

"He's out at the moment, would you like to come in for a squash and a biscuit?"

"Er, yeah, thanks."

Dungl thinks that he might as well, now he's here, and maybe he'll learn some things about Billy.

"Sit down, dear. Are you a friend of Billy's?" says Nan. "What's your name?"

"Erm, sort of. My name's David."

"Well, David, you can call me 'Nan' like Billy does, that would be nice."

"Alright, Nan."

Nan makes an orange squash drink for Dungl and opens a tin of biscuits. "There you are, help yourself."

"Thanks."

"Are you in Billy's class at school?" asks Nan.

"No, same class as Larky."

"Larky, yes, she's a lovely girl."

"I don't really know 'er," Dungl mumbles through his biscuit.

Nan can see that David is nervous. She wonders about his black eye but decides that it might be best not to ask about it.

"Do you know where Billy is, Nan?" Dungl asks eventually.

"They went to the woods, it's such nice weather."

"Who's 'they'?"

"Oh! I'm not sure, David, because they were meeting someone, but he went off with Larky and Penny."

"Right-oh, Nan, thanks. I'll go lookin' for 'em."

Dungl goes on his way, Nan watching him from the doorway. As he walks towards Tillings Wood, he remembers how he'd spied on Billy and Larky. He realises now, having met the mouse and the woodpecker, how they must have been feeling. He feels a kind of ache inside; he doesn't know if he's sorry for what he did, or if he's longing for something, or what. Maybe both. Yes, definitely longing for something.

Arriving at the woods, Dungl goes directly to the bivouac where he first spied on Billy and Larky. He's surprised to see the bivvy broken up and the sticks scattered about all over the place. There's no sign of Billy and the others, so he walks on into the woods, often stopping to listen in case he might hear them. He hears birds and squirrels and other woodland sounds, and he smiles, remembering how much he likes being in the woods.

After walking for a long time, he stops for a rest and another 'listen'. He's about to move on again when he hears a distant sound of a girl laughing.

"That'll be Larky, I reckon!" he says out loud, setting off in the direction the sound came from. Within a few minutes he hears voices; he moves closer slowly and quietly, careful not to tread on twigs that would snap and give him away. When he's close enough to make out what's being said, he hears Penny's voice.

"Stomper Jack, will you come with us on Sunday to Donna's?"

"Would that be alright?"

"Course it's alright!" says Billy. "It'll be good. There's loads o' wool so you can 'ave some 'n make your own krochettin'."

"Ha-ha! Billy!" says Penny, playfully. "It's 'kroshaying', not krotchetting. I think it's a French word."

Dungl knows that he must show himself. If he hesitates now, his courage will fail him. He steps forward from the bushes into the clearing. The children stare at him in astonishment while the sound of Penny's laughter fades away to silence.

Penny notices Dungl's discomfort and she can see that he hasn't come to pick a fight. She wants to help him.

"Dungl?" she says, gently. "Are you alright? Come, join us."

Penny's gentleness eases the tension in the air and Dungl moves a few paces towards them. His voice is unusually wobbly.

"Erm, I er, I wanted to see you, Billy. I went to your place 'n your Nan said you'd be 'ere. I's spent ages lookin'."

Billy is looking uncomfortable too. He notices Dungl's black eye straight away, seeing that it's more yellow and purple now, so it's healing all right.

"I 'ope your eye's alright," says Billy. "I's sorry I 'it ya."

Dungl is silent.

"What do you want to see Billy about?" asks Penny, her voice again soothing the tension.

"I's met the mouse 'n the woodpecker."

Billy squares up to Dungl, a fierce jealousy erupting inside.

"What do you mean you met the mouse?" he demands.

"Billy, it's alright," says Penny. "What happened, Dungl?"

"I was up by Blackstone Farm smashin' up that car wreck, 'n the mouse was 'overin' over'ead 'n 'e talks to me 'n gets me to follow 'im to the woods…"

Dungl tells the whole story of the woodpecker and the acorn, and then he pauses; the children see tears in his eyes.

"I plants the acorn in a special place," he continues. "The woodpecker was right, it's in me 'eart as well 'n I don't know what's 'appenin' to me, 'n I's 'appy 'n I's un'appy at the same time . . . 'n I's feelin' sick . . . 'n I's 'opin' you'd understand . . ."

Dungl falls silent, too emotional to say any more.

Billy walks slowly over to Dungl. Billy's jealousy and anger drain away into the ground, leaving him light and free. He wants to give Dungl a hug but thinks that might be a mistake, so he puts an arm around his shoulders.

"Come and join us, Dungl," he says, quietly.

"Welcome, Dungl!" chorus the girls.

"What a surprise!" says Stomper Jack. "In at the deep end, Dungl, just like me. I haven't even met Emmy yet."

"I don't understand," says Dungl, looking puzzled.

"Dungl," Larky begins to explain. "It's a long story about the mouse. None of us understand any of it really, but we know what we feel. Pip has invited us all round to his place for stories about the mouse. Will you come too?"

"Good idea, Larks!" cries Billy. "Pip invited you 'n your Mum 'n Stomper, 'n now we's invitin' Dungl. Pip'll love it."

"Who's Pip?" asks Dungl, feeling overwhelmed.

"Pip's the gardener," says Penny. "He's writing the mouse's story. He reads us chapters of the story so that we can understand what's happened. Emmy calls the story 'Wot 'Appnd'."

"Let's go to Pip's after school tomorrow!" cries Stomper Jack. They all agree except Dungl, who remains silent.

"Dungl, will you come too? We'd like you to," says Penny.

"Er, yeah, where?" says Dungl hesitantly.

"Come to my place," says Billy. "We'll go from there."

"Alright, thanks."

~

Dungl visit's Billy after school the next day and they walk together to Pip's place.

"What 'appened to you when you met the mouse?" asks Dungl. Billy describes his first meeting with Emmy, saying 'sorry' to a bramble, and getting angry. Dungl wants to know more.

"But 'ow was you *feelin'*?" insists Dungl.

"After meetin' Emmy? It was like bein' ill; I didn't know what was 'appenin'."

"So, does you know what's 'appenin' now, 'cos I's feelin' sick 'n all? What's 'appenin' to me, Billy?"

"Did Emmy ask you 'What's in your 'eart'?"

"Yeah, that's when I starts feelin' like pukin'. I was angry."

"Me too. Dungl, you 'n me's the same, ain't we? It's stupid fightin' each other."

"Yeah."

"These stories Pip's tellin', they'll 'elp you feel better."

"'Ow's stories doin' that?"

"'Cos of Emmy. You'll see. It's somethin' about 'ow our 'earts'll grow bigger 'n we won't 'urt as much."

Dungl shrugs his shoulders. "I don't get it."

Billy puts a hand on his shoulder. "It'll be alright."

When they get to Pip's place, they find the others already there: Stomper and her mother Linda, and Larky and Penny.

Pip and Linda are introduced to Dungl, who mumbles a 'hallo'; he's feeling shy and uncomfortable with so many grown-ups about.

"I'm glad you've all come," says Pip. "Let's go out to the back, it's such a lovely warm day. Larky and Penny, would you grab some cushions and a blanket or two from the sofa, thanks."

Pip's back garden is small and overgrown and looks like the edge of a bit of woodland with a scraggly bit of grass in front. But it's not the edge of woodland at all; the next-door gardens are just a few feet away. Everyone gets settled on the grass while Pip sets up a folding chair; he sits with the orange ring binder on his lap.

"We should start at the beginning," Pip suggests. "That way Stomper, Linda and Dungl can understand how it all began. I hope you don't mind."

"No, Mr Pip, we'd like to hear it again, it always helps explain things when we hear it again," says Penny.

Pip reads 'Typhoon', ''Allo', and 'Time Capsules', and then there's questions and talk. Billy, Larky and Penny answer the questions that the others come up with. Dungl remains silent.

"Lots of your questions will be answered in the next stories, so do be patient," says Pip. "I'll read some more and then we'll leave it until tomorrow. Emmy likes to sleep on things to see how he feels later, perhaps we'll do a bit of that ourselves."

Pip reads several more chapters until he's tired and has to stop.

"O-w-a!" cries Penny. "Please, Mr Pip, just one more."

"No, Penny, I'm tired and you should probably all be getting home now."

"Thanks, Mr Pip," says Stomper. "I'm really glad to be hearing Emmy's story, I can't wait for tomorrow!"

"Thank you, Pip," says Linda. "I'm glad I came along. Is it alright if I come again tomorrow?"

"Yes, Mum, of course!" says Stomper.

"Yes, Linda, Stomper's right, you're very welcome," says Pip.

They go, leaving Pip sitting in his chair. He watches the birds return to the feeders hanging from the bird table. Having so many people around had frightened the birds off and they chattered in the bushes making little 'go away, this is our patch' sorts of noises. They don't mind Pip sitting there, and soon they are all back squabbling over the sunflower seeds. Pip smiles sleepily, watching their antics for a while before closing his eyes.

~

The next day is chilly and when the children and Linda arrive at Pip's, he directs them to the front room where it's warmer. He reads more of 'Wot 'Appnd', getting to the wool gathering and Muffin's death.

Linda and Stomper cry their eyes out when Pip reads 'Silk and Sad', and they cry their eyes out all over again at the end of the wool gathering when Muffin dies.

Dungl has been silent all along and to everyone's surprise, he suddenly bursts out with an angry question.

"I don't get it. What's we goin' to *do*?"

Billy is quick to answer.

"I's like you, Dungl, I's been angry 'cos we can't do anything. But we can! I's always liked bein' outside with nature 'n livin' things, but I's never thought nothin' 'bout it. Nor 'as I ever been told anythin' real by anybody 'till Emmy comes along, 'n I's learnin' real stuff 'bout nature 'n what's 'appenin' 'n what 'umans is doin'. What I's feelin' is that what's 'appenin' ain't alright, 'n my 'eart's 'urtin' 'n I 'as to do somethin' to 'elp. I wants to be learnin' from wild things 'n I wants to be learnin' the wild talk 'n I wants to be purlin'!"

"Well said, Billy!" says Pip. "Quite a speech!"

"What can we do straight away?" asks Linda. "I want to do something too."

"Hooray! That's great, Mum, so do I," says Stomper.

"The first thing to do is to get a bowl of things sorted out," suggests Penny. "Come with us to Donna's on Sunday and we'll begin making pouches; there's loads of wool, so you come and make pouches too."

Dungl is fidgeting and looking uncomfortable.

"'Ow's all this wool stuff goin' to 'elp?"

"It's fun, Dungl, you'll love it, I bet," says Larky.

"Remember the chapter called 'Pouches and Things,?" Penny asks Dungl. "Well, the pouches are a way to be closer to the invisible ones. We have to make a special effort to gather the wool, card it and spin it, plait it and crochet the pouches with the heartstrings; and to do all that, we have to really want to. Emmy's said that it's something to do with getting ready for purling."

"You's rite, Pennee."

"Emmy! Where did you spring from?" cries Larky.

"'Allo, Linda, 'allo, Stomper Jack, 'allo, Dungl," Emmy says in greeting. Linda and Stomper stare at him in surprise.

"Wen you's wantin' a littl majik to come, you's 'avin' to be makin' space for majik to be livin' in. Wot you's doin' wiv wool iz makin' space in your 'earts. You's bein' re-knittd."

"Why does it 'urt?" asks Dungl. "I's 'urtin'."

"Feelin' wot'z real iz 'urtin' 'till yor 'earts iz fully big. You's needin' currij to be 'oldin' troof in yor 'earts."

"We all feel it, Dungl," says Penny. "We understand how you feel. We've had a bit more time to get used to it than you, and we've had each other too. Now you have us to help you."

"It's 'appened so sudden," says Dungl, his voice a bit croaky.

"I's sorry you's 'urtin, Dungl. You's wiv frendz now who's kno-in' wot'z in yor 'eart. You's nevva to be wurryin 'bout doin', you be simplee bein'."

Emmy hovers close to Dungl as he says this, looking into his eyes for a long time. When he turns away, Dungl closes his eyes and smiles.

Emmy then moves close to Stomper, and to Linda, looking deep into their eyes, and soon they are smiling too.

"I's 'opin you's all comin' to Donna's to be makin' pouchiz. You'sll be purlin' before long, n I'sll be wiv you."

Emmy slowly fades and as they watch, he disappears with a pop.

"It's confusing for us all, Dungl, as Penny's said," says Pip. "Emmy is pushing us to get on with making our pouches, because he knows that when we're purling, we'll understand lots of things that we can't understand now. If LuLu were here she could tell us about purling, because she has been purling, a lot since Muffin died. Let's all go home now and get ready for Sunday. We'll meet up at Donna's and get on with making our pouches."

"Right-oh, Mr Pip!" says Billy. "Come to Nan's on Sunday, Dungl, and we'll go together."

"Thanks, Billy."

There's a lot of chattering as everyone gets ready to go home, but Pip is not listening. He's tired from the reading, and he's remembering how hard it was for him when he was being 're-knitted'. He looks at Dungl with admiration.

Pip is looking forward to Sunday and looking forward to purling. He hasn't been strong enough to begin yet, except for the time when Emmy had to rescue him, and he was a bit see-through.

He says goodbye to everyone as they leave, and when at last he's alone again, he puts his feet up on the sofa and is asleep before you could say 'Batz iz sleepin'.

~

When Sunday morning arrives, Pip is reluctant to wake up.

"Be wakin', Pippee! We's goin' to Donna's!" cries Emmy.

There's no response, so Emmy climbs onto his chest and bounces about, singing a 'bouncing about' song.

"Fridee sox, bloo sox, stripee sox, blak sox, smellee sox, knee sox, Thursdee sox, pink sox."

"Stop! Emmy, alright — enough, I'm awake! Please stop!"

"Ha-ha!"

"That really was a test of endurance."

"You's rite, Pippee. It's tee oh eee numba three!"

"You rascal, Emmy."

"You's luvin' it."

"What's a 'tee oh eee'?"

"Term of Endearment iz tee ohh eee numba one."

"Ah! Of course! Alright, time to get up and get going. Emmy, are you coming with me, or purling?"

"I'sll come wiv you."

"Good. Let's go."

"I's reddi!"

~

"Hallo, Pip! Hallo, Emmy!" Larky greets them when they arrive. "Everyone's here now except Billy and Dungl."

"Is Dungl coming? How odd!" says Pip.

"Dungl and Billy are friends now," Larky explains. "Don't you remember? Dungl was at your house just the other day."

"Remarkable. Yes, I remember now."

"'Allo, Larkee, I's wantin' yor 'and," cries Emmy, as he jumps from Pip's shirt pocket towards Larky. She shrieks as she jumps to catch him.

"Oh, Emmy, your feather's a bit battered, I'll find a new one."

"Larkee, fankz, n I's needin' an 'eadband wot'z made wiv 'eartstring n fredz."

"Emmy, I'll make you one, and find you a new feather."

"Fankz, Larkee."

In the kitchen, busy people look up from what they are doing, say hallo and straight away go back to their carding or spinning or plying or plaiting. There's lots of chatter going on and Donna has to call out to get attention.

"Who wants to start making a pouch?"

"Me!"

"Me!"

"I see! Everybody wants to start making a pouch. LuLu, you're good at crocheting, aren't you?"

"Quite good, Donna."

"Would you teach people who aren't so good?"

"Yes, of course."

"Could you start with Linda and Penny, please? They should get the hang of it quickly and then there'll be three able to teach."

Penny and Linda go with LuLu to the front room, taking their plaited 'heartstring' with them. It's a bit quieter, so they'll be able to concentrate better. LuLu gives them each a crochet hook and shows them how to start. Making a pouch is like making a spiral, starting at the bottom and going around and around; the trick is in how many stitches you add or take away to make the growing pouch get wider or narrower. LuLu had learned how to make the right shape when she made the first three pouches with the wool sent by Pearl from Emmy's home world.

"I've written out a pattern," explains LuLu. "Once you get the hang of the crocheting, the pattern will remind you about the number of stitches. I've done enough copies for everyone, so you can keep these."

"Thanks, LuLu."

A little later, Larky hears a knock on the front door and she runs to open it.

"Sorry, Larks, we got talkin'," says Billy.

"It's alright, Billy. Hallo, Dungl, glad you could come."

"'Allo, Larky," says Dungl, smiling shyly.

Billy notices Emmy tucked into Larky's T-shirt

"Hey, Emmy! What's you doin' 'idin' there?"

"'Allo, Billee, 'allo, Dungl, I's very 'appy you's 'ere. Larkeez makin' Emmy an 'eadband wiv 'eartstring."

"I ain't even made an 'artstring yet," says Billy, with a laugh.

"I 'ain't done none of it yet," says Dungl.

"That's remindin' me, Emmy," says Billy. "I's got loads of wool so Dungl could be usin' mine. Alright?"

"Orite, Billee."

"Thanks, Em."

They go to the kitchen and Donna quickly organises them somewhere to sit and shows them what to do.

Dungl watches Bernie carding wool, and Donna spinning wool, and he watches Larky plying two threads together, and he watches

Stomper plaiting a heartstring.

"Billy, can I do spinnin'?" he says.

"Yeah! Donna'll show you 'ow."

"I'll show you, Dungl, bring some of Billy's carded wool and come over here," says Donna.

She teaches Dungl the basics, which he gets the hang of very quickly. Donna is surprised, but not as surprised as Dungl. He's really enjoying himself. Who would have thought it?

When he's got going enough to be left on his own, Donna makes up a tray of drinks and biscuits for the pouch-makers in the front room.

"How's it going?"

LuLu sighs. "Well, Donna, we have a little problem."

"Problem?"

"The heartstring is much too thick to use for making an Emmy-sized pouch. I should've realised sooner. It's because we can't spin the wool fine enough. Anyway, we decided to use the single-ply, spun wool, it's perfect — look at these!"

Donna examines the pouches they've been working on. "Oh! LuLu, they're beautiful! And nearly finished!"

"Linda and Penny are both good at it and can teach the others. I just need to show them how to finish off."

"Donna," says Linda. "When we've finished these, I'd like to do some spinning, I've always wanted to have a go at that."

"Of course, come to the kitchen when you're ready. I'll go and talk to Emmy and the others about the heartstring being too thick."

"Alright, see you later," says Penny. "Thanks for the drinks."

Donna finds Emmy tangling himself up in the candyfloss clouds of carded wool that Dungl is using. He's laughing and making Dungl smile.

"Emmy, can I ask you something?"

"Ha-ha! Iz Emmy needin' choklit?"

"No, Emmy, chocolate comes later. Emmy, the heartstrings are too thick to make the pouches. LuLu and Penny and Linda are making lovely pouches with the single-ply wool, is that alright?"

Emmy is quiet. "Donna, please be carryin' Emmy to LuLu. C u inna mo, Dungl!"

"Later, Emmy," says Dungl.

Donna frees Emmy from the carded wool and carries him to see LuLu who has just finished a pouch. She helps him to climb in.

"LuLu, you's done good, pouch iz perfik."

"Thanks, Em. So, it's alright if we don't use heartstring?"

"Pouchiz iz nevva mindin'. Wot'z matterin' iz you's made

'eartstring wiv luv in yor 'earts n you's all bein' re-knittd."

"So, we don't need to ply the wool or plait the heartstring?"

"Plyin' n plattin' iz for yor 'eart's eeze."

"Oh, Emmy," says Penny. "The magic is growing!"

"You's 'xaklee rite, Pennee, you's feelin' great wave."

"I don't know about that," says Donna, re-tying her apron. "It means we've got miles of heartstring we won't be using."

"We can use it for other things, Donna," Penny suggests.

"Of course. LuLu, I'll send two others in here for their first crochet lesson — is that alright?"

"Fine."

~

Things settle down as everyone gets busy with something; there's lots of joking and teasing — Pip gets teased because he's not very good with the wool and when it's time for his crochet lesson, he can't get the hang of it at all: he's all thumbs.

"I'll never get this!" he grumbles, dropping another stitch. He goes on trying, but it doesn't get any easier.

"I know what!" he says happily. "Instead of trying to crochet I'm going to read stories. If anyone wants to hear a chapter of 'Wot 'Appnd', I'll read it! I've got a pouch already, the one LuLu made using the wool from Emmy's home world; it's extra magic!"

The others have a good giggle about Pip being beaten by a crochet hook, but soon the requests for chapters of 'Wot 'Appnd' are called out and Pip gets reading. Between stories there are questions and lots of talk; there's a good feeling in the room as everybody is happy to be working together and listening to stories.

The next time Donna makes a snack, they stop and relax.

"Larks, where's Emmy gone?" asks Billy.

"He's asleep in Donna's bowl of things."

"Where's it at?"

"On the dresser over there," says Donna, pointing.

Billy goes to look, seeing Emmy curled up like a dormouse, fast asleep. He notices shells in the bowl, and dried flowers, and some small black-and-white photographs of Donna's family.

"I's not wakin' 'im, 'e might be purlin'."

"If he's purling, you wouldn't be able to wake him," says LuLu.

"Is that really true?" says Stomper.

"I think so, but I'm not certain."

"I's not riskin' it," says Billy. "I'll be askin' you all instead."

"Ask what, Billy?" says Pip.

"I's thinkin' of givin' me Nan some 'artstring — I's meanin' wool now we's changin' the plan — so she can make pouches for Grandpa 'n 'erself, 'n I's wonderin' if it'll work 'cos Nan 'asn't found the wool nor done the spinnin' nor nothin'."

"Billy, I think it will be fine and it will work," says LuLu.

"Why do you say that?" asks Penny.

"Because Billy is so close with his Nan and Grandpa, Billy's heart is big enough for all of them!"

"Thanks, LuLu," says Billy. "I's thinkin' Grandpa's already purlin' 'n if 'e can be in a pouch 'e'll be 'appy as a skylark!"

Pip reads 'Wot 'Appnd' from the beginning to help Bernie, Linda, Stomper Jack and Dungl to catch up. It's a busy day, and later, when they get tired, they sit down comfortably to listen to the stories.

Pip gets tired of reading, so he stops after 'Snow!'. Emmy is awake again now and singing quietly.

"Batz iz wakin', batz iz wakin', batz iz wakin' . . ."

The others join in with the 'Up from the day' bit and sing along with Emmy until the song is ended.

Stomper sighs. "I love the way the song slows down at the end! I could go to sleep right now," she says dreamily.

It's time to bag up what they want and get ready to go home.

"We'll need a few days like this before we've all finished our pouches," says Donna. "Please come back next week if you can."

"When's we purlin', Emmy?" asks Dungl, who's done so well today he's already started to make his own pouch.

"You's nevva kno-in', till great wave 'appnz. You'sll be purlin' wen you's ready."

Billy turns towards Emmy. "I's makin' extra wool 'n 'artstring for me Nan, so she can make a pouch for 'erself 'n Grandpa — is you 'appy I's doin,' it, Emmy?"

"Perfik, Billee. Wot Nan 'as to be doin' iz makin' 'eartstring bracelit like Pippeez."

"You mean a friendship band, like Mr Pip's?" cries Larky.

"Yip, 'n for Grampa too."

"Alright! Thanks, Em."

"Could I do that for Sarah too?" asks Larky, thinking of her sister.

"Yip, n you's needin' Emmy's 'elp 'apnin'."

"Thanks, Em!"

"Alright, folks," says Pip. "It's a few weeks until school finishes for the summer, so let's all get ready for purling at the beginning of the holidays."

"Thanks, Donna!" says LuLu. "Thanks for looking after us all and teaching us so well. We would never have done so well without your help."

"Bye, everyone," says Donna.

"Bye!" cries Larky. "See you soon."

Donna and Larky stand at the door watching their friends leaving; they go back inside together, closing the door softly.

~

Billy works hard with the wool-spinning because he wants enough wool for three pouches — wool for his own pouch and wool for Nan to make pouches for herself and Grandpa. He also wants to give her plied wool so that she can plait some heartstring, enough to make a friendship band for Grandpa and herself.

The crochet lessons with LuLu get him started and she has explained the pattern to him; he's taken his wool home ready to ask Nan to help him.

After tea he helps clear the table and opens his school bag to do some homework. It's not easy to concentrate.

"Nan?" he says.

"Yes, Billy," says Nan.

"Come 'n see what I's got 'ere."

"What's that, Billy?"

"Look, I's got four balls o' wool, a crochet 'ook 'n a pattern what LuLu drawd."

"'Drew', you should say, Billy. Who's LuLu?"

"She's my special friend. The pattern is for the egg-cosy thing I was tellin' you about 'n I 'ad some teachin' from LuLu, but I's needin your 'elp, Nan."

"I'm happy to help, Billy, what shall I do?"

"If you've got a crochet 'ook, Nan, could you crochet a pouch 'n I can watch 'n do mine the same?"

"Pouch?"

"Oh, that's what we's callin' 'em."

"Who?"

"All of us, all my friends, everyone's makin' a pouch."

"Ah."

"'N, Nan?"

"Yes?"

"Please will you make one for Grandpa, too?"

"Why would he want one of these things, for heaven's sake?"

"Nan, I's really wantin' you both to 'ave one. Look at this wool I made! Look!"

Nan looks at the four balls of wool. Two of them are hand-spun wool, single-ply, one ball is two-ply, and one ball is plaited two-ply.

"This is lovely, Billy. You must have worked hard at this. Did you really do all the spinning?"

"Yep, Nan, 'n collectin' the wool 'n cardin' 'n everythin'."

"Very impressive."

"Nan, lots o' love 'as gone into this 'n I wants to give it you so's you can be makin' a special pouch."

"Thank you, Billy, that's lovely, I'd like to do that."

"Can we start when I's done this 'omework?"

"Yes, I'll go and see to Grandpa."

Billy does the best he can with his homework, then packs away his school stuff to clear the table.

"Grandpa's alright," says Nan, coming into the kitchen. "He's talking to someone I can't see, as usual, and he's smiling. Shall we do some crocheting? I brought my crochet hook."

"Yes, please, Nan, but first would you make some 'artstring?"

"Heartstring? What's that?"

"It's the plaited one."

"Alright, how long shall we cut the plied wool?"

"You'll need enough to make two bracelets."

"A bracelet? What for?"

"One for you 'n one for Grandpa."

"Oh, Billy, I don't know what the world is coming to!"

But Nan is not complaining, she loves making things and she loves this closeness with Billy. She cuts the three lengths of wool and ties a knot to join them together at one end. Billy moves his chair closer and holds on to the knotted end while Nan plaits the heartstring.

She's quick, and in no time at all she's finished the first one, and Billy helps her tie it to her wrist.

"Now, one for Grandpa, please, Nan," says Billy.

"You could do this one, Billy."

"Not really, Nan. It should be 'im what does it, but you're the nearest to 'im."

"'Should be 'im what does it'?" says Nan, mimicking Billy. "Whatever next, Billy. Well, here goes."

Nan makes another heartstring just like the first.

"Well, what now, young man?"

"Let's tie it to Grandpa's wrist!"

They go through to the front room where Frank is sitting.

"'Allo, Grandpa!" says Billy. "We's got a present for you!"

Nan takes Grandpa's left hand in hers, starting to wrap the heartstring band around his wrist.

"What? What's this? What's this?" he cries out in panic.

"Grandpa!" says Billy. "It's a special friendship band that'll 'elp you talkin' with invisible ones."

Grandpa turns slowly to look at Billy, his eyes wide. His face slowly creases up into a great big smile.

"Yes, yes, that'll be it for sure," he says, and turns to look at his new bracelet admiringly.

"He's very happy with that, Billy. I've no idea what you said to him, but it worked!"

"Could we start the crocheting now, Nan?"

"Yes, Billy, but not for long as it's nearly bedtime. We'll finish tomorrow, or the next day."

Back at the kitchen table, Nan has a close look at the crochet work Billy has already done, and she hums a tune to herself while she's working out how to copy it. Then she looks at the pattern from LuLu and nods her head.

Nan is quick to begin a new pouch and catch up with Billy.

"Alright, Billy, now watch me closely and do the same."

They work together, Billy feeling happy to be close to his Nan, and he feels happy to be bringing his new life home and sharing it with her. Nan feels happy that Billy is with her, that he's spending time with her and talking. He's changed so much recently.

Over the next few days they finish the first two pouches, and Nan begins another one for Grandpa. Billy puts his pouch into his bowl of things in his bedroom. In bed that night he can't stop thinking about the pouch; he reaches over to pick it up and snuggles down, holding the pouch in his hand all night.

~

In the next few weeks, Billy finds it hard at school. Like all the children, he is thinking about purling and can't concentrate on anything else. They sit in their classrooms looking out of the windows at the sunshine outside, imagining the adventures they will be having when the holidays come. It won't be long now, just another week or so.

They think more and more about purling. When will it happen? What will it be like? Will it be scary? All the pouches are made now, and each person's bowl of things is filled with loved objects; they have done everything that Emmy has asked them to do — and nothing has happened.

In the playground, Dungl keeps to himself but Bottl is always pestering him, trying to find out what's going on and why he isn't his friend any more. Bottl has followed Dungl every day, spying on him, but so far has never seen him meet up with anyone.

Dungl has to be very careful. He knows that Bottl is following him and spying on him, but he knows more about spying than Bottl does. When Dungl wants to go to Pip's or to Donna's, he takes great care to make sure Bottl loses track of him. That can take a long time and a lot of walking.

It would be good if they could talk and sort it out so Bottl could join in too, but Dungl knows Bottl too well, he knows that Bottl is more proud and angry than he is himself and will never change. *I should ask Emmy about it,* thinks Dungl to himself, *Emmy did change me after all.*

Billy, too, keeps to himself. He's feeling unhappy and he's not sleeping well at night and he's getting tired and irritable. Larky can read the signs and she warns the others to leave him alone. "He gets like that sometimes, you have to leave him alone," she tells them.

Billy's nights are restless and uncomfortable, and he dreams all sorts of not very nice dreams. One night he is feeling sort of stuck and wondering what to do when he suddenly remembers his Nan suggesting he talk to his Mum. Of course! He thinks about his Mum and the things he wants to say to her, but before he gets to say them he falls asleep — with a smile on his face.

His dreams change after that. He dreams of a place in the woods that he's never seen before, a clearing in the trees dotted about with mossy rocks and branches fallen in years gone by. Growing amongst the rocks and logs are tree saplings and ferns, great woodrush and wild flowers. Billy likes the place. It makes him feel happy.

The next day, Saturday, Billy goes to Tillings Wood to look for the clearing that he saw in his dream; he sets off with food and water in his backpack. He reckons that he knows the woods very well but try as he might, he can't find the clearing anywhere. He comes to the conclusion that the woods he saw in his dream are not the same as Tillings Wood: they must be somewhere else or not real at all.

Later, he dreams of the same clearing — waking in the night with a jolt, feeling as though he's actually been there. Dozing off, he dreams of it again and this time the clearing is much closer. He feels drawn towards it. It's the same the next night, but he doesn't ever quite get there.

I'll 'ave to 'ave Emmy's 'elp, thinks Billy, sighing as he turns over to go back to sleep.

~

Emmy has been thinking a lot about Billy recently. Ever since the fight with Dungl, Billy has been edgy. Since he and Dungl have 'buried the hatchet', you know, become sort of friends, they've both changed a lot. Emmy reckons that Billy will be ready for purling very soon, but it might not be easy for him to get started.

Emmy's purling adventures have taken him to many places and he's met all sorts of creatures. Often, he has been told about a place called the Glade, a meeting place where the creatures gather for special occasions. They have a gathering at the turn of the year in mid-winter when the sun is at its lowest. This is the moment to celebrate the sun returning; from this day on, the sun will be a little higher in the sky every day. There's another party in mid-summer to mark the day when the days begin to get shorter again. The creatures also have meetings in the Glade when there is a crisis if something terrible happens, or when somebody is in big trouble.

He asks Priklstik about the Glade one day, because it seems a funny thing for creatures to meet in one place when they spend the rest of the time trying to eat each other. Priklstik explains that it's only possible when there is a truce, and this means a very special event. The word 'truce' comes from 'truth', and when there's something important to talk about, all the creatures are bound by the rules of truce.

The Glade is invisible to humans, not because it really is invisible, but because it is cloaked in a 'glamour'. 'Glamour' is when something is not what it seems to be, and once upon a time, when there were wizards in the world, they would cast spells to make a glamour spell if they wanted not to be seen. But the Glade is not invisible because of wizards; it is so because of the invisible ones who make it so. No one knows how this happens, but it does.

While Priklstik talks about the Glade, Emmy becomes more and more thoughtful as an idea begins to arrive.

"Fankz, Priklstik, you's givin' Emmy 'xaklee wot 'es needin'. Iz Emmy abl to be seein' Glade now?"

"I would like to take you there myself, Mowzl Emmy, but it's too far away from here and would take me a long time to get there."

"Wot direkshn iz it?"

"That way," says Priklstik, pointing with his snout.

"Fankz, I'sll be callin' Rattltap for 'elp. Bi, Priklstik!"

Emmy purls his way in the direction that Priklstik had shown him, and after a while he hears a 'tchack' as Rattltap draws near.

"Hallo, Mowzl Emmy! How good it is to see you. What's happening this fine day that causes you to summon me?"

"Rattltap, I's very 'appy to be seein' you. Pleez be takin' Emmy to Glade where creechaz iz meetin'."

"Ah! I've wondered when you'd ask. Follow me!"

Rattltap flies off through the wood, clinging to trees here and there to wait for Emmy to catch up. Emmy could go more quickly but he wants to go slowly so that he can remember the way.

"Iz Emmy seein' the Glade? 'Coz it's invizibl," asks Emmy, when he's caught up.

"Ah-ha! You've been talking to Priklstik, have you not? You will see the Glade, Mowzl Emmy, because you are a wild creature; even if in this world you are a toy mouse, truly you are a real mouse with real feelings, as you know all too well."

"I's seein' sumfin'."

"Yes, we have arrived."

Emmy sees at once that the Glade is a special place. He likes it here. Purling over to a rock, his pouch settles between the unfurling fronds of a fern. Emmy rests, closing his eyes and listening to the sounds of insects and birds. Rattltap flies to join him, perching on a log lying nearby.

"Well? What do you think?"

"I's bizzee feelin'."

"Ah yes, of course. What do you feel?"

"I's wishin' I's come sooner," he says, happily. "Rattltap?"

"Yes, Mowzl Emmy?"

"Oomans iz 'avin' to be comin' 'ere; we's callin' oomans to be comin' 'ere, pleez."

"Er . . . which humans do you mean exactly?" says Rattltap.

"Ooman cubz n Pippee n LuLu."

"Ah! That's all right; you had me worried for a moment. You see we can't just invite any old humans here."

"They's nevva any old oomans. 'Ow iz creachaz decidin'?"

"You mean who can come here and who can't come here?"

"'Xaklee."

"If a human can see the Glade, they are made welcome," says Rattltap. "If they could see it at all, we would welcome them."

"Good, I's gettin' it. Iz it orite for Emmy to be stayin' a bit?"

"Yes, Mowzl Emmy, you can stay. I am sorry to have to leave you, but I must return to my beloved."

"Fankz for yor 'elp, Rattltap, I's needin' loneniss."

"Then I shall leave you. Goodbye, flying mouse! Tchack!"

And away he flies.

~

Emmy stays there in the Glade for a long time purling around, exploring and talking with creatures that come and go, becoming more and more certain that this is the place to call his human purlers to. He tells the creatures he meets about his plan; some are worried about humans coming here and it takes a lot of explaining before they understand that the Glade will help humans to learn the wild talk.

When the creatures at last agree to the idea of human cubs coming to the Glade, Emmy feels that it's alright now for him to call the humans and he begins to do exactly that. His pouch comes to rest in the fern fronds once more and he settles himself to wait.

"Billee," says Emmy out loud. "You's ready for purlin', I's kno- in' it. Be comin'!"

Of course, Emmy is calling Billy with his heart as well as speaking the words. He yawns, closes his eyes and settles down to listen to the woodland sounds that surround him.

~

Billy dreams of the clearing again, and this time he gets closer. It's strangely familiar — he recognises some of the rocks and their positions. Sunlight filters through the fringe of leaves high up on the surrounding trees creating dancing shadows; insects zoom in all directions filling the air with their sounds, and he smells damp earth and the leaves of plants.

"I feel like I's really 'ere," he says out loud.

"'Allo, Billee!"

"Emmy? Where's you at?"

"I's in front ov yor eyz."

Billy can't really see Emmy except for a fuzzy patch in the air in front of him, which he hadn't noticed until now.

"You'sll 'ave to be wakin' up, Billee, if you's wantin' to be seein' Emmy."

"But I's dreamin'. I'll wake in me bed."

"'Xcept you's purlin'. 'Ave a look at yor pouch."

Billy tries to look downwards, but his neck won't bend. He tries again and sees only fuzzy air; he can't see his pouch!

"Billee, be lookin' at yor 'andz."

Billy puts a hand out in front of him.

"'Ere's me 'and — what now?"

"Be rubbin' yor tummee wiv yor 'and flat n be rubbin' in sirklz. Now be lookin'."

Billy looks down and sees his hand rubbing the pouch that he so recently made. The pouch is enormous — it's as big as he is and he's inside it! He feels queasy and dizzy, he's falling, and he can't keep steady.

"You's orite, Billee, be lookin' at Emmy, look at Emmy."

Billy looks up to see Emmy floating in the air beside him. Seeing Emmy reassures him, and he stops falling, but then he looks again and is frightened — Emmy is the same size he is!

"Emmy, is you giant or is I little all of a sudden?" he cries.

"You's littl, you's got littl 'coz you's purlin'."

"Ooo. Emmy! Ooo, I's feelin' sick 'n dizzy — I's fallin'!"

Billy tips over, falling to the ground.

"Billee, pleez be lettin' yor pouch be carryin' you."

"'Ow does I do that?" says Billy, groaning, unable to move.

"Be trustin', simplee."

"Emmy, trustin's 'ard for 'umans."

"You's already trustin, you's forgot. You's 'avin to be wakin' 'ere, Billee, where we's iz."

Billy feels sick again; when he tries to look at Emmy, all he can see is a fuzzy patch of air.

"Billee, you's sleepin' in yor bed n you's purlin' 'ere. Be wakin', Billee, be wakin' 'ere."

Billy is being stretched. Realising that he's purling makes his tummy tighten with fear and the stretched feeling gets worse and worse. Suddenly he snaps back, finding himself in his bed at home, wide-eyed, sweaty and frightened. Something hurts, he can't quite find where, it's inside. He lies awake wondering. *Did I really see Emmy? Was I really almost purling?* He drifts off to sleep with a smile on his face, thinking: *yes! I was purling!*

~

Emmy isn't at all surprised that Billy didn't manage purling the first time. Purling is a bit more complicated than he has let on. He decides to make sure that Rattltap is here to help next time.

Over the next few days Billy walks out of town after school every day to get away from everyone. He's been sullen recently, and hasn't talked to anyone, not even his friends. *Why can't I do it?* he asks himself, meaning why can't he do purling.

One afternoon he's sitting in the corner of a field, looking down into the valley. He hears a familiar sound.

"Laaa La Laaa La Laaa Laaa."

"'Allo, Emmy. I's sorry, Em, I just can't do it."

"Wot, Billee?"

"Purlin'."

"Billee, purlin's nevva eezee n you's doin perfiklee."

"But — "

"I'sll be 'elpin' n I's wantin' you to praktiss sumfin'."

Billy feels encouraged. "What's I practisin'?"

"Meremba to be lookin' upwudz from yor fawtz; be slippin' 'tween fawtz n lookin' to sky. Be seein', take notiss, be seein' sky n clowdz n leevz n treez. N then be lookin' down n be seein' all wot'z 'appnin' wiv littl plantz n insektz, n yor footsez."

Billy stands up to begin practising as Emmy is talking.

"Be slippin' 'tween fawtz," Emmy reminds him.

"I gets what you're sayin', but doin' it is somethin' else."

"You'sll be orite, I'sll be leavin' you to praktiss. Bi."

"Bye, Emmy, thanks!" calls Billy, as Emmy disappears.

Billy goes on practising until he gets a headache from the effort of concentrating, and then he sets off home. Nan has finished making the two pouches, one for Grandpa and one for herself, and they're in the bowl of things. Billy has moved the bowl of things down from his bedroom to the dresser in the kitchen because he feels that the kitchen is the heart of the house and he wants his Nan and Grandpa to be purling too, one day.

He hasn't talked about purling yet, so Nan knows nothing about it. Now that he's having difficulties with purling, he's feeling a bit worried for them. *I'll 'ave to ask Emmy 'bout that,* he thinks.

That night Billy doesn't sleep much. He dreams he's looking at the sky and bumping into lamp-posts because he isn't looking where he's going, and then looking at his feet and bumping into lamp-posts again. *Why lamp-posts?* he wonders, when he wakes.

Things go on like this for the next few days and nights, while Billy works at his practice after school. He goes for walks, practising looking up and noticing things, like the very high clouds that are moving a different way to the clouds nearer the ground. He looks down and notices things like the print of a leaf on the pavement; he sees it clearly even though the leaf isn't there. He watches ants scurrying along twigs searching for aphids, drinking from the beads of honeydew the aphids squirt out of their abdomens.

Sometimes he gets a feeling there's been a gap between his thoughts… but it doesn't last any time at all; *Maybe I's gettin' what Emmy's meanin',* he thinks. But straight away he's in his thoughts again and he has to do the practice: looking up and looking down, like doing push-ups.

One afternoon he has a nap and dreams about the woods again. He sees the clearing in the woods that has already become familiar to him. He's being pulled closer until he sees the rocks that he recognises, and he sees Emmy there, purling, and Rattltap too clinging to the rock. They are watching him, silent.

Billy gets close. He tries to rub his tummy and to look down at his hand, but he can't seem to move his hands at all.

"Billy," says Rattltap. "Remember the sky."

Billy looks up to the sky; he hears a strange, faraway tinkling like a pin falling on a tiled floor, and then his ears pop just like when he's been swimming under water. He swallows hard and blinks, seeing the leaves of the trees silhouetted against the sky and he notices the curious high clouds that have wavy stripes like the patterns on a mackerel's skin.

"Welcome, Billy!" says Rattltap.

Billy looks down to see Rattltap and Emmy in front of him. He looks at his hands and then sees the pouch; he is in his pouch floating in mid-air, and he feels warm and alive and wide awake!

"Thanks, Rattltap! Thanks, Emmy! I's 'ere at last!"

There's a lot for Billy to get used to. For one thing, he's very small. Imagine, suddenly you are the size of a mouse! How different the world would look! Everything seems very strange; he has to get used to being almost weightless floating about in mid-air, not knowing how to move.

"Emmy, 'ow does I move?" asks Billy.

"Pouch iz movin' you."

Emmy and Rattltap move to a tree at the edge of the Glade.

"Be comin', Billee!"

Billy wants to move but doesn't know how.

"I's tryin', but I ain't budgin'."

"Remember the sky, young Billy!" says Rattltap.

Billy remembers his practice: look up at the sky and down to the ground, up again, down again, noticing little things. His panicky thoughts slow down and a new feeling grows — is it a feeling? It's odd, very odd indeed.

He wants to move over to where Emmy and Rattltap are, but he can't move; his legs don't even twitch when he thinks of climbing out of the pouch and walking. He thinks about normal walking, he's never thought about it before, how to do it or anything, walking just happens. Maybe purling just happens.

At that moment he moves, or his pouch moves with him in it. The pouch turns gently, moving towards Emmy and Rattltap.

"Good, Billy, what are you feeling now?" asks Rattltap.

"Somethin's carryin' me," says Billy. "It's like I asks 'n somethin' does the movin'."

"That's right," says Rattltap. "The 'something' carrying you is the invisible ones; they will move you, but your intention must be heartfelt."

"What's 'intention', Rattltap?"

"'Intention' is what you want to happen. It's the wish of your heart. You will move if the wish of your heart is for the good of all, but if it isn't, you won't move at all."

"Blimey. 'Ow's I knowin' if I's gettin' it right?"

"You don't have to think about it, young Billy, you'll know when you move and that's all that matters."

Rattltap shinters up the trunk of the tree. "Follow me!" he says, flying high up into the tree.

"Be comin', Billee!" says Emmy, following Rattltap.

"Wait for me!" cries Billy, having trouble getting going.

"You'sll be orite!" calls Emmy, purling into the leaves above.

Billy begins to move. He is so thrilled to be moving he quite forgets where he's going, but it doesn't matter: the pouch carries him through the woods faster and faster, catching up with Rattltap and Emmy. He finds them high in the trees; Rattltap has flown to a broken branch where the splintered wood sticks up in jagged spikes — his favourite place for drumming in this part of the wood. As Billy draws near, Rattltap begins to drum. The noise is deafening.

"Cover yor eerz, Billee, kwik!" cries Emmy, when Rattltap pauses for a moment.

Billy covers his ears, watching as Rattltap drills into his drumming board. He watches Emmy too, and he looks up at the sky seeing a swift flying over, and he looks down at the ground far below. He doesn't feel sick or dizzy from the height: he feels happy and at peace for the first time in his life.

Chapter Four

Tooby

"Where are you, Emmy?" calls Pip. "A new story has arrived!"

"'Oorayee! Wotz it callin' itself?"

"It's called 'Tooby'."

"Uncle One-Eye! 'Oorayee! 'Ow's it 'appnd, Pippee?"

"It's a puzzle, Em; the pages arrive in the night while I'm sleeping, as they always do, except you haven't told this story yet! The story of 'Ocean' was the same. How is it possible, Em?"

"Invizibl ones iz 'elpin' n great wave iz 'appnin'."

"I don't get it, what do you mean?"

"We's all feelin' great wave n 'uman cubz iz nearly purlin' n majik's growin'."

"I sort of see what you mean. What shall we do with this story, do you want me to read it to you?"

"Ha! Let's be 'avin' a storytellin'!"

"I could read it next Sunday at Donna's, I think everyone's going to be there."

"Perfik, Pippee, n we'sll be seein' wot 'appnz."

"But, Emmy! Don't you want to hear it now? Don't you want to know more about 'Wot 'Appnd'?"

"You's rite, Pippee, I's needin' to be kno-in'. Pleez be tellin' story to Emmy."

"Right now, this minute, Em?"

"Yip."

Emmy settles himself in the Gypshun Bowt while Pip opens the orange ring binder on his knee.

"Here we go, Em: 'Tooby'," says Pip, beginning to read.

~

When Emmy and Scraggy are late home, their family and friends at Burrow Cave start to worry. Three of the older mice are talking about what might have happened to them. Digga Bill, always down to earth, gets impatient with all the talking.

"Maybe this, maybe that! What we need is facts," he booms. "We should send out a search party straight away."

"Digga," says Scribbla patiently. "We can't search the whole wildwood, we need to start somewhere; we need some clues."

"What were they up to today, anyone know?" asks Burrow Bill.

"Mowzl — I mean Emmy — said that they might have a look at another tree he wants to mark on his map," says Scribbla. "We should ask Tooby, he'll probably know."

"I'll fetch him," says Digga.

"How about we all go to see him?" Scribbla suggests.

"Good plan, let's go!" agrees Digga.

As they get close to Tooby's den, they see the faint glow from the lantern. Even though they've seen it many times before, they still feel goosebumps, and as they draw near, their voices drop to a whisper.

"I'll never get used to that light thing of his, it's not natural," mutters Burrow Bill.

"It may be more natural than the fur on your back, Bill, we just don't know," replies Scribbla.

"Hallo, Tooby!" booms Digga. "Are you at home?"

"I is, I is, do be a-comin' in," says One-Eye, as the young mice know him. "I be 'earin' Digga Bill if I be 'earin' right, eh?"

"You're right, Tooby, and it's Scribbla and Burrow Bill too."

"Come in, come in, what a pleasure indeed, and what can Tooby do bein' for ye all?"

Between the three of them, they tell Tooby about Emmy and Scraggy not coming home and how worried everyone is getting. They want to send out a search party but need some clues to follow.

Tooby listens, his face growing more serious by the minute. He tugs at his whiskers, remaining silent for some time.

"Well?" says Digga, getting impatient already.

"Mowzl Emmy, as I finds I's 'avin' to call 'im," says Tooby.

"Mowzl Emmy is 'avin my permission to be keepin' 'is maps in this very chamber. Let's see now what we's 'avin'…"

Tooby goes to the shelf Emmy uses for map-making stuff. Bringing a map tube back to the table, he pops out the plug and teases out the roll inside, unrolling it carefully on the table.

"Be 'oldin' 'em down flat, lads, that's the way. There be a few of 'em, but this 'ere top 'un is the newest map — see 'ere, Emmy says to me this be where 'e's exploring next.

"'E's explorin' north-west from Burrow Cave. See there, they's goin' further 'n a bit westerin', look at this 'ere, where it says 'Map', send our search party that way, 'n tell 'em to visit the 'Ollo Cherry on their ways 'ome. Take this 'n let Star 'ave a peek at it, 'e'll know."

Back in Burrow Cave a search party is quickly organised. Star, Acorn and BillBill will travel together; Star has a backpack of his own in which he carries his navigating equipment and some food.

One look at the map is enough to tell Star where to go and how to get there. The distances are marked on the map with little dots, and Star remembers the way to Tumble Cave. They'll need to go nearly as far as the 'wet place' and then turn westwards.

The three mice set off into the night, following the scent trail left by Emmy and Scraggy. Now and again they lose the trail and have to do a 'sweep' — going in a circle sniffing the ground — to find it again. The scent has grown faint and can be hard to find, but BillBill manages to find it, and they carry on.

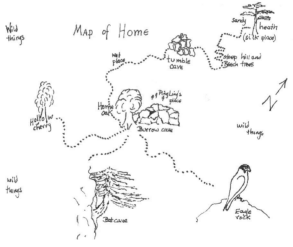

Since the time he was on lookout duty and saw the fox hunting in the snow for Star and Mowzl (as Emmy was called then), BillBill has worked hard learning about scent trails and becoming a tracker. He has a very good 'nose', and now, following the trail tonight he can smell the scent of different creatures that have passed this way. He can smell hedgehog, shrew, and weasel! He is relieved to know that the weasel scent is very faint, suggesting that it passed this way some time ago. Emmy and Scraggy's scent trail is familiar and easy for BillBill to recognise, so he has no trouble knowing which way to go.

The trail does indeed lead them to a big old tree that One-Eye said they should find, and it shows that they climbed the big old tree and climbed down again, going off through the woods towards the south.

"Let's follow and see where they went," says Star. "I have a feeling they went to the Hollow Cherry."

Star is right: the trail leads the three mice straight to the Hollow Cherry; Emmy and Scraggy must have been measuring the distance between the two trees to mark onto the map when they got home.

The search party arrives at the Hollow Cherry to find the scent trail goes up the inside of the tree, but they can find no sign of it coming down again and no sign of a scent trail leading back towards Burrow Cave or anywhere else.

"Up we go!" says Acorn, climbing up with Star and BillBill close behind.

Star has visited Waggl before, but neither Acorn nor BillBill have ever seen Waggl. When they arrive at the ledge where Waggl's nest had been, they sniff around, discovering that Emmy and Scraggy had a bit of a lie-down and then gone to the hole in the tree to look out, but there the trail ends.

"Maybe Gabbee came back and carried them away on her back!" BillBill suggests.

"Or Waggl! Ha! Imagine that," says Star. But then he remembers that the others have never seen Waggl. "When I saw Waggl, he didn't have any feathers!"

"They couldn't have fallen out, could they?" suggests Acorn. "Emmy and Scraggy, I mean, not Waggl's feathers."

"Their scent trail ends before the edge, they would've had to jump," says BillBill.

"Alright," says Star, decisively. "We must report back to Burrow Cave, but keep alert, there may be more clues!"

They climb down the inside of the Hollow Cherry and set off home along the trail familiar to Star. They find no new clues on the way until they are nearly home. A new day is dawning, and birds are waking up, preening and chattering. Our travellers hear a jay screeching, it's Dappa, warming up his voice in case he should need it in a hurry.

"Hallo, Dappa!" calls Star.

"Ah-ha! Hallo, my friends. Are you coming or going?"

"Well, Dappa, that's an interesting question! We could happily talk about that all day long but we need your help."

Star explains that Emmy and Scraggy disappeared from Waggl's nest in the Hollow Cherry, yesterday before dark.

"Ah, yes!" cries Dappa. "I wonder, hmm. I saw a flash of lightning yesterday about that part of the day and in that sort of direction, and I remember thinking it was very strange because there was no thunder, none at all. Very strange."

"Oh dear," says Star. "I'm not at all sure that this is good news, Dappa, but thank you. We must get back to Burrow Cave and tell what we've found out."

"Good luck!" calls Dappa, as he flies off, and the three mice head for Burrow Cave as fast as they can go.

~

In One-Eye'd Tooby's den, Star describes everything they have found out so far in their search for Emmy and Scraggy. Tooby gives him a quill and ink and Star draws arrows on the map to show the way that the search party went, and dots to show the scent trail that Emmy and Scraggy left behind. One-Eye listens intently, his face serious, a frown forming on his brow when he hears what Dappa the jay had seen. He gazes at the map, and into the light of the lantern, and is silent for a long time. At last he straightens himself up and heaves a deep sigh.

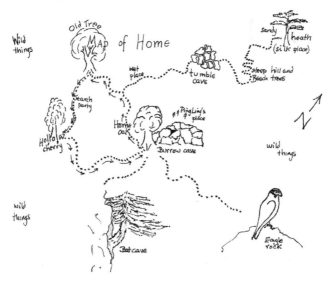

"I thank ye, all three; you's findin' all the clues I's needin' for guessin' what's 'appened. Get to your rest now, 'n please send Flimsy 'n Dreamer to be 'elpin' me."

"Alright, Dad," says Star. "Do you know what's happened? Where are they?"

"That ain't an easy thing to be tellin', lad, give me a little time, a little time. Be off now, I thank ye for all you's done."

One-Eye gazes into the lantern light for a long time after the three young mice have gone. Shaking himself out of his reverie, he goes over to the shelves to gather a few things, putting them in a basket. He inspects the contents of the basket by the light of the lantern, selecting one map tube and a small wooden box. He puts the basket on the floor.

He looks at the map tube and wooden box sitting there on the table and heaves a deep sigh; a tear wells up in the corner of his eye, glinting in the lantern light.

"Daddy, may we come in?" calls Flimsy, softly.

"Aye! Come, please."

"Hallo, Uncle," says Dreamer.

"Hallo, Daddy," says Flimsy. "What's it all about? Star was a bit mysterious when he told us you wanted to see us."

"There be a mystery 'ere, Flimsy. I's in need of your 'elp, ye both, you with your seein' 'n Dreamer with 'is dreamin'."

"Daddy, is this to do with the Island of Mist?" asks Flimsy.

"Aye!"

One-Eye is finding it difficult to speak. His throat is tight.

"Daddy, you're crying. What is it? What hurts you?"

One-Eye tries to speak and stumbles with the words but finds his voice at last.

"It'll be down to me that young Mowzl Emmy 'n Scraggy 'as disappeared."

"Down to you, Uncle? How can that be?" says Dreamer.

One-Eye speaks hesitantly.

"It's . . . It's a long story . . . a bit of a saga, 'n a confession too. I's never spoke a word of it before."

"A word about what, Daddy?" asks Flimsy.

"'Bout stealin' the light."

Flimsy looks deep into One-Eye's eye.

"Daddy, the light cannot be stolen, it gives of itself or not at all."

He looks at Flimsy, impressed by her quiet confidence.

"And this you know? How so?" he asks her.

"I have been to the centre of darkness where the light is born, and I know it is so. Daddy, you shouldn't keep this locked in your heart for a moment more, you must speak of it. Will you speak?"

"Aye, I will."

"Will you speak it now to Dreamer and to me, or will you speak it to everyone?" Flimsy asks him, gently.

One-Eye hesitates again.

"What be your advice?" he says at last, looking to both Flimsy and Dreamer.

"Tell it to everyone, Uncle," says Dreamer.

"Yes, I agree," says Flimsy.

"So be it," says One-Eye, slumping down, exhausted. "I's been 'idin' for so long, dreadin' this moment, 'n now 'tis 'ere I's relieved."

"Daddy, do you want Dreamer and me to get everyone gathered in Burrow Cave?"

"That's 'xactly right, my dear, but don't be leavin' me alone just yet or else I's runnin' from me own shadow. 'Ere, lad, carry this."

One-Eye puts the map tube and the little box back into the basket and hands the basket to Dreamer.

"Carry the lantern, lass," One-Eye says to Flimsy.

"Lean on me, Uncle," says Dreamer, and they set off for Burrow Cave.

~

Burrow Cave echoes with the sound of young mice calling out for more stories. Ping Ling has been telling a story and now that it's over, the young mice want more.

"Please, Ping Ling, tell us more about when you were little!"

"My dear ones, you must remember that I am very old, and one story at a time is plenty for me! We will have more another day."

"Ping Ling needs to rest now, let's leave her in peace," says Pearl, who has been looking after the youngest mice.

"Daddy!" cries Violet, spying One-Eye, Flimsy and Dreamer arriving. "Will you tell us a story? Please, pleeeez!"

"Violet," says Flimsy. "Yes, One-Eye will tell us a story, but he wants to tell a very special story and we need to fetch everyone to come and listen. Scarlett and Violet, please will you fetch Captain Blunda and Elfrida, Fivrit, Forby, Threeda and Wunda; Marigold and Ruby, please run and find Digga Bill and Messy Nell, Burrow Bill and Bess; Little Garnet, please go with Sapphyr to find Scribbla and Bookworm Bernie."

The young mice set off in great excitement to do as they are bid, and while they are gone Flimsy and Dreamer set about organising things for Ping Ling and One-Eye to be comfortable. Flimsy then goes to the Mouseum to fetch Star, Acorn and BillBill, where they had gone to learn what they could about lightning.

One-Eye settles himself on table rock with the basket and lantern next to him. The mice arriving from the burrows gather round, making themselves comfortable; they are excited to see the mysterious light of the lantern and their whispering sounds like wind rustling leaves in the trees.

The last to arrive are the oldest mice and when Messy Nell appears there is a buzz of excitement. Many of the younger mice have never even seen her before; Messy Nell hardly ever comes to Burrow Cave. She isn't messy at all in fact, and now she appears on Bookworm Bernie's arm with a fine shawl around her shoulders. She smiles as she looks at all the eager faces, nodding her head in greeting towards each mouse in turn.

Knowing that it will be hard for One-Eye to get started, Flimsy goes to table rock and patiently waits for everyone's attention. When the cave is quiet, and all eyes are on her, she speaks.

"One-Eye has something he would like to tell us. Please be patient and quiet while he prepares himself."

Flimsy sits down close to One-Eye, touching him as though to say, *I'll be here, with you.*

"Thank thee, lass," One-Eye murmurs.

Burrow Cave becomes so quiet that the young mice hardly dare to breathe. It's quieter than if there had been nobody there at all. The lantern casts its curious light into the cave, chasing shadows into the corners.

At last One-Eye speaks and to everyone's astonishment, his voice has changed: no more pirate-talk with funny words and accents; instead, it is the voice of Tooby as it was before his pirate adventures began.

"I'm not really a pirate," he says, pausing to gather himself while a ripple of whispers sweeps round his audience. "I have not told my story before because I'm ashamed of something I did a long time ago. But now I must tell you because I believe it will explain what has happened to Mowzl and Scraggy, and it might help us to find them and bring them home.

"It all began a long time ago when I was called Tooby and I still had my two eyes. Back then I spent a lot of time in the Mouseum, and one day I came across a stone shaped by human hands many winters ago when humans still existed. The stone had a simple shape and looked like a little head with a hint of a face."

One-Eye takes the wooden box from the basket next to him, opens it carefully and takes out a small stone. He looks at it for a moment before passing it to Flimsy.

"This is one of the little heads that I found, and I found many more afterwards. Flimsy, would you pass it on so that everyone can see and hold this stone? I have another one here, which I will pass round the other way — Violet, please hold this for a while and pass it on.

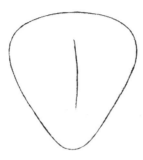

"There was something special about the first little head and I took it with me to my chamber; I looked at it a lot and kept it near me while I slept. I found more like it in the Mouseum and I took them to my chamber until I had a collection which I kept in a bowl on my table.

"I dreamed more often from that time onwards, and the dreaming got more real and more powerful as time went by. I dreamed of monsters underground; I was running away from them, but the burrows were so many I got lost. I'd find myself waking up in a frightened sweat, hearing the roaring of a monster in my ears.

"I dreamed of ships sailing on the sea, human ships, and I could see the rows of oars sticking out the sides and humans working the oars to the rhythm of a drum.

"I started to dream of the sea, just the sea, with no land to be seen. Then a large human ship appeared, sailing, always sailing, and finding no land.

"In my dreaming, I saw the sea from high in the sky, so high that I could see the roundness of the world below, a world entirely covered with blue water.

"The ship sailed on and nothing changed until a cloud of fog appeared, making a dark patch on the ocean below me; the ship sailed towards the fog and disappeared into it. Later the ship sailed out from the fog and continued to sail round the great, blue ocean world. The fog had disappeared.

"One day, or one dream, when I watched the ship sailing towards another patch of fog, I saw a flash of lightning illuminate the fog just as the ship disappeared into it and in that very moment I woke up — on board the ship!"

One-Eye stops speaking and surveys his audience. The younger mice are gazing at him with wide eyes, waiting to hear what happens next. Some of the older mice have smiles on their faces; they are thinking, *here we go, another of One-Eye's yarns.*

"In the years that followed," One-Eye continues, "things happened that would make good stories for many a long winter, but now I shall cut a long story as short as I can.

"I was found and captured by the ship's mice, a bunch of cut-throats, or so I thought, whose chief, or Captain, as they called him, was Whip-Tail Jack. It turned out that they were a good bunch and when we got to know each other we all became friends.

"It didn't take me long to discover from Whip-Tail Jack that the humans were enchanted, sailing their ship endlessly across the ocean looking for the fog and looking for the Island of Mist, which lay somewhere hidden in the fog. The mice, too, were enchanted; I had to work hard at keeping myself awake and one of the ways I used to keep myself sharp was to talk to my new friends and try to keep them awake too; you see they'd been there so long they'd forgotten all else. I slowly won their trust and they let me into their secrets more and more, until, at long last, Jack admitted that he could remember being awake before finding himself on this human ship but had forgotten how to stay awake. We made a pact to help each other find a way out of the enchanted ocean world.

"Time was measured by the ship's bell, by the passing days and nights, and by calm and storm; we watched as the ship sailed round and round the world until the fog appeared, once every six or seven moons. We watched as the human sailors sailed the ship into the fog and searched for the Island of Mist, and when the Island appeared they'd anchor in a sheltered bay. We watched the sailors row their longboat from the ship to the shore loaded with barrels, crates and guns; they returned with the barrels filled with fresh water and the crates stuffed with the strangest creatures we'd ever seen.

"The humans seemed to be daydreaming — each day doing whatever they had to do as though yesterday hadn't happened. They looked like ghosts, always sailing, always searching.

"Whip-Tail Jack told me that the humans hoped to find treasure; they searched for the Island of Mist because they believed there is treasure there, a treasure that will satisfy all their desires.

"I was getting restless on the ship and I worried that I would fall under the spell of the enchantment. I *had* to go to the Island of Mist; I had to have earth under my feet and trees around me, I had to go. But when I told Jack, he begged me not to go; he said that I would never return, and he would blame himself for letting me go. When I asked him to come with me, he said that he had a duty to his comrades and that if I must go, I would have to go alone.

"My plan for going to the island was simple: I would sneak onto the longboat in the night and hide there and go to the island when the sailors rowed there. I told Jack and the others about my plan and asked them to help me look for things I could take with me.

"The human sailors spent time making models of ships and the little things that go inside them. These model ships were cunningly pushed inside glass bottles, the masts and rigging pulled up with a thread. We could climb into the bottles — before the model was finished and there was still no cork — and find very useful things to take back to the Hideout. We found a canvas bag and bits of string that I used to make a backpack — the first one! — and a miniature dagger that I could use for cutting things. That's where the cutlasses came from that the pirate mice have stuck in their belts.

"My friends were helpful in finding bits and pieces but they didn't want me to go and were not enthusiastic about it. I told them that I would be back and that they must do everything possible not to fall under the spell again. At last everything was ready and all we could do was wait for the fog.

"As soon as we saw the fog, I stowed away in the longboat while it was still lashed down on the deck covered over with a tarpaulin. I had with me my new backpack with the useful things that we had found or made, and some seeds and nuts to eat. There was a long wait before the Island of Mist revealed itself, but at last the ship anchored and the longboat was winched over the side and down into the sea. I was excited and scared, especially when the human giants lumbered into the boat; I thought my time had come and we would all sink to the bottom of the sea.

"But in their clumsy, noisy way, they were good seamen and they loaded the longboat with barrels, crates and guns, just as we had seen happen before, and rowed ashore. I stayed hiding while the sailors unloaded the cargo, carrying everything up the beach to stack up under the cliffs. I had to wait while they ate and rested; at last they picked up their guns and strode off up the river valley into the heart of the island where they would hunt for food and search for treasure. I watched from the bow of the longboat where the anchor rope fed through a cleat; I hid behind the rope until the sailors were safely gone.

"When they were gone, and I didn't have to worry about being seen by them, I began to notice other things. Looking back at the ship, I thought of Jack and Kate and the others. I thought about how I must explore the island as quickly as possible and then get back to the ship; I didn't want to let them down.

"I decided to run along the anchor rope rather than jump down to the sand, but hearing the waves breaking I stopped to look. I wanted to go nearer, so I jumped down onto the sand and ran towards the sea. The sand was smooth and cool, scattered with bits of shell, everything sparkling and colourful; the waves pounded rhythmically onto the beach, sucking back into the sea like a great creature breathing, and all the time sparkling fragments of shell rolled and hissed at the water's edge.

"I did get too near and got wet when a bigger wave came, catching me by surprise, but I liked the taste of the salt and didn't mind getting wet. That woke me up and I ran up the beach. I loved the beach and could have stayed exploring the rock pools and the seaside plants growing on the cliffs, but I had to get safely away before the humans returned.

"Climbing the cliff was good fun. I went that way so that I'd get away from the humans quickly. They wouldn't be climbing cliffs. I found a snug little cave in the rock and sat down for a rest looking out over the bay. As the sun went down and the daylight faded, the sailors returned, laden with the creatures they had shot with their guns. They loaded everything into the longboat, including two barrels of fresh water, and rowed back to the ship for the night.

"At last I felt free and, in the night, I climbed the cliff and into the jungle. By the time the sailors returned, I could hear them shouting, but I couldn't see them, and they couldn't see me.

"The Island of Mist is mountainous and covered with huge trees and tropical plants, but it's not like our wildwood here at Burrow Cave because the trees are different, and the thousands of plants that grow among the trees — and up the trees — are all different too. It's hot, and every day thunderclouds build up in the sky until rain falls, and after the rain the sun shines again, making the air steamy. Everything grows and grows, and millions of insects and creepy crawlies thrive in the undergrowth, and birds of many colours and shapes make strange noises as they fly about.

"Some of the nuts and seeds I found were tasty and some not nice at all. The good ones I stuffed into my backpack. I came across a big grass-like plant and some of the stalks had been broken, perhaps by a storm or a big animal. The broken stalks were hollow, and I thought how useful these would be back at home.

"Thinking about this distracted me and for a moment I wasn't alert; the next thing I heard was a voice. 'Hallo, you must be new around here,' it said, speaking slowly.

"I turned towards where the voice was coming from only to find myself staring at a rock, or so I thought. 'I didn't know rocks could talk, but this is a very strange island,' I said.

"The voice said, 'I think the problem is that you can't see me, I'm sorry about that, I'll just move myself a bit, that'll help.'

"Whoever owned the voice moved a little and suddenly I could see the shape of it — a giant creature, so big that I had been unable to see it! I still couldn't see the head and when the voice came again it said: 'I'm up here, look up a bit.'

"I looked upwards, realising that what had seemed to be a tree trunk was in fact the creature's neck; now I could see his great scaly head looking down and his big, sad eyes regarding me solemnly.

"When at last I found my voice, I said: 'Hallo, my name is Tooby and I'm a wood mouse.'

"'Hallo, Tooby, my name was Lonely, and I was a tortoise,' replied the enormous creature, reaching up for some leaves.

"'Why do you say that your name *was* Lonely?' I asked him and he said: 'Because I was the last of my kind and when I died there were no more like me.'

"'But here you are! You are a tortoise!'

"'You are new around here, aren't you, my little friend,' said the tortoise. 'I am extinct, by which I mean, of course, that my kind are extinct. In fact, everything on this island is extinct, even the old volcano upon which we stand.'

"'Am I extinct too? Am I dead?' I asked the tortoise. He replied, 'Perhaps not, it depends.'

"'Depends upon what?'

"'How did you come here?'

"'I came on the ship with the human sailors.'

"Lonely paused, shaking his head slowly. 'Ah,' he said. 'Those restless creatures that kill everything in their reach, and everything that isn't in their reach too. It was humans that killed all my kind before they kept me as a trophy, because I was the last one.'

"'It must be terribly sad being the last of your kind. I can't imagine it. I'm so sorry for you, Lonely.'

"'You're right, Tooby, it was terribly sad, but beautiful too.'

"'Beautiful? How could that be?' I asked.

"'As the last one of my kind, I was aware of the world in a new way because there was no longer a future, and when that feeling happened, the beauty of the world was revealed to me.'

"'I don't understand, Lonely, but I'm glad it was beautiful for you. Why is this island here if everyone is extinct?'

"'None of us know, except we hear the singing.'

"'What singing? I don't hear singing,' I said.

"'That's because you aren't dead,' said Lonely, in a matter of fact sort of way.

"'Who is it singing?'

"'The invisible ones. If you try really hard to be quiet inside, you might hear them.'

"'What does it mean?'

"'The singing? The singing means that this place is a song.'

"'But I can't hear it!' I protested.

"'But you can see me — and the jungle and the mountain and the sea — it's a good song, isn't it?'

"'Oh, Lonely, I'm confused now. Can you tell me which way to go next?'

"'You can only go the right way.'

"'But which way is that?'

"'Whichever way you go.'

"'How is that possible?'

"'Because you are here; you are not extinct, you are not enchanted as the humans are, and you have wonder in your eyes and in your heart. The invisible ones may have been waiting for you — not that the invisible ones wait at all, but you know what I mean. The great wave moves slowly except when it doesn't move slowly.'

"'Lonely, you are talking in riddles and giving me a headache, let's talk about something else. Can I ask you a question?'

"'You are a most inquisitive mouse; of course, you can ask me a question, but the only thing is it has to be the right question.'

"'How do I tell if it's the right one or not?'

"'You'd better ask me!'

"'Lonely, what does dying teach you?'

"'Ah! That's a magic question, isn't it? I like magic questions.'

"'If it's a magic question, will it have an answer?'

"'Patience, little one, I am merely waiting for the wave.'

"'Wave?'

"'Dying teaches me that awareness and the wave are one.'

"'Wareniss?'

"'Ah! How marvellous to have a student who knows nothing of death! It's really very exciting. I think you should ask another question, and then another, and eventually one will be the right one and you will say "Ah!" as well.'

"'Do we grow "wareniss", whatever that is?'

"'We grow isness, awareness grows us.'

"'Ah! — oh dear.'

"'What happened, Tooby?'

"'For a moment I understood something important, but then it slipped away again.'

"'Hmm, very good. It will not have slipped far away.'

"I watched as the giant tortoise raised his head up on his long neck and peered through the tangle of jungle plants. 'Those humans will be hunting for me,' he said. 'We may not meet again although I hope that we do. It has been a pleasure to meet you, Tooby, and I wish you long adventures that fill your heart. I shall leave you now.'

"He moved his great legs very carefully so that he didn't crush me, turned, and moved away; his weight pushed aside the stems of plants as he moved, cracking some open, revealing the hollowness inside. So, it was Lonely that had squashed the plants!

"I climbed a bit further up the mountain before beginning to look for somewhere to sleep. I saw plants that I'd never seen before, and one of them looked like a giant version of the one Lonely had just squashed. I wondered if it was hollow too. Lots of insects buzzed about making a cloud around my head, so I looked for an opening in the rock to climb in and find a place to sleep.

"Not finding any caves or openings in the rock straight away, I stopped for a rest and sat to look out over the bay. The day was ending and in the growing twilight, the sea was shining with the last light in the sky. There was the *Wreckless* at anchor, and the longboat being rowed by the sailors, from the island to the ship, for the night. I could just make out the barrels and crates on board the longboat. I thought of Whip-Tail Jack and the other mice on board the *Wreckless*, my new friends in this strange world. I shivered as a ripple of fear overtook me, sweeping down my body, and I jumped up, scattering the thousands of insects that had gathered around me, and a renewed determination drove me on to climb higher up the mountain.

"I found a crack in the rocks eventually and it led into a small cave which was perfect for sleeping. The crack was quite narrow, and I had to take off my backpack to squeeze through and pull it along behind me. I thought I'd better explore a bit before settling down for a nap and went to have a look in the darkness at the back of the cave. The passageway reminded me of the burrows here at Burrow Cave, except there were no familiar smells of family and friends. The passage had some squeezy bits and soon I heard water trickling. I went forward carefully so as not to fall in, and as I got near, I could see light shining through a gap in the rocks where the water flowed through. I wanted to see what was the other side in case there might be dangers coming from that way.

"I put my backpack down in a dry place and walked along the edge of the water until the stream disappeared underground. I had to dive into the water and swim towards the glow. The tunnel through the rocks was quite long and narrow and I was bursting for breath by the time I got through, but I got there and surfaced, gasping and coughing, and for a moment I didn't notice what was around me. When I'd recovered my breath and stopped coughing, I saw the beauty of the cave I found myself in.

"It was the most beautiful sight I have ever seen. A round pool in the middle shone with the strange light, and this light reflected in crystals that sparkled in the walls and ceiling of the cave and even on the floor, where many had fallen down.

"The light itself was soft and pale and had a soothing effect on me. I was drawn irresistibly towards it and I sat on the cave floor, leaning against the low rim of the pool. I stayed there for I know not how long, having lost all track of time. Sometimes I woke up enough to be aware of being there, but mostly I was in a dream. One of the times I woke up, I poked at the light with my finger and a grain of sand fell from my finger into the light. The light wrapped around the grain of sand, making a ball about the size of my head and it floated in the air in front of me. I looked into it feeling at peace and wanting for nothing; I felt no cold or hot, no hunger or thirst; and time drifted along its way.

"All of a sudden, I heard a 'pop' in my head and I came to my senses with an idea happening. I could see my brain working, very slowly, like time was slowed down, and I remembered the talk with Lonely, the giant tortoise, and I remembered the ship in the bay, and then all the memories flooded back, and the idea arrived — take some light away with me.

"I didn't know why, or what the light might be for, it was just an idea. And then, with another 'pop', a second idea arrived: it was a picture in my head of the hollow plants I'd seen on the mountain, showing a bit of hollow plant stem with a plug in the end. I could keep the light inside the tube!

"I plunged into the stream and swam back through the underwater tunnel, this time going against the current of water, but I knew what to expect and had filled my lungs properly before diving. I picked up the backpack that still lay waiting and squeezed through the passage to the open air. It was a bright sunny day and I was dazzled for a moment, but when I could see again and looked down into the bay, I saw no ship. The *Wreckless* had disappeared!"

One-Eye pauses to rest his voice and to compose himself. Memories have been flooding back, affecting him deeply; it is such a long time ago that he was there on the Island of Mist, but now he feels it as though it were yesterday.

Flimsy puts a hand on his shoulder.

"Rest, Daddy, take your time," she says gently.

"I must speak it all and have it done," says One-Eye. "But I thank you, Flimsy."

One-Eye looks at the expectant faces all round him. He feels strengthened to be with his family and friends and is encouraged to go on with his story.

"For a time, I stood gazing at the bit of empty sea where the ship had been. My thoughts were full of worry for my friends on board and worry for myself. What now? Was I trapped forever on the Island of Mist?

"These worries faded when I remembered the light and the plan to make the tubes to put some light in. I had no idea what I was going to do, but it felt right. I thought of Lonely's words, You can only go the right way.

"With a light heart I set off down the mountain to the place where the big grasses were growing. I found some bits of stem lying about and gathered them together where I could sit comfortably and work with my knife, whittling and scraping, and with my teeth, gnawing and chewing; I learned how to work with the giant grass stems and how to make tubes and plugs.

"The grass stems had bulges in them where leaves had grown when the plant was young. I discovered that if I cut through the stem next to a bulge, it was not an open tube but closed and strong. I didn't need to make a plug for both ends, only the open end. I decided how long the tube should be and cut through it using the knife and my teeth. Then I made a plug that fitted tightly in the open end, but not so tight that I couldn't get it out again.

"When I'd got the hang of it, I set about making a set of tubes: some fat, some thin, some short and some long. I had no idea what I was doing, but it was fun. This all took a long time, about as long as the moon takes to go from full to nothing and back to full again. I went to a cave nearby to rest when I got tired and searched the jungle for food when I was hungry.

"I had quite a collection of tubes in the cave, and one day I felt the time had come to take them to the Crystal Cave. I was feeling alright about it by then, and my doubts had disappeared. I carried the tubes up to the Crystal Cave tunnel. It turned out to be really difficult to get the tubes through the underwater bit because they were full of air and wanted to float; their buoyancy made the swimming harder. I took them one at a time, resting each time to catch my breath.

"It was magical being back in the Crystal Cave. The small ball of light that had gathered around the grain of sand was still there waiting for me, and I sat for a while looking at it and at the marvel of the light pool. It wasn't really like a ball because it had no visible surface and was mysterious to look into. I thought of it as an 'Orb'. I would probably still be sitting there still if there hadn't been a nagging somewhere inside me, a nagging that reminded me to wake up and do what I'd come to do. I looked at the ball of light floating in front of me, thinking that it was too big to fit in any of the tubes that I'd made. I tried anyway, holding an open tube close to the Orb, and to my amazement it made itself smaller, threading itself into the tube just as smoke moves in the air. I couldn't believe my eyes!

"Next, I tried the fattest light tube that I'd made and, taking out the plug, I held the tube close to the light pool. A wispy thread of light rose up from the light pool and poured into the tube, filling it; this happened again with some smaller tubes, but then it stopped happening. Whatever I tried, the light would not go into the tubes any more. 'This must be all that's needed!' I said out loud, the sound of my voice echoing in the Crystal Cave in an eerie way, sending a shiver down my spine. I began to carry the tubes out through the underwater tunnel, one by one, taking the empty ones too as they would be useful for keeping maps in.

"When all was done, I went back to Crystal Cave to say goodbye and to thank the light. I sat for ages with my hand dipping in the pool, just feeling good and not wanting to go anywhere. I thought about how magical it was that the light had gone into the tubes by itself. This made me feel happy because it meant the light wanted to come with me and that I wasn't stealing it. But I have worried ever since that I did steal it, because in all the time I've had the light, I've done nothing with it but keep it locked up.

"At last I felt ready to go; I spoke to the pool of light, thanking it for the peace that it had shown me and for the light I was going to take away. I left the cave, making my way through the narrow passage back into the world. The sunlight outside was dazzling after the soft light in the cave and it took a few moments for my eyes to adjust. Looking towards the bay I could see the *Wreckless* at anchor; I must have been in the Crystal Cave beside the pool of light for at least six moons!

"I watched the sailors come and go while I made some small tubes for maps. My backpack was now crammed full but not as heavy as I thought it would be, perhaps because of the light in the tubes. Making my way down the mountain, I said goodbye to everything as I passed by, hoping to see Lonely again, but I didn't see him. When the sailors had gone off hunting, I returned to the beach and climbed into the longboat using the mooring rope. After hiding the backpack behind the seat-locker in the stern of the boat, I climbed up and sat on the prow to look at the bay and the beach and the mountain clothed with trees; I said my goodbyes. Never again would I see a place so magical and strange. Or so I thought then.

"I quickly hid when I heard the sailors returning from their hunting. They loaded the boat with barrels of fresh water and crates containing animals or fruits. Some of the animals were alive, to be kept on board the *Wreckless* until the sailors killed them and ate them. I felt very sad for them, thinking of what Lonely had said about being extinct. At last the longboat was rowed back to the *Wreckless* and unloaded, but then straight away it was rowed back to the beach for another load. This happened a few times and I was getting really seasick with all the banging and rocking about, and the shouting of humans. I realised that they were bringing everything back to the ship from the beach, so this must be the end of their hunting and time to sail away. I am lucky to have been in time.

"At last the job was done. The longboat was hoisted up out of the water, unloaded, turned upside down and made fast to the deck of the *Wreckless*. I nearly fell out of my hiding place and had to hold on to the backpack as tight as I could to stop it falling and giving me away. When all went quiet in the deep part of the night, I crept out from under the boat and towards the Hideout. *How long has it been?* I wondered. *Are they still here? Are they alive?*

"They were still all there, thank goodness. Cutlass Kate was on sentry duty and when she saw me moving in the shadows, she hissed a challenge: 'Password or die!', and all I could think to say was 'It's Tooby, Kate!' She must have been confused because the password wouldn't have been 'Tooby'. Anyway, she said, 'He's dead,' so I stepped forward saying, 'No I'm not! Look, it's me!' She recognised my voice and smell, greeting me with a hug. We went on to the Hideout, meeting Stumpy on the way.

"When we got near the Hideout, we had to go through some

holes too small for my backpack to fit through. I took everything out, explaining to my friends that the tubes must not be opened, and we carried them, one by one, through to the Hideout.

"Whip-Tail Jack was very happy to see me, they all were. They thought I might have died on the island, but they hadn't given up hope. We had a celebration and they told me some of their adventures on the *Wreckless* as she had sailed around the world. They had been about twelve moons at sea before entering the fog and finding the Island of Mist again. I had spent all that time sitting in the Crystal Cave! Jack said that nothing very unusual had happened and they had just followed the usual routines. There had been the occasional tussle with the rats, but nothing much.

"I told them of my adventures and discoveries on the Island of Mist. I told them everything except that some of the tubes that I'd brought back contained light taken from Crystal Cave. I explained that I had spent a lot of time making the tubes because they would be so useful, and I opened an empty one to show them.

"Later, when I had time alone with Jack, I told him that I had taken some of the light. We opened a tube, releasing a small Orb which hung motionless in the air; the room seemed to move around it as the ship swayed this way and that in the ocean swell. Jack was astonished, and spell bound, just as I had been, and I had to call him back or he would have stayed like that forever. I opened the tube again and asked the light to go back in, which it did, shrinking down until it was small enough to enter. 'It's like a livin' creature that light is,' whispered Jack, in awe. 'Yes, Jack, it is. I don't understand what it is or how it works or what we should do with it, but I know that its magic is beyond anything we have seen before.'

"Jack looked at me with a puzzled expression. 'I thought you'd 'ave a plan, Tooby,' he said, and I replied: 'I don't have a plan, Jack, only a feeling. We will have to wait to see what happens.'

"I asked Jack to protect the light tubes if I went away, with his life if necessary, and to swear to it; he agreed and swear to it he did. Later he asked Stumpy to find some materials to make a sea-chest to store the tubes in. Stumpy enjoyed the task, finding bits of wood and some leather, tacks and black paint; he made a sea-chest with the lid on a leather hinge, and with black lines painted on pretending to be iron straps, and a pretend lock painted on too, so it looked very proper. The sea-chest ended up in the corner of the Hideout, out of the way, and was soon forgotten about by all except me and Jack. I took out some empty tubes for maps and things, and one small tube with light in it, and put them in my backpack; I took to wearing it all the time, just in case.

145

"We got back to normal duties while keeping an eye on the sailors, hoping that something would happen, but it never did. We had a lot of fun telling stories and singing, but at the back of our minds was always the question: how are we going to escape the enchanted world? I didn't know the answer, and I told them so.

"One night we were ambushed by the rats. The battle raged for hours with neither side having any particular advantage. The rats were much bigger and stronger, but they couldn't get through the small holes that we used and so we could escape them.

"There was a moment of 'stand-off', when we were separated from the rats by a massive oak wall and the only hole through it was mouse-sized. I thought I would try to parley; you know, have a talk and try to make a truce. I shouted through the hole 'Let's talk! Let's stop fighting, and work together to escape this enchanted world!' A roar went up as the rats laughed themselves hoarse, and we could hear them saying things like 'Work with mice! Ha-ha! Would you believe it! Never in a winter of winters.' I waited a moment before shouting again: 'If we find a way to escape this world, would you like to come too?' and again the rats roared their disapproval, clashing their cutlasses and banging on the wall, calling us cowards for hiding. So, I gave up trying.

"Later, things went badly wrong; me and Red-Belly Ron got separated from the others, cornered on deck and were about to be overpowered by the rats. I shouted to Ron to jump up into the rigging and climb and we both did, but the rats were quick, being so much bigger, and they caught up with Ron and killed him and his body fell back to the deck. I had no time to think about him as I had two rats closing in on me. I rushed to reach the crow's nest thinking I would have to leap into the sea — when suddenly an idea came. I was good at getting things out of my backpack without taking it off and I quickly reached in and pulled out the tube with light in it. I opened the stopper just a crack, letting out a tiny bit of light. In a flash, I found myself all of a sudden on the floor in my den at Burrow Cave, the light tube still in my hand and my other hand pushing the stopper in tight.

"One of my eyes was hurting and felt wet and sticky, I had the taste of blood in my mouth; I'd been wounded. In the very last moment, a rat had struck with his cutlass and cut my face and blinded an eye."

Tooby slumps down, exhausted. Burrow Cave is quiet. Elfrida walks slowly over to Tooby, putting her hand gently on his head.

"Tooby came to find me that night," she says in her softest voice. "He needed me to clean and bandage his terrible wound and he needed to ask questions. I made him lie down while I washed and dressed the wound as best I could in the dark, but I would need daylight to examine the wound properly.

"Tooby kept asking me how long he'd been away, and I said that I didn't know he'd been away at all. Tooby often disappears for half a moon or more, it's not unusual, we are all used to that. So that's what I told him, but he wouldn't believe me. He asked when I had last seen him, and I said it must have been at Violet and Scarlett's birthdays, about a half moon past.

"Tooby didn't believe me or was confused by the shock of his accident. Anyway, he went away when I'd finished dressing the wound and he didn't come back for me to renew the dressing. Eventually I went to visit him to look at his wound in daylight. When I went in to his den, a strange light shone from a thing above the table. 'What's all this, Tooby?' I said to him, but he wouldn't say anything. I checked his wound by the strange light, seeing that an eye was missing and there was a great gash across the eye socket and his face. I cleaned it all very carefully and redressed it, putting healing herbs in the bandages. 'It will take a long time to heal, Tooby, but it is clean and healthy. Mind you keep it that way! I will make you an eye-patch for your blinded eye.'

"I used a piece of thread to measure round his head, tying a knot in it to remember the right length. I left him to be miserable and silent on his own while I made a nice eye-patch."

Elfrida strokes Tooby's head for a moment before walking slowly back to her place. Tooby raises himself, takes a few deep breaths, clears his throat and is ready to speak.

"Thank you, Elfrida," he says. "You saved my life that night, and you've never said a word about it. I thought that I had been away for about four winters and that everybody at home would have given up hope and thought that I had died somewhere. It was a great shock to realise that I had not even been missed!

"You will want to know why I kept all this secret for so long. There are a few reasons. One reason is that I feel it was wrong to steal the light, and I don't want anything bad to happen to my family, so I carry responsibility for that.

"Another reason is that by spilling the light to save myself from the rats, I may have done something terrible.

"Also, I feel bad because I don't know what to do with the light. Why did I take it? Why lock it up?

"Even though I have these doubts, I do still feel that the light is important and maybe it's not for me to know what to do, but for somebody else to know. So, I have kept quiet, waiting, spending my time making things and looking at the little heads. From time to time I've dreamed back onto the *Wreckless* and spent many moons with Whip-Tail Jack and the others, but we have so far not come up with a plan. It is always good to see the light that is kept in the other light tubes in the sea-chest, and Jack and I let them out and ask them what we should do, but they have never said anything or made any sign, except that they went back into their tubes again as if to say, 'Not time yet.'

"Where was I? Ah yes. When Gabbee and Waggl appeared here, I began to think that there must be a hole, like a leak between the worlds. I must have caused a leak between the worlds when I spilled the light to save myself from the rats. I feel bad about that. Why Gabbee and Waggl ended up in the Hollow Cherry and not in my den, I still don't understand, but it's just as well as they are too big to fit in my den.

"When they disappeared again I reckoned the hole must be wobbly; now that Mowzl Emmy and Scraggy have gone too, I reckon it's the same hole they leaked through. They're on board the *Wreckless*, that's where they are.

"That'll be the ending of my little story and we come to the present time. I should go through the portal to find 'em!"

"What's a portal, Uncle One-Eye?" asks Sapphyr.

"It's a human word, Sapphyr, meanin' gateway, or doorway, 'tween worlds. You could say sleep is the portal to dreamin'.""

"Daddy, may I speak?" asks Flimsy.

"Aye, lass."

"Before you try to go diving back through a leaky portal, we should do all we can from here, from this world, where we are strong in our hearts. There is a great mystery happening, even now, and we must not be too hasty, but allow it to unfold as it will."

"Whatever can we do from here, child?" asks Captain Blunda, gruffly.

"Well, Grandpa, we have One-Eye's light and we have the bowl of little heads; we also have the shell and the light tubes which come from the Island of Mist. With these we can do 'seeing' and 'dreaming' and we must learn everything that we can learn. Maybe then we will know what to do."

"Yes, I agree!" says Dreamer. "We'll do whatever we can, so please don't go disappearing tonight, One-Eye!"

"Well said," agrees One-Eye. "I's not rushin' to go back, but I's worried for Emmy 'n Scraggy."

"Grandpa," asks Ruby. "Is that when you were called 'One-Eye'?"

"You're right, lass! 'Twas Burrow Bill, he calls me 'One-Eye' when he sees me all bandaged up." One-Eye gets up stiffly and stretches. "I's talked enough. Flimsy, Dreamer, come 'n see me when you's ready."

He walks away slowly, disappearing into the burrow leading to his den. Burrow Cave is quiet and still.

"Oh dear," says Dreamer, breaking the silence. "I've never seen him like this before, looking so unhappy."

"He's very worried," says Elfrida. "He's worried that he's done something bad by taking the light, putting us all in danger."

"I don't think he has," says Flimsy. "But he won't listen to me. We must do whatever we can to help."

"He does listen to you, Flimsy," says Dreamer. "Maybe his worry is that things are not right, and something is going to happen. It would be natural to worry about that."

"You're right there, Dreamer," says Burrow Bill. "What adventures! I'm glad I'm on solid ground."

"Did you know about all this, LaLa?" asks Bess.

"Only a little," replies LaLa. "One-Eye hasn't talked much about it. He's never talked about the Crystal Cave before. I think he's worried because he doesn't understand any of it and has kept it all inside and not talked to anyone. He might begin to feel better now that he's talking to us."

"Well, what I think," says Elfrida, cheerfully, "is that Flimsy and Dreamer should do their best to help One-Eye, while the rest of us stay out of the way and prepare for visitors!"

"Visitors? Who do you mean, Elfrida?" asks Acorn.

"We shall know when they arrive!"

~

After giving One-Eye time to rest and recover from the storytelling, Flimsy and Dreamer visit him in his den. He welcomes them and they gather round the table with the lantern hanging above.

"Daddy, thank you for telling your story to us all, it must have been a hard thing to do," says Flimsy.

"'Twas 'arder than I did expect, you're right," admits One-Eye, his pirate's accent back again. "Now then, m'dear, I beg you, do your deepest seein', 'n you Dreamer, I beg of you, dream your deepest dreamin'."

They are quiet for a time; Dreamer closes his eyes, slipping into his dream sleep, while Flimsy looks at the glow from the lantern. She is fascinated by the way the light is shining onto the bowl of things. The little heads are glowing, and she is drawn into the glow and she finds herself in a swirling mist that gets thicker every moment until it is a dense fog — she is 'seeing'. She feels squashed; the fog is heavy, pressing on her, making it difficult to breathe. She hears a sort of click, or pop, and finds herself looking across the table at One-Eye.

"Something's stopping me seeing through the fog," she says.

"Something's not working for me, too," says Dreamer. "I dreamed the fog too, but it was like a dead thing."

One-Eye goes over to the shelves in the corner.

"I's 'avin' a chart or two to be showin' ye," he says, bringing a few thin map tubes back to the table. In the light from the lantern, he opens each one and looks inside.

"I's remembrin' one specially, but it ain't 'ere. It'll be on board the *Wreckless*, I'll be bound, in the sea-chest, it'll be. I'll 'ave to be drawin' it again."

He fetches birch bark, a quill feather and a pot of black ink.

"I's puttin' the Island o' Mist in the middle like; 'n 'ome, where we now be, I's puttin' over 'ere, floatin; ocean be floatin' likewise over 'ere. Then I's thinkin' there 'as to be an 'uman world too, 'umans that's left their time capsules, so I's puttin' that over 'ere, floatin' likewise. 'n for all we's knowin' there's other worlds we's not even imaginin', so I's puttin' question marks for them. There! 'n what you 'as to be remembrin' is, this be no map, 'tis a way o' imaginin', 'n a way o' thinkin'.''

"What's the wiggly lines meaning?" asks Dreamer.

"Them's the fog."

"Why wiggly?"

"That'll be lightnin'."

"But isn't the Island of Mist in the ocean?" asks Flimsy.

"It be 'n it be'nt. There be not a scrap o' land in that there ocean, 'n that 'uman ship'll be sailin' for all time lookin' for what ain't there; only within the fog will the Island o' Mist be seen."

"I've tried with all my might to see through the fog!" Flimsy cries. "I thought the fog's a barrier but now it isn't; the fog is the key, it's what we want! I'll do seeing again looking *into* the fog, not trying to see through it."

Again, they are quiet, gazing at the lantern light shining onto the bowl of things; Flimsy picks up the shell from the Island of Mist, closing her eyes and holding the shell to her ear. She speaks with her 'seeing' voice.

"I hear the sounds of storm and howling wind, I see fog swirling, spiralling, and objects rising into the sky: I see shards of wood, broken barrels, seaweed, fishes and birds, all lifted into the sky by the spiral of wind. I see the seaweed wrapping around the bodies of the fishes and birds, the birds' wings hang limply at their sides; I see seaweed carrying the birds and fishes, holding them."

Flimsy slumps down, tired from the effort of 'seeing'. "What do you think it means, Daddy?" she whispers.

"Typhoon, it be. A great wind that spins round 'n round, suckin' everythin' to the sky. The *Wreckless* may be smashed to bits and sunk, but I reckon not so."

"Flimsy," says Dreamer. "Are you seeing what's happened already, or what's going to happen?"

"No — well — yes; I don't know. It might not have happened yet, but I feel that it has."

"Never mind when it be," says One-Eye. "Can you make out what the seaweed be doin'?"

"Uncle," says Dreamer. "I will see by dreaming but I will need to sleep on it, and now I think Flimsy should rest."

"Aye, you both be goin' to rest. I thank ye."

"Daddy, you seem lighter, not so worried," says Flimsy.

"Thanks to you. Your seein' tells me all is not lost."

~

Flimsy is very tired after her efforts to do seeing and she sleeps deeply. Dreamer sleeps a restless sleep, dreaming of the ocean and the typhoon; he sees a great whirlwind lifting wreckage and creatures high into the sky. He sees seaweed strands wrapping around the bodies of creatures and now Dreamer himself is wrapped in seaweed too!

The word that comes to him is 'pouch', and he looks around at the birds and fishes floating in the sky, all shapes and sizes, each wrapped in a seaweed pouch; the fishes are drifting gently back down to the sea. He looks carefully at every creature he can see but there is no sign of Emmy or Scraggy.

When they've slept, Flimsy and Dreamer meet up with Pearl in Burrow Cave. Dreamer tells everything that he has dreamed, and Flimsy describes the seeing she did in One-Eye's den.

"I like your word 'pouch', Dreamer," says Pearl. "From what you've seen it looks like these pouches are helping the fishes to survive and get back to the sea and helping the birds to survive the battering of the wind."

"Elfrida says that seaweed is healing," says Flimsy.

"The seaweed needs to get back to the sea too," says Pearl. "But how does it move? How does it wrap itself around the fishes and birds?"

"In my dreaming, I could feel the seaweed," says Dreamer. "It felt special. A bit of seaweed isn't going to make much difference after all, is it? But it did make a huge difference, like the difference between being safe and falling from the sky!"

"It sounds very mysterious," agrees Pearl. "I wish we could make sure that Emmy and Scraggy have seaweed pouches."

Dreamer looks thoughtful.

"Hmm. I wonder," he murmurs.

"Wonder what, Dreamer?" asks Pearl.

"You know that 'portal' thing that One-Eye talks about?"

"Sort of," says Flimsy. "What about it?"

"Could we send a parcel?"

"Send a parcel?" exclaims Pearl. "Where to? How?"

"What about: 'To Horatio Mowzl, also known as Emmy, who got sucked up by the typhoon', or something like that," suggests Flimsy. "And we could mark the parcel 'Portal Post' as well."

"Sounds good to me," says Dreamer. "But what to put in it?"

"Leave that to me," says Pearl. "I've got some ideas about that already! You two had better get back to One-Eye and tell him what you've told me. I'll find some things to send and see you there."

"Alright, Pearl, see you later!" cries Flimsy and she and Dreamer run back to One-Eye's den.

They find him staring at the Orb which is now floating in the air just above the table. Hanging from the ceiling, the lantern is dark and empty.

"Daddy?" says Flimsy. "Daddy?"

One-Eye is startled and cries out — "Ah! Ah, there ye be, there ye be. Aye, good!"

"What is this beautiful light, Uncle?" asks Dreamer.

"This be light from the lantern, 'tis an Orb. I did let it out 'n it'll 'elp with thy seein' 'n dreamin'.'"

"Let it out! You make it sound like it's alive!"

"It be as live as ye 'n, me, lad, 'n more besides."

"Daddy?" says Flimsy. "It really is alive, isn't it? You aren't joking, are you?"

"'Tis true, as we live 'n breathe, lass, 'n I should never 'ave stolen it nor locked it up."

"But, Daddy, you said that the light went into the tube by itself in the Crystal Cave. It chose to go with you! Maybe it wanted you to take it!"

"You's thinkin' it could be so?"

"Yes! I feel it. I know it in my heart!"

Responding to her, the Orb moves towards Flimsy, stopping close to her face. She gazes into it, eventually speaking with her 'seeing' voice.

"I see the pool of light in the Crystal Cave; there are two mice there sitting down back to back, leaning against the rim of the pool. The mice are asleep, or so it seems, and they are smiling. It's Scraggy — and another, but the other is not Emmy."

"Aha!" cries One-Eye. "That'll be Whip-Tail Jack with our Scraggy. Good! Well done, Flimsy! They be there already at Crystal Cave. Well, now I's thinkin' on it, it might 'ave been a long while for them, years even. Flimsy, lass, can you wake 'em?"

"No, Daddy, I have tried, my seeing talk doesn't reach them, I don't know why. Dreamer? Might you be able to do it?"

Dreamer too has been gazing into the Orb. It's the nicest feeling, warm and inviting. He hears Flimsy's words, but he doesn't reply. He is already falling into dream sleep and he finds himself inside Crystal Cave; he touches Scraggy, speaking to him in dream talk but he can't wake him. He feels himself slipping deeper into sleep, but something pulls at him; he resists the pulling because it is so nice slipping away into sleep, but the pulling gets more insistent and he wakes in One-Eye's den.

"Dreamer! Dreamer!" One-Eye is calling, over and over again. "Ah! Welcome home."

Dreamer yawns and rubs his eyes.

153

"Oh, what heavy sleep that was. How did you manage to wake up when you first went to Crystal Cave, Uncle One-Eye?"

"I's not really knowin'. I's wakin with a sort of 'click' in my 'ead, 'n the notion of takin' the light was there in me 'ead already. It come with a click or a pop, that's what wakes me."

"Daddy," says Flimsy. "Something, or someone, woke you up and wanted you to take light back to the world, but who, and why?"

"Or what," says Dreamer. "Could it be the light itself? Could the light have something to do with the invisible ones?"

"Whoa there, lad! What's we knowin' 'bout invisible ones? That's not for us to be knowin'."

"We don't know, Uncle, you're right," says Flimsy calmly. "We do know that we can't wake Scraggy and Jack. What should we do?"

"I's avin' to go 'n wake 'em meself," says One-Eye. "With you two 'elpin, I can do it."

Flimsy and Dreamer look at each other, alarmed at the idea of One-Eye disappearing.

"But we don't know where Emmy is, Uncle!" says Dreamer. "We need you here."

"Well, you'll just be 'avin' to find 'im yourselves!" says One-Eye, going over to the shelves in the corner and returning with his backpack, wriggling it onto his shoulders.

"Now then, Flimsy, Dreamer — set your 'eart's eye upon the *Wreckless* . . ."

"Daddy!" Flimsy cries, as One-Eye picks up a little head; she watches, mesmerised, as he lifts the little head until his hand touches the Orb, and then, in a flash, he vanishes.

Flimsy and Dreamer, shocked and speechless, continue to sit staring into the light where One-Eye disappeared. After some time, Pearl's voice comes from the burrow outside the den.

"Hallo, can I come in?"

Flimsy manages a hoarse whisper. "Yes, Pearl, come in."

"What's the matter?" says Pearl. "You two look as though you've seen an invisible one!"

"One-Eye has just disappeared," says Dreamer.

"How? Where's he gone?"

"We can't be sure," Flimsy explains. "He wanted to go back to the *Wreckless*." She and Dreamer describe to Pearl what just happened. Pearl is quick to see what they need to do now.

"If Uncle One-Eye can rescue Scraggy and the ship's mice, then we must get on with helping Emmy. Let's try sending the parcel, as you suggested, Dreamer. I've brought some things for you to look at, and then we can decide if we should send them. I went to see Threeda and Ping Ling to tell them what's happening, and they gave me this!"

Pearl shows them a ball of the finest heartstring they have ever seen. Ping Ling made it a long time ago for no purpose in particular, she just wanted to make it. She's been keeping it safe until it might be needed, and she knew at once that it's needed now. Pearl told Threeda and Ping Ling about the seaweed pouches, seen by Flimsy and Dreamer in their visions; Threeda suggested that the best thing to copy the seaweed pouch would be to knit or crochet a pouch using Ping Ling's heartstring.

"That's it, Pearl!" cries Flimsy. "We can send the heartstring and a drawing of a pouch as a pattern!"

"But if Emmy was sucked up by the wind, won't he have a seaweed pouch like all the other creatures we saw?" asks Dreamer.

"I've wondered about that too, Dreamer," says Flimsy. "But we didn't see Emmy and he may not have a seaweed pouch. Now that you two have had this idea, we should send it anyway."

"Let's make a drawing," suggests Pearl. "I'll draw, and you tell me what you want me to draw."

Flimsy describes how she thinks a pouch might look, and Dreamer describes how the pouches looked in his dreaming; Pearl makes sketches and soon her sketches are looking just right, and she draws a neat drawing of the 'just right' sketch of a pouch.

"That's lovely, Pearl," says Flimsy.

"Thanks, Flimsy. Look, I've brought some more birch bark to wrap it with, and we need to make a label and tie it all up."

"What else should we put in?" asks Dreamer.

"A message? And what about a crochet hook?" says Flimsy.

"Have we got one?"

"I forgot to ask for one," says Pearl. "Dreamer, would you go and ask Ping Ling? We'll get on making the labels."

Pearl and Flimsy carry on making the label and writing a message to go inside the parcel. The message says:

'dear mowzl emmy
please come home quick
we're missing you
luv from us all x x x'

The message is written on a small roll of birch bark. Pearl and Flimsy are pleased with their preparations and when Dreamer returns with a small crochet hook, the only one that Threeda or Ping Ling had, they are ready to make the parcel. The crochet hook is a curved twig with a small notch at one end. Dreamer brings some more heartstring too, to tie the parcel up with.

Pearl flattens out some birch bark, and Flimsy lays out all the things to go: the heartstring wool, the folded-up drawing of a pouch, the crochet hook and the message.

"Is this crochet hook useable? It's very small," asks Flimsy.

"Hmm, maybe not, but let's put it in anyway," replies Pearl. "Let's put two layers of birch bark on the parcel, shall we?"

After tying it up and writing on it until it looks right, they sit in silence with the parcel in the middle of the table. They look at it and at each other, wondering what to do next.

"Are we ready?" asks Flimsy.

"Yes."

"Yes."

"Let's all stand up. Pearl, you should hold the parcel, Dreamer and I will be touching the parcel as well, just lightly. Now, let's have Emmy in our hearts and may our love give wings to this little bundle of hope."

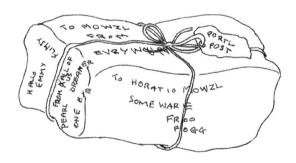

156

As Flimsy speaks, they slowly raise their hands towards the Orb. Suddenly their hands are empty.

"It's gone!" gasps Pearl. "The parcel has gone! Oh, Emmy! Come back soon, dear brother!"

"Please can we stay with the Orb for a while?" says Flimsy.

They settle down again, sitting quietly.

"Thank you, mysterious light," says Flimsy. "We don't know what you are, but we know that you awaken love in our hearts and we are sure now that Tooby has not done a bad thing in taking you from Crystal Cave. Please help him to do what he has to do and please help Emmy in whatever he has to do, and please bring them all back home when it is the right time.

"We are now going to Burrow Cave, please come with us if you would like to. If it is your wish to stay here, we'll come back to see you often."

Flimsy, Pearl and Dreamer go quietly out of One-Eye's den; the Orb remains, perfectly still, floating in the air below the empty lantern.

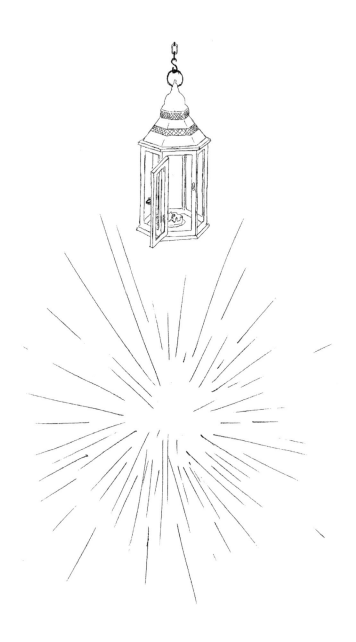

Chapter Five

First Purlings

Pip feels sleepy after reading Tooby's story to Emmy, and he begins to nod off.

"We's findin' out wot 'appnd littl bi littl," says Emmy from the windowsill where he sits in the Gypshun Boat. "I's unda standin' fingz a littl betta."

Pip yawns and stretches, trying to wake up. "Emmy, do you think LuLu and the human cubs should hear Tooby's story?"

"Yip. I's needin' evrywun to be kno-in' kwik, n I's finkin' we'sll be 'avin' storytellin' in the wudz."

"Alright, let's call them all for Saturday to meet here, and then we'll walk to Tillings Wood."

"I's 'appy. Emmy's purlin' p'raps."

~

On Saturday afternoon they are all there in Tillings Wood: Billy and Larky, Penny, Stomper Jack and Dungl; and LuLu of course. Emmy weaves between them, purling, and Pip has just finished reading the 'Tooby' story, about the *Wreckless* and the Crystal Cave, the story that arrived without Emmy knowing how.

"Emmy, the story's so complicated I've got no idea what's going on any more," Pip moans.

"Ha!" says Emmy. "You's rite, none ov us iz kno-in'."

"How can you be so relaxed about it, Emmy?" says Penny.

"I's arrivin' in world ov 'umans sum 'ow, Pennee, n I's trustin' great wave'll be gettin' Emmy bak 'ome."

"At least we know how the parcel was sent," says LuLu. "The parcel with the wool and drawing of the pouch. Where would we be without that? And it's good to know that One-Eye has gone to rescue Jack and Scraggy."

"I'm fed up," grumbles Larky. "I'm fed up because we've made our pouches and we can't do purling. We've been waiting ages, and nothing happens! The pouches are a waste of time."

"Purlin's 'appnin' inna bit, Larkee. I's sorry you's feddup, but you's 'avin to be findin' a littl payshntz."

There's a fed-up sort of silence, then Billy speaks quietly.

"I's done purlin'."

"Billy! What? You never said!" cries Larky.

"I's said it now."

"What's it like, Billy?" Penny asks.

"It was really 'ard, 'n I was sick. Emmy 'ad to 'elp me learn 'ow," admits Billy, shy to own up to just how hard it was.

"Oh dear! I hope I don't feel sick too," says Penny.

The children have been waiting for weeks since finishing their pouches, and nothing has happened. They've waited for term to finish and for the summer holidays to start, and now they're impatient for something to happen. Emmy hasn't said anything about it, except that they have to be patient. In fact, Emmy doesn't know what to say, because he knows it will be more difficult for them to learn purling than he's been letting on. But he has a plan.

"I's 'avin' ideea wot'll be 'elpin'. Pleez be comin' wiv Emmy to speshl place, n meremba, we's 'avin' to be kwiet."

Emmy purls to the edge of the clearing where they have been sitting and makes his way through the trees while the humans quietly follow. Billy, who knows Tillings Wood better than anyone, notices that Emmy is taking them to a part of the wood he's never seen before. They come to a clearing that he recognises from his dreams — this is the Glade! This is where he did his first purling! He wants to shout out with excitement but remembers just in time not to make any noise.

Emmy waits in the Glade for the humans to catch up.

"Pleez be seein' wiv yor 'eartz n merembrin' evryfin' wot'z 'ere. Meremba treez, n rokz n furnz n sunlite, n be merembrin' feelin's wot'z livin' in yor 'eartz."

The magic of the Glade opens their hearts, and they look in wonder at the beauty of the place. The plants are lush with early summer growth: mosses and ferns, bushes and trees with sunlight bathing everything in warm light. The air is alive with the sounds of insects and birds.

"I's wontin' you to be sayin' no wurdz, simplee meremba where we's iz. Meremba where we's iz wen you's dreamin', n pleez be goin' 'ome wiv izniss ov where we's iz in yor 'eartz."

Emmy purls close to each of them in turn, gazing deep into their eyes; he then fades away, disappearing with a pop.

Without saying a word, Pip, LuLu and the gang slowly walk back the way they had come. The spell of the Glade stays with them as they walk on home and when they finally go their separate ways, they smile to each other; something is changing. The fed-up feeling fades and excitement quickens their hearts.

~

Early the next day, Billy is in his room trying to sort stuff out. He still hasn't finished clearing up since he dumped all his things on the floor, asking his Nan to leave it for him to do it later. He hears a bird singing outside and turns to gaze out of the window. There's not much to be seen outside Billy's window, mostly walls, roofs and a bit of sky. He sits on his bed gazing at the bit of sky and he pictures the Glade in his imagination, remembering smells and the coolness of the plants and hearing Emmy's voice. Billy is purling.

"'Allo, Billee, I's 'appy you's 'ere to 'elp, let's be callin' evrywun to be comin'.'"

"'Allo, Em, course I'll 'elp, but I's needin' to whizz about a bit first!" says Billy, and he whizzes about like a bee let out of a bottle, so happy is he to know that purling can happen — just like that.

"Hallo, human cub!" says Rattltap, arriving in response to Emmy's call. "It is good to see that you have mastered the art of flying in your pouch."

"Rattltap, I 'asn't got a clue 'ow it works, but it's workin'!"

"Sumwunz comin'!" says Emmy.

Billy and Rattltap move closer to him.

"Who is it?" Billy wonders out loud.

"We'sll be seein . . ."

Pop! Out of thin air Larky arrives, already laughing, and when she sees Billy she shrieks — she hasn't seen him as small as a mouse before! She's a natural purler, straight away at ease being tiny and floating in the air; she can twist and turn without feeling dizzy or sick.

"'Allo, Larkee," says Emmy. "We's very 'appy to be seein' you purlin', welcum to the Glade. Pleez 'elp us callin' evrywun wiv our 'eartz. I's 'opin' theyzl be purlin' eezia'."

Larky comes closer to them and talks all in a rush.

"Emmy, this is so much fun! I know what you mean now, everything's clear now I'm purling. Oh, how stupid I've been . . ."

"Slow down, Larks, you're makin' me 'ead spin," says Billy.

"How can calling them make it easier?" asks Larky.

"Thought you said everythin's clear now?"

"Well, not really."

"Emmy reckons the more of us is purlin', the easier it'll be."

Larky fidgets about, bobbing up and down, whizzing off and back, round and around.

"Come on, Rattltap, let's fly!" she cries, speeding away, with Rattltap chasing as fast as he can.

"It's just you 'n me, Emmy, let's do some callin'."

"Fankz, Billee."

They settle themselves comfortably into the fern fronds.

"Open yor eerz to soundz, Billee."

Billy listens to the birds and insects and to the wind humming through the trees; from far away he hears Rattltap drumming and Larky's delighted shrieking.

Pop! Pop!

"'Allo, Pennee, who's we 'avin' 'ere?"

"Am I really here?" says Penny, happily. "Am I really purling? I can't believe it! Nosey, this is Emmy."

"Hallo, Emmy, my name is Nosey and I'm a mouse."

"'Allo, Nosey, I's a mowse too, n I's very 'appy to meet you."

"Penny!" cries Billy. "It's triffic seein' you purlin'. Looks like you's findin' it easier 'n wot I did."

"Not hard because you and Emmy called, it was like being pulled."

"Pull'd bi a fred frew a fog!" cries Emmy.

"But no fog," says Penny. "Nosey wanted to purl too, so I made him a pouch. Emmy, is it alright for a wild animal to purl?"

"Nosey's orite, Pennee. N you's 'avin' to be merembrin', Emmy's a wild creacha too."

"I didn't forget that, Emmy."

"Pennee, you's a nachral purla."

"Thanks, Emmy."

"You're a natural purler too, Nosey, eh?" says Billy.

"I am, Billy, and now we can talk to each other!"

"So, Emmy, is this the wild talk?" asks Penny.

"You's rite," says Emmy. "It's wild talk for 'umans who's forgot unwurdz."

"Wild talk for beginners, is it, Emmy?" says Billy.

"Ha-ha! You's 'bout rite!"

"So, where's you been, Nosey? It's ages since I saw you in school," asks Billy.

"I've been helping my family. They live under the shed at Penny's place."

"Is Penny mindin' when you's disappearin'?"

"I heard that!" cried Penny. "Nosey comes and goes, he's wild."

"That's so good. C'mon, let's practise movin'," says Billy.

Penny, Billy and Nosey begin a game of tag, quickly learning how to move and chase each other. Soon they are whizzing about all over the Glade. Rattltap and Larky come back, Larky laughing and excited.

"Hallo, Penny! Hallo, Nosey! Bet you can't catch me!"

They chase after Larky, disappearing from the Glade, leaving Emmy on his own resting quietly in his clump of fern fronds; he's calling the others to come to the Glade.

~

Dungl is really fed up. For weeks, he's been waiting for term to end and the holidays to start — and for purling to start! Bottl has been pestering him and being really annoying.

He's glad when Billy comes looking for him to tell him that Pip will be reading a new story tomorrow.

"Come by Nan's place, we'll go togevva," says Billy.

Dungl has missed his new friends and has felt lonely. He's so impatient for tomorrow to come it takes him ages to get to sleep. When he does sleep, weird dreams happen; he sees children he doesn't recognise climbing out from manholes in the streets. He sees the covers being pushed up and children climbing out covered in mud, their eyes shining like diamonds in their muddy faces.

They move swiftly towards him, frightening him, and he runs

away only to wake up sweating and confused.

"What was all that about?" he says out loud.

The next day, Dungl walks to Billy's place, taking care that Bottl isn't following him. He and Billy walk to Pip's place and they are surprised to hear Pip saying they're all going to Tillings Wood for the story.

Dungl enjoys being with the others and he feels much less lonely. He listens to his friends talking about purling and why it isn't happening. He doesn't say much, but he's glad to know that he's not the only one feeling bad about it.

There's talk too of the story about Tooby and how complicated and far away it seems; it's hard to remember that it's all about how Emmy came to the human world in the first place, bringing purling magic with him.

When he hears that Billy has already been purling, Dungl feels envious and it worries him to hear that it had been difficult for Billy and made him feel sick. When they go to the magic place in the wood and everyone has to be quiet, all Emmy says is to remember the place and to dream about it and this will help them do purling. Dungl hopes it will help. He's all wrapped up in himself and even when Penny talked to him earlier he hadn't said much, but he did glance shyly at her because he likes her and admires her dark eyes and pale face, framed by black hair.

Later, when he's alone and has a chance to think about what's happened, he slips into proper daydreaming and is soon imagining the clearing in the woods. He sees it for a moment, but then the muddy children come up out of the ground again. He is about to turn away from them when he hears a voice.

"We can see all that is hidden from your eyes."

Dungl looks at the muddy children more carefully. They're not moving, just watching him, waiting.

"We could show you what we see," the voice says.

Dungl thinks of what Emmy would say; he would say something like, 'Fankz, I's 'opin' to be seein' wot you's seein'. Dungl hears himself saying to the children in the dream: 'Yes, please show me what you see.'

The children smile and slowly fade away. As they fade, Dungl sees more clearly until he sees the Glade right there in front of him, real and vibrant. Trembling with excitement as he is drawn closer, he finds himself looking into Emmy's eyes.

"'Allo, Dungl, I's very 'appy to be seein' you."

Dungl tries to speak, but his mouth is full of mud.

"You's 'avin to spit owt mud, Dungl," advises Emmy.

Dungl spits and chokes and coughs, and spits some more, and at last he's able to breathe again.

"Thanks, Emmy, I's chokin' on that."

"It's dream stuff wotz stoppin' you seein'."

"I's seein' now."

"Be lookin' at yor legziz."

Dungl looks down but can't see his legs; instead, he sees a pouch. His head spins and his tummy churns as he realises how small he is; he is the same size as Emmy and he is purling. For a moment he's dizzy and his pouch wobbles, but he looks at Emmy again and the spinning slows; he begins to feel better.

"Be lookin' all around n listnin'."

"Emmy, I's purlin'!"

"You's purlin', Dungl, n I's very 'appy."

Dungl feels more awake than he ever has before. He loves being so small and light, and he notices the tiny things, like the moss growing on the rocks under the ferns that Emmy is resting in. He sees a wren clinging to the moss, looking at him. The wren rustles its wings, looking straight at Dungl.

"Hallo," says Dungl.

"My name is Rindill, welcome to the Glade, David."

"Thanks, Rindill, my name is Dungl."

"Yes, your name has been Dungl until now, but from this day on you will be called David."

"I don't get it; how do you know my name, 'n why shouldn't I be called Dungl no more?"

"You will understand, David. Today you have changed, you are no longer Dungl."

Rindill sings his wren song, which, as you may know, is very shrill, and David and Emmy have to cover their ears. Rindill finishes his song and slips away into the undergrowth.

"Dayvidd," says Emmy. "You's 'ad a treat to be welcumd bi Rindill."

Rattltap swoops down. "Hallo, David who was Dungl, welcome to the Glade and the wild talk."

"Hallo, Rattltap, thanks. How did you know?" says David, his voice no longer quite the same.

"You will discover, one day, how the unwords tell us what we need to know. But now I must go to my beloved Tattlrap. Mowzl Emmy, I have left the other tiny humans playing with Twitchy and Skip."

"Fankz, Rattltap, see you innabit."

"Tchack!" and off he flies.

"Who's Twitchy and Skip?" asks David.

"They'z skwirrlz."

"Who's the tiny humans?"

"'E's meanin' purlaz. We's 'avin Billee n Larkee, n Pennee n Nosey, n you, so we's doin' orite."

"How do I find them?" David asks, wanting to explore and find his friends.

"Meremba, you's nevva finkin' ov yor footsiz wen you's walkin'. Be lettin' pouch be movin'.'."

David hesitates a moment then smiles as the pouch rises, gliding towards the trees.

"See you later, Emmy!" he calls, leaving Emmy among the fern fronds calling purlers to the Glade.

~

Donna, Larky's mum, calls upstairs to Larky. "Would you like to come shopping with me, Charlotte?"

No answer. She goes upstairs, thinking that Larky will be listening to music with her earphones on. She knocks on the door, calling again.

"Charlotte?"

There's no reply and straight away Donna is worried enough to knock again and open the door.

"Charlotte?"

She sees Larky asleep on her bed with her pouch in her hand;

she has a mischievous smile on her face. Donna touches her gently, and then a bit more firmly, but she doesn't wake up.

Donna spreads a blanket over her and goes quietly from the room thinking: *She's purling! Well done, Charlotte, I wonder if I can too?*

Donna has never been good at sleeping in the daytime, except when she's ill, but she is determined to try purling. She goes to her room, gets her pouch from the bowl of things she keeps there, and sits at her mirror. *What am I doing!* she thinks. *I must be a bit mad to think that I could fit into this little woollen bag.*

Looking down at the pouch in her hand she smiles, thinking of Emmy and of the wonderful times she's had since she met LuLu and everyone; she remembers the wool gathering, the spinning, and making pouches — it's all been such fun — but it's been disappointing that nothing has happened, nobody is purling yet. Emmy says that 'Purlin' 'appnz wen purlin' 'appnz, n'll nevva be 'urrid,' but that hasn't been very reassuring.

She looks up at the mirror again and to her amazement she sees the clearing in the woods. She looks closer, squinting her eyes, and the clearing seems to get closer. She smells the damp earth and hears birds singing, and there . . . she can see Emmy! Emmy is in his pouch snuggled in amongst the ferns. He's looking at her, smiling. *He's calling me!* she thinks, coming so close she could touch him.

"'Allo, Donna, iz you kno-in you's purlin'?"

"Hallo, Emmy. I went to look for Charlotte in her room and found her asleep on her bed."

"Larkeez purlin' 'ere wiv frendz. She's 'appy, n you's not 'avin' to wurree."

"Emmy, I'm not worrying, but I do feel strange. Am I really so small? Am I truly here? It's wonderful! I love it!"

Emmy purls over to the edge of the clearing, calling back for Donna to follow him.

"Donna, be comin'."

Donna tries to follow him, but her body won't move.

"Be like a rivva flowin'."

Donna imagines she is in a boat floating in a river, and she imagines untying a rope that's holding her back and she begins to move — it feels just like floating down a river!

"You's lernin' kwik, Donna, now pleez be findin' purlaz n be bringin' 'em all bak 'ere."

"How do I find them, Emmy?"

"Larkee'z in yor 'eart. You's flowin' to 'er like a rivva."

Emmy watches as Donna purls away into the woods. He returns to his place in the ferns, listening to birds singing and butterflies making rustly whispers with their wings; he can hear the earthworms pushing their casts of soil out of the ground; and then he hears the sound of a big animal making a racket as it pushes through the undergrowth, sniffing and snorting.

Purling higher for a better view, he sees a badger emerge from the bushes.

"'Allo, Mista Badja, mi name's Emmy n I's . . ."

"A mouse — yes, yes, I've heard of you. I've got no time for pleasantries, I'm looking for my young ones, they've been missing too long."

He keeps on going, stomping through the Glade, disappearing into the trees again. Emmy follows at a respectful distance.

"Iz you lettin us all be 'elpin'?"

"Who's 'us all'?" says Badger grumpily.

"Emmy n frendz."

"That would be kind, yes. Two young badgers, Firkin and Budge, missing since morning. Things are all wrong since their mother died."

"We'sll be findin' Firkin n Budj."

Emmy fades, disappearing with a pop. The badger stops to turn and look, grunts, and walks on.

Emmy reappears in the middle of the purlers playing tag with Twitchy and Skip. When Larky sees Emmy, she shouts out.

"Emmy's here!"

They slow down, gathering round. Donna is with them, having had such fun she completely forgot to say that Emmy wants them all back at the Glade. Twitchy and Skip cling to the nearest twigs.

"I's 'appy you's 'avin' fun but we's 'avin to 'elp Badja who's littl wunz iz missin'."

"Can we help look for them?" asks Donna.

"What's their names?" asks Penny.

"Them's Firkin n Budj."

"Come on, gang! Let's find Firkin and Budge!" cries Larky.

168

Billy, Larky and Donna race off.

"Wait a minute!" says David. "We need a plan!"

"Well, they've gone now, so we should just go a different way," says Penny.

"This way!" cries Nosey, purling away at top speed with David and Penny close behind. Twitchy and Skip follow but they are not so quick, because they have to find branches to leap along from tree to tree. Nosey seems to know where he's going and soon slows down to look carefully at the ground.

"There!" he cries. "Down there — under that oak tree, a trap!"

Budge is caught in a wire cage; Firkin scratches at the cage from the outside, but it is too strong for her to get into and Budge can't get out. Penny, Nosey and David hover in the air nearby.

"Who are you? Can you help? Please help, please," pleads Firkin, very frightened.

"We are Penny and Nosey and David," says Penny. "Yes, we can help, but we'll need to get more help to open the trap."

"Please hurry," says Budge, his voice desperate.

"We are too small to open the cage, we need a full-size human," Penny says, sounding worried too. "Dungl — I mean David — do you think you could purl to fetch Pip?"

"I'll have a go."

David stops moving and closes his eyes to concentrate; he fades a little, then comes back, then fades a bit more, finally disappearing with a pop.

"Well done, David!" cries Penny.

Nosey has been talking with Firkin and Budge, trying to comfort them a little. Twitchy and Skip arrive; they already know the young badgers and are very upset to see Budge caught in the trap. They inspect every bit of the trap to see if there is anything they could chew through or unclip, but it's too strong for them, and the latch too stiff for them to undo.

Emmy arrives, then Billy, Larky and Donna. Penny explains about David going to fetch Pip.

"You's clevva, Pennee. I's finkin' Billee should be 'elpin' n purlin to Pippee's."

"Emmy," says Billy, looking at the cage. "If I just stops purlin, so I's my 'uman size, I'll 'ave it open in a mo."

"Billee, you's 'avin to be merembrin, you'sll be wakin' at 'ome in yor boddee wen you's stoppin' purlin'. Pennee'z ideea iz good."

"Alright, Emmy, 'ow does I do purlin' to Pip's?"

"You's wantin' to be at Pippee'z 'ouse so you's lettin' great wave be carryin' you."

169

Pop! Billy's gone.

"Let's be callin' Badja," says Emmy.

"We've been calling him for a little while now," says Twitchy. "Here he comes! He's called Trundlweed."

Trundlweed arrives, looking tired and worried. He glances up at the cloud of five purlers.

"Hmm," he grunts. "Where are my cubs?"

"Here!" cries Skip. "See if you can open this thing."

"Hallo, Budge; hallo, Firkin; I'm glad we've found you. No, I'll not be able to open this trap, I've seen such things before many times and I know it's too strong for me. Have you got any ideas?"

Penny explains about David going to fetch Pip, and she says that Pip is a full-sized human.

"A human?" says Trundlweed, worried and suspicious.

"You have nothing to fear from Pip. He'll be able to open the cage and let Budge out," says Donna. "It'll be alright, so now you could comfort your cubs and tell them help is coming."

Trundlweed hesitates, unsure if he can trust these newcomers. He shrugs and grunts, turning his attention to the cubs. "Budge, we'll have you out in no time. Firkin, my dear, help is on the way." He nuzzles Budge through the wire mesh to reassure him.

Up in the trees, Twitchy and Skip hear alarm calls in the distance; they can hear jays screeching and squirrels scolding. It's coming from the direction of the road at the north edge of the woods. They scamper down to tell Trundlweed.

"There's a gate up there," he says. "There may be humans coming, we need to hurry."

"I's'll be 'avin' a look," says Emmy, disappearing in an instant. A few moments later he's back, saying that he's seen two humans with guns climbing over the gate by the road.

"Let's distract them away from here," suggests Donna.

"What? And let them see us?" cries Penny.

"Donna's xaklee rite," says Emmy. "We's needin' lot's ov creachaz to be makin' big noyz n get 'umans to be followin' 'em."

"Alright," says Trundlweed. "It's worth a try, I'll get help."

"We will too!" cry Twitchy and Skip, leaping away.

"I's callin' Rattltap," says Emmy.

Creatures start turning up at once; maybe it's the wild web, maybe the unwords — whatever it is, creatures are gathering: Natty and Flashy the jays; two ravens, Krunk and Kronk, who were flying over and heard Emmy calling; two magpies, Rachet and Racket; two blackbirds, Chink and Plink; two mistle thrushes, Thistl and Throstl — all creatures that can make lots of noise.

The plan is to make a big fuss a little way ahead of the humans, arouse their curiosity and so lead them away from where Budge is caught in the trap. The humans are likely to think that if they follow the commotion, they'll be able to shoot some fancy creature.

The plan works. The humans follow the mobbing creatures, and no wonder! With all that screeching and kronking and chinking, it's a show not to be missed!

Meanwhile, Pip, with Billy purling along beside him, rushes to Tillings Wood as fast as he can go. It's just as well that Billy went to get Pip because David wakes up in his own home, not at Pip's at all, and then he forgets to go to Pip's. Instead, he walks to LuLu's, and they set off for the Glade on foot.

Billy leads Pip to the trap. When they get near, they cause a bit of upset because Trundlweed is not used to allowing humans close to his cubs; some explaining has to happen before Pip can come close enough to open the trap. When he is freed, Budge runs to hide behind Trundlweed.

"Thank you," says Trundlweed. "Now we must go to the Glade and wait for the hunters to leave the wood. You, human, are invited too."

He disappears into the undergrowth followed by Firkin and Budge. The creatures making the mobbing noise hear the call to go to the Glade and they fall silent, slipping away into the trees.

"Who knows the way to the Glade?" asks Pip.

"We all do," says Penny.

"Will you show me the way, please? I wish I was purling too."

"This way, Mr Pip!"

~

Flashy and Natty, the two jays, stay on guard to keep an eye on the humans with guns; they silently follow them to know where they go and to be sure when the woods are safe again.

The two jays watch the humans scratch their heads in puzzlement when the mobbing noise stops; they watch them walk back to the badger trap and inspect it. Seeing that something had been caught but has escaped, they scratch their heads in puzzlement once again before walking on through the woods. At last they get to the gate by the road, climb over and drive away in their truck. Flashy and Natty fly to the Glade with the news that the humans have gone — for now.

"Good," says Trundlweed, and he climbs on to the talk-stone to speak. The talk-stone is just a rock, but tradition has it that anyone who has something to say should stand, or sit, on this particular rock. Trundlweed coughs a few times and begins.

"This may be the first time ever that we've invited a human to the Glade. I know that many of you will be feeling uncomfortable about this, and about the curious tiny humans floating about, but we all know that these humans have helped to rescue Budge from the human's trap, and for this we are grateful.

"I'm sure I'm not the only one who wants to know what these humans are doing here in the Glade, and how they are able to understand the wild talk. Would someone please explain to us?"

Emmy purls over to the talk-stone as Trundlweed steps down. He floats in the air, turning slowly, looking at the creatures all about him, one by one.

"Fankz for lettin' us all be 'ere. You's kno-in' a littl 'bout tiny flo-tin' 'umans, n now we's xplaynin' more . . ."

Emmy tells the creatures about how he came to their world from the future, and about how he needed Pip's help to write down 'Wot 'Appnd' so that he could find his way to get home again. He explains how he met the children, and about the wool gathering and making the pouches, and how the invisible ones are helping the human cubs to understand the wild talk. The human cubs want to learn from creatures about the wild web, so that they can tell the grown-up humans about all the things that are hurting the wild web so that they can stop doing them.

Emmy explains that Pip is his full size because he was needed to open the trap that Budge was caught in, and also to be able to write things down in his notebook. It's only because of the magic of the Glade that Pip can understand the wild talk.

When Emmy has finished, a rustle of whispering ripples through the assembled crowd of creatures. Emmy purls back to his fern fronds as Trundlweed returns to the talk-stone. He doesn't say anything, but his presence is enough for the moment. More creatures are arriving while whispered explanations are given.

LuLu and David arrive; they are not purling — they are full size. Some creatures are frightened and protest, and Trundlweed calls for silence.

"Welcome, one and all," he says in his gruff voice. "We are all feeling a cold wind in our bellies, for these are strange times, but let us hold our fear at bay while our hearts welcome the newcomers who want to learn the wild talk.

"We creatures have known for many winters that a day would come when we would all agree that enough is enough. You know what I mean. We have had enough of waiting for humans to awaken to the harm they do to the wild web. We have had enough of seeing our homes and families destroyed and the wild lands and seas reduced to deserts.

"Never before have we had humans in the Glade, and today the flying mouse is asking us to teach them about the wild web and the great wave.

"A few of us have been getting to know these newcomers over the last few moons, and I ask those who know to speak to us and tell us what it is that these humans want."

"Well said, Trundlweed!" kronked Kronk the raven from a nearby tree. "Who will speak first?"

Rattltap ruffles his feathers and flies to the talk-stone as Trundlweed steps down.

"Tchack," he says, to clear his throat. "I first met the flying mouse, whose name is Mowzl Emmy, before the winter — maybe seven moons past. He has been learning from me and my beloved Tattlrap, and many other creatures, about the wild web and what is happening in our world because of the things that humans do.

"Mowzl Emmy comes from the future. Where he comes from there are no humans and the wild web is not torn. He does not know how or why that is so.

"He is teaching the human cubs, and he brings a little magic so that they can understand the wild talk. This magic can only work because their hearts are open to seeing.

"I've wanted to help the flying mouse since the first day we met, and I want to help the human cubs too. Humans have forgotten how to feel the wild web and now they have a chance to discover it once again."

Rattltap looks around at the many faces watching him, then he flies to a tree and clings to the trunk.

"Thank you, Rattltap," says Trundlweed. "Who's next?"

"I'll say a word or two," says Priklstik. "Just to agree with Rattltap really. Life has been such fun since the flying mouse appeared. There is magic happening and we can all help!"

"Next!" calls Trundlweed, a trifle impatiently.

"May I speak too?"

All eyes seek out the owner of the voice, wondering who it is. One of the purlers moves to the talk-stone.

"My name is Nosey, and I'm a mouse; because I'm purling — that's what the flying is called — you all thought I was not a wild creature; I am a wild creature, just like you all.

"I have a special human friend — this is Penny." Penny waves, and smiles; Nosey continues. "Penny can feel the unwords, and from her I have learned that many humans have a great hurting in their hearts because they are so far from feeling the wild web and the great wave, and they would change the way things are if they could. Many humans try to save creatures and their homes, and many humans want to help but don't know how.

"It's time for us to teach the humans all that we can."

Nosey returns to the group of purlers gathered around Emmy. Trundlweed calls out.

"Next!"

There is a long silence.

"I's 'avin' a littl more sumfin' to be sayin'," says Emmy, rising up from the fern fronds and purling to the talk-stone. "Wot I's learnin' from creechaz iz makin' mi 'eart be 'urtin'. 'Umans iz too mennee n too greedee, n they's like dizeez wot'z killin' wild web."

He pauses, feeling the Glade and all the creatures there.

"We's 'avin' to be doin' sumfin' kwik n we's not kno-in' wot, so we's 'avin to be talkin' 'bout wotz rite n wotz rong, n 'avin' Pippee 'ere, who's good wiv lysts, to get all wotz said rit on paypah wiv majik ov ritin'."

"What use is a list?" says Budge, feeling fed up because he was caught in the trap and he's bored with all this talking even though he knows it's important. He's also fed up because he won't be able to eat anything until midnight.

Rindill the wren flies to the talk-stone as Emmy purls back to the fern fronds.

"The tiny creatures have asked me to speak for them," says Rindill. "The ants and woodlice, the mites and hoppers, beetles and centipedes, everything that lives in the soil and the leaf mould and the undergrowth. They want me to say that they may be little, but there's a lot of them and everything depends upon them; they say that the lists are a good idea and they've got a lot to say."

"Thank you, Rindill," says Trundlweed. "Anyone else want to say anything?"

Silence.

"May I say something?" says Penny, purling to the talk-stone.

"Of course, Penny Unwords," says Trundlweed.

"Thank you. I need to speak for all the trees and plants and growing things that are not creatures like us and they do not have the wild talk in the same way, but they do have the unwords.

"It is the growing things that grow the homes where we all live, and the wildwood where our hearts are nested, and they grow the food that we eat, and they make the soil rich and the air pure. Everything depends upon the growing things and we must all speak for them."

"Good words, Penny, thank you," says Trundlweed. "We will all speak for the plants and growing things. There are birds that live in the tops of the trees, and there are Rindill's tiny creatures that live in the earth itself and know about the roots of plants and the secrets of the soil. We will all speak for the growing things and honour them, because it is they that feed us with their abundance."

Trundlweed pauses for a moment. He's thinking that it's time to bring the formal bit of the gathering to an end so that all the creatures in the Glade can chat with each other.

"Anyone else?" he calls.

"May I speak?"

The creatures gasp at the sound of a human voice — LuLu's voice. She stands up slowly, aware of her great size compared to most of the creatures. She can sense their fear.

"Speak to us," says Trundlweed.

LuLu speaks very softly.

"My name is LuLu, I am a full-sized human. I know that you have listened to Penny speaking, and you were not afraid even though she is human. She is small, and I am sorry that you feel frightened of me. I do understand, because I, too, am frightened by the human world. Thank you for allowing me to be here at your gathering, and for letting me listen to the wise things that are being said. If you will allow me to say more, I would like to speak for the oceans and all the creatures and plants that live in the seas and rivers and lakes of the world. Their homes are being destroyed, just as our homes on the land and in the air are being destroyed, by the things that humans do; we must find creatures that come from the oceans to speak for all their cousins."

"That is well said, LuLu, thank you," says Trundlweed. "We will call our sea friends with the unwords and they shall speak. This gathering is now finished, and you are all free to get to know each other, but please remember the Code of the Glade — we all fast until midnight."

His job done, Trundlweed moves away, disappearing into the undergrowth.

~

Now that the gathering is officially over, the creatures chatter excitedly, exclaiming about how unusual it all is and how scared they were at the beginning to have humans so close. The purlers start chattering too.

"What does 'fast until midnight' mean?" asks Larky.

"Meremba, Larkee," says Emmy. "Lotz ov creechaz iz eetin'

each uvva, so they's 'avin truce."

"So that's why there's a code, I s'pose," says Penny.

"You's rite, Pennee, Trundlweed mite be eetin' Priklstik uvvawize."

"Oh, Emmy! You don't mean it, do you?" cries Larky.

"It's true, Larks," says Billy. "But Priklstik'll keep out of Trundlweed's way so long as there's enough 'abitat."

"Ooo! Get you with your fancy words, Billy!" teases Larky.

"It's true alright," says Budge, the young badger. "We badgers eat worms and slugs, fruits and roots, anything we find when we're rootling about. Trundlweed says that sometimes there's not enough to eat, especially when the ground is frozen or very dry and hard and we have to hunt other things. If only the wood was bigger . . ."

"Budge," says LuLu, sitting in the ferns near Emmy, trying to be as small as possible. "If you don't mind my asking, what happened to your mother?"

"Bundl she was called, and we miss her. Humans with guns killed her. Trundlweed says the humans blame us for their cows getting ill so they hunt us. We moved away, but too late for Bundl. I hurt for her."

"I'm so sorry, Budge."

"Budge, me Mum died 'n all when I was a nipper," says Billy. "Five I was. I knows what it's like."

"Was she hunted?" says Budge.

"No, she 'ad cancer."

"What's that?"

"She 'ad somethin' in 'er body what growd and growd 'n she died, 'n I 'urts for 'er too."

Billy purling in his pouch seems very small compared with the badger, but they look each other in the eye and they are united, recognising that they share the hardest feelings of all.

"Budge, this is the best — talkin' 'bout this with you — it's the best."

Budge feels a warm glow inside.

~

The purlers move about saying hallo to creatures, feeling happiness overflowing in their hearts because their dream has come true — they can understand the wild talk! After all the serious talk of the gathering, when everyone that spoke had to use the talk-stone, this is more like a party and it's fun.

The purlers say hallo to birds and caterpillars, greenflies and earthworms, rabbits and frogs — every sort of creature that you can imagine — and many more! Soon the purlers are feeling the unwords; they are beginning to understand without words. They begin to feel the plants and what they're saying; the plants are telling them how it is to be a plant and what the wild web feels like for a plant.

The full-size humans, Pip, LuLu and David, feel disappointed at first that they aren't purling too, but because of the magic of the Glade, there is so much wildness that they do understand the wild talk and even begin to feel the unwords. They stay sitting down, making themselves as small as possible, and the creatures and purlers come to them.

The purlers are learning about the wild web without noticing it happening. It's like having another five senses switched on all of a sudden. Little by little the creatures stop feeling quite so wary of the humans. There are so many creatures now that it's not possible for everyone to meet everyone else, but by the end of the afternoon the creatures agree that they want to help to teach the humans about the wild web. They begin to leave the Glade, flying away through the trees or creeping through the undergrowth or burrowing into the ground. The purlers disappear too, one by one, each one fading and vanishing with a little pop, leaving only the full-size humans, Pip, LuLu and David.

"Where's Emmy?" says David.

"Gone already, I think," says Pip.

"I's 'ere, talkin' wiv Rindill," says Emmy from the shadows.

Rindill flies up to the talk-stone and sings. Emmy purls up from the ferns that had hidden him.

"Rindill iz keepa of the Glade 'n 'e 'as sumfin' to be sayin'. I's bein' pulled, so I's 'avin' to be sayin' bi!" He disappears.

"Bye, Emmy!" sings Larky.

"Hallo, Rindill," says LuLu. "Thank you, and all the creatures, for letting us be here in the Glade."

"We creatures share an ancient memory — humans once could feel the unwords. We are happy that it is your wish to feel the unwords again."

"Why did humans stop feeling the unwords?" asks Pip.

"Human isness changed. As they became clever at thinking, isness changed to I-ness and the unwords faded from their hearts. It is time for the I-ness of humans to return to the whole. That is why we creatures welcome you here."

"Blimey," says David. "I don't get all that."

"I don't understand either, David," says Pip. "But it sounds right, if only we knew how to do it."

Rindill flies up into the air and down again, trilling his piercing song, and he has more to say.

"The human return is beyond your seeing, only your hearts will lead you," he says mysteriously.

"That's what Emmy teaches us too, Rindill," says LuLu.

"Now you must go from this place," says Rindill. "Prepare yourselves for the solstice gathering, in the winter. Until then, farewell!"

Rindill drops from the talk-stone, vanishing into vegetation.

"Wow!" says Pip.

"What's all that about?" says David.

"LuLu? Are you alright?" says Pip,

"The Glade is telling me something," LuLu whispers.

"Have you gone bonkers? The Glade can't talk," cries David.

"It's a feeling, David — the unwords. How can Rindill know about history? I'm feeling that this place holds the memory and the wisdom. It's the isness of this place, and it's this that Rindill feels; it's part of his isness, and part of his knowing."

"LuLu, you've lost me there," says Pip. "Come on, I'm tired, let's go home."

"LuLu, I do get that," says David. "Thanks! Isness of a place! I'm loving that."

"You're welcome, David. Come on then, let's go home!"

~

Early one morning, Billy's Nan goes downstairs to check on Frank in the front room. He doesn't sleep in a bed any more: he prefers his armchair. There he is, fast asleep, smiling.

Nan goes to the kitchen to start making breakfast; she picks up the kettle to fill it and is just about to turn the tap when a voice behind her stops her in her tracks.

"Wuzzie, I'm in heaven!"

She stands stock still, her hand on the tap. She hasn't heard her nickname 'Wuzzie' for years. The only person in the world to call her Wuzzie is Frank and he's asleep in his chair in the front room.

Nan slowly turns around, her eyes growing wide with surprise.

"What . . .?" she says, gasping.

Moving towards her, floating in his pouch, is Frank. He is as small as a mouse and looking like a child, a very happy child.

"Wuzz . . .?" begins Nan, her voice trembling and not able to form any words. She remembers how they used to call each other

Wuzz or Wuzzie, and it didn't matter which because they were alone and didn't get muddled up, but when Billy came to live with them it got a bit complicated and they stopped calling each other Wuzz or Wuzzie. After that, Frank began to talk to the fairies.

"Wuzzie," Nan manages to say. "Are you dead? Is that what you mean by 'I'm in heaven'?"

"No, no, I'm not dead, far from it!"

"Whatever happened to you?"

"Ask Billy, Wuzzie dear, he knows."

"Knows what, for heaven's sake?"

"About the invisible ones."

"Invisible whats?"

"After you and Billy tied the special bracelet on to my wrist the invisible ones began to tell me about the pouch in the bowl of things. You and Billy hadn't told me, so I didn't know what they were on about, but they showed me in a dream and here I am!"

Nan stares in astonishment. Frank hasn't talked like this for years, and never so many words at once.

"Frank, you really are off with the fairies now, you've got me really worried."

"You can do this too, Wuzzie."

"Do what, exactly?"

"Fly in your pouch, you've got one too, you know!"

"And why, exactly, would I want to do that? Someone around here has to keep their feet on the ground!"

"Because it's . . ." but Frank is interrupted by Billy's voice.

"'E's purlin', Nan, Grandpa's purlin'. Well done, Grandpa!"

"You see," says Grandpa. "I've always said they're here."

"What's he on about now, Billy?" says Nan, sounding irritated.

"Look, Nan," says Billy, walking over to the bowl of things on the dresser and picking up the three pouches. "'Ere's all three pouches. Grandpa's dreamin' into 'is pouch, so what you's seein' is 'is dream pouch, I'm 'oldin' the wool one."

"What's it all for? What are you talking about?"

"It's magic, Nan, it's so we can be near the invisible ones."

"Why? And what are they?"

"Nan, it's 'ard to say it, you'll 'ave to be purlin' to get it."

"I'm not sure that I want to . . . to be as small as a mouse? I shudder to think . . ."

"Nan, I's been purlin' lots. I's purlin' far away 'n talkin' wiv creatures 'n learnin' lots."

"Wuzzie, please stop your worrying!" says Grandpa. "You'll be purling soon and then you'll understand."

"I shall do no such thing!" cries Nan, truly frightened.

"Nan, no one's goin' to make you do anythin'," says Billy. "Come on, let's take 'im outside."

Billy opens the back door and Grandpa purls out into the early morning light. Billy follows, leaving Nan standing in the kitchen with her hands on her hips.

"Come on, Nan!" calls Billy, bright and cheerful; Nan softens, and her curiosity moves her feet for her as she goes outside too.

Grandpa purls about in the little garden, inspecting everything and greeting the plants and woodlice and spiders — and a passing bumblebee that's up so early that it's only just warm enough to fly.

"Billy," says Nan. "What about Grandpa in his armchair?"

"'E's alright, Nan, 'e won't wake up 'till 'e's done purlin'."

"Will he be able to find himself?"

"Yes, don't worry, Nan, 'e'll be fine."

Grandpa completes his tour of the little garden and purls over to Nan. They look into each other's eyes. Nan sighs.

"That's good, Wuzzie!" says Grandpa. "You needn't worry so." And he fades away, disappearing with a pop.

Nan shrieks, rushing into the house and through to the front room, where she finds Grandpa asleep in the armchair snoring and muttering as usual.

"Billy?" she calls.

"Yeah, Nan?"

"You've got some explaining to do."

~

Stomper Jack sometimes goes for a walk close to home along the footpath beside the railway line. There's a bit where the railway goes through a cutting and the footpath goes uphill steeply. On one side of the path fence panels close off people's back gardens, but on the railway side there's a strong fence made with upright metal strips with spiky tops. It's called palisade fencing and it's really hard to climb over unless there's something to stand on to climb up — and something to climb down again on the other side. There's nowhere to do that.

Near the top of the slope the fence has been bent by a branch that fell from a tree that used to grow on the railway side of the fence. The tree was cut down to a stump after that. The vertical metal strips in the fence got bent and two of them bent different ways, making a squeezy gap that Stomper Jack can just get through. One day when she is out on one of her 'being alone' walks, she squeezes through the gap in the fence and wriggles her way through the tangle of undergrowth growing on the slope of the cutting.

She goes to the big tree stump where she has a den. It's all that remains of the tree that was cut down after the fence got damaged. It's still alive and growing, but the railway people come every few years and cut the new growth, so it never gets tall. You can see some of the tree roots above the ground because of the steep slope of the railway cutting; the rain and burrowing creatures have washed and scraped the soil downhill, bit by bit, exposing the roots more and more. The roots are entwined together in a lattice, but there is a gap where Stomper can wriggle through to get inside. There she can sit or curl up, but not stand.

Stomper loves this place. She thinks of it as her lair. A lair is like a den but wilder. Even though it's close to the path she can't be seen by anybody, especially now that it's summer and the leaves protect her. Stomper loves to feel safe like this, and alone, so that she can daydream properly.

Today she sits in the lair enjoying the secure feeling that she has surrounded by the roots; she likes the smell of the tree and the rich, earthy smell of the ground. Looking out through the lattice of roots she watches the wind moving twigs and leaves in the bushes; she listens to the secret sounds that come from the wind, and from birds and insects all around. She can make the town noises disappear when she's in her lair, but not the trains. When the trains come they are too loud to make disappear, but she doesn't mind; they are dragons passing by.

A dunnock appears, flicking from twig to twig close to the ground. Some people call this bird a hedge sparrow, but it isn't a sparrow; it's got a thin, sharp beak for eating insects, not like a sparrow with its strong beak for eating seeds.

The dunnock sees Stomper and comes right up close to have a look. Stomper notices that the feathers aren't all brown; when the light moves on them they are blue, the breast and the head are blue-grey and the legs are pink. *It's gorgeous,* Stomper thinks, as she gazes in wonder at the little bird as she begins to do what she calls proper daydreaming.

"Hallo, little bird, you are very beautiful. I've never seen a bird like you before."

"I've never seen a whatever-you-are before!" says the dunnock. "My name is Tinkalin, what are you?"

"My name is Jackie," says Stomper. "I'm a human."

"A human! Ha! Humans are big and clumsy and break things, but you are no bigger than me and you can fly without wings!"

Stomper Jack is shocked to hear this and she backs away from Tinkalin, bumping into the roots of the lair. She turns to see what she's bumped into — and gasps.

"What's happening to me?"

The tree stump is right in front of her, and sitting inside is a girl, daydreaming. The girl looks exactly like Stomper. It is Stomper!

"I must be dreaming," she says.

"Are you alright?"

"Yes and no, Tinkalin. What do I look like to you?" says Stomper, turning to look at the bird.

"You look like a fairy with red hair and green eyes, but you haven't got any legs that I can see."

Stomper looks down at her legs — and sees her pouch!

"Tinkalin, I'm very alright! I'm purling! Hooray!"

She turns back to look at herself sitting in the lair, purling closer to examine herself. "Do I really look like that? Ha-ha! Hallo, me, are you awake? Hmm, if you wake up I'll disappear, won't I?"

The life-sized Stomper that she's looking at doesn't move or talk. It's a shock. It's not like looking in a mirror, not at all. A mirror makes everything the wrong way round, so this is a bit like looking at a stranger. Purling Stomper sees that full-sized Stomper is a bit scruffy and wild-looking; her red hair and the determined look on her face make her look fierce!

"I like you!" says purling Stomper to full-sized Stomper. She turns back to Tinkalin.

"I'm alright now, Tinkalin. I just had to say hallo to myself."

"Hmm. Strange indeed," says Tinkalin. "What are you feeling now, Jackie?"

"Different, light, excited! I don't know 'me' any more, but I feel at home."

"The heaviness is your full-sized human body," says Tinkalin. "You are light now because you are all heart-thought."

"Is that why my fingers don't really touch anything? Look! If I try to touch your feathers, it's like my fingers are *seeing*."

"Yes! You are seeing in a new way. You're lucky, Jackie!"

"Except it will end, and full-size Stomper will wake up."

"You must go to the Glade, Jackie, before you wake up."

"The Glade? That's miles away in Tillings Wood!"

"You will be taken there by your heart-thoughts. Go now!"

"I'm being pulled! Oh, Tinkalin, what's happening?"

"Jackie, be like the wind! Goodbye!"

"Bye, Tinkalin, thanks . . ."

Stomper is moving — well, her pouch is moving and she's inside it, rising out of the thicket of bushes on the railway embankment. She can see the railway lines below glinting in the sun, and she sees houses with small gardens backing onto the railway. She gets higher, seeing more of the town spread out below; she sees the network of little roads that join up to bigger roads, and she sees parks with swings and slides and grass to play on.

"There's my house!" she cries out loud. "There's Mummy in the garden! Hallo, Mummy! Oh, she can't hear me."

Stomper looks down at the familiar roads that she often walks along to get to school, and to the local shop, and she sees the park where she goes to play with school friends sometimes. Maybe purling does give a new way of seeing. Whatever it is, she looks down on the patchwork pattern of her hometown, and she feels for the first time that she is beginning to understand what Emmy has been saying about the wild web. She looks harder, trying to put her finger on what it is but can't quite get it.

She sees the labyrinth of roads and houses and she sees how tidy it all is; every scrap of space has been built on or covered in concrete or tarmac for cars to park on, except for little bits of mown grass beside the roads, and the gardens at the back of the houses. Some of the gardens are empty, just a lawn or paved patio or gravel, and some of them are planted with fancy things bought in pots from the garden centre; just a few gardens, here and there, are little jungles where you could hide and play and make a den and daydream properly.

The pouch carries Stomper on towards the edge of town and towards open country, crossing bigger roads and roundabouts, purling over factories and huge car parks next to supermarkets and warehouses. There are little patches of grass here and there and a few shrubs and trees dotted about, but that's it really. At the edge of town, she sees whole fields being bulldozed and roads being built for the new houses and shops and factories that will be built.

Purling on into the countryside, Stomper looks down on a beautiful tapestry of fields divided by hedgerows and country lanes. Some fields are brown earth with crops just beginning to emerge, other fields are shimmering with luscious grass or young wheat or barley. She sees the wind writing secret stories into the young barley, the wind-words rippling across the silvery fields.

She purls on, lower now, and she feels the truth of Pip's 'ecology lesson'. She can see that these fields have only the crop that is grown for humans. She can see that there is no room for wildness and because she is purling, she can feel how wildness is squashed down; the wildness is trying to push up towards the sun again, but is always cut, or ploughed or poisoned. Even the hedgerows are trimmed, like in a town garden, and will not make fruit or seeds for the birds and creatures in winter.

The farmland is nearly as tidy as the town! she thinks. *Wildness is squashed . . .why do we humans do that? It's like humans want to get rid of nature. It hurts me . . .*

The pouch carries Stomper on across the fields, past small copses and stands of trees on ground too steep for tractors to plough. From a distance they look nice and it's a relief to see some trees, but when she gets close up, she sees that beneath the trees nothing grows: there are no homes for creatures at all. The land is used for what humans and their farm animals need.

Stomper purls on with a heavy heart. She has never seen the world like this before and she feels a terrible sadness because wildness is missing. It's so bewildering. Everything looks right and normal and she realises that it *would* be right and normal to her if she hadn't met Emmy. Humans have to grow food to eat, and need homes to live in. What's the problem? *Humans are just taking too much, that's what it is, 'cos there's so many of us,* she thinks. *What was it Mr Pip said? Give land back to Nature, that's what he said, but how can we do that? Oh dear.*

She sees woodland in the distance — Tillings Wood — and she remembers how good she always feels when she's there. She frowns, thinking of the network of roads she has just been flying over. Why can't there be a network of wild woodland coming right into the heart of the town, bringing the wildness of Tillings Wood right to her own street?

The instant that Stomper has this thought, she finds herself in Tillings Wood. The wild web is strong and fills her heart with happiness, and yet she bursts into tears because of the sadness she has been feeling.

"So, purlers can cry real tears!" she says, laughing and crying at the same time.

"Yes, Stomper Jack, welcome to the Glade; my name is Rindill."

"Thank you, Rindill," says Stomper, watching Rindill flick his body from one position to another, as wrens do. "I don't quite believe this is happening, perhaps I'll wake up in a minute."

"You won't wake up yet, you are purling. This is the Glade, you've been here before, do you remember? What do you see?"

"Yes, I remember the Glade, Rindill, and I remember you and the gathering of creatures, but now everything feels strange — I'm *feeling* everything I see — it's like — it's like I haven't got any skin, and instead of touching things I'm joined to them. It's making me dizzy."

"You're feeling the wild web, Stomper Jack, and your human I-ness is melting. You are feeling the isness that you are."

"Emmy didn't say that it would be like this, that it would hurt."

"He didn't say anything because every human will find their own way to isness, and it will be different for each one. For some it will be harder than it is for you."

"Why does it have to be so difficult?"

"For a long time, humans have been so clever that they have thought themselves to be separate from the wild web; humans believe that everything in Nature is for humans to control, and to take, and to use. Humans have become separated and can think 'I am' as though they exist without the wild web, but that is an illusion. We don't know if all this is good or bad, or right or wrong, but we do know that humans are destroying the wild web. Humans are not noticing because they are thinking without their hearts.

"Stomper Jack, it is difficult and painful for you to feel the wild web, but you can do it. Your I-ness will melt, and you will learn how to be a human with I-ness and isness together."

"Rindill, your words float through me and disappear, and I don't know where they go but the meaning just happens inside like the sun coming from behind a cloud."

"That's the unwords. You are learning fast, Stomper. You should return now and rest. This place is where you will come to when the gathering is called."

"How will I know?"

"You will know."

"Goodbye, Rindill, thank you."

"Thank you, too, little human isness. Until we meet again."

Rindill flies up to a favourite high twig and trills his trill so loud that Stomper covers her ears. She watches as Rindill drops down, disappearing into the undergrowth. She heaves a great sigh, and as her breath flows out, she vanishes with a little pop.

~

Stomper Jack wakes from her daydreaming in her lair under the tree roots by the railway. She can hear Tinkalin singing a little way off in the blackthorn scrub, the sound clearer and sweeter than she has ever noticed before.

She crawls out of the lair, feeling the earth and stones under her hands and smelling the sweet smell of the ground. She rubs her hands into the earth and touches the bark on the roots of the tree, feeling the texture and the life surging inside. Her body is seeing as though she is still purling, her senses alert as never before.

Standing up, she looks at the sunlight cascading through the leaves above her, making many shades of green. Pushing through the bushes, she scratches a forearm on some thorns; beads of blood appear on her skin and she sucks the wounds clean, relishing the metallic smell and taste of her blood. The crisp pain reminds her that she has skin again.

Memories of purling come flooding back and she laughs out loud in her happiness to be alive. Squeezing back through the palisade fence, she runs down the footpath beside the railway embankment heading home. Hungry and thirsty, she's looking forward to a snack. She is amazed, when she arrives home, to discover that she has been out for only half an hour.

~

Pip usually does one day a week working in Mr Wylder's garden. One day he turns up for work to see a familiar old and battered off-road vehicle in the drive.

"Emmy!" exclaims Pip. "Tom's home! This should be fun."

"Iz Emmy 'idin' or sayin' 'allo?"

"Emmy, he's used to all sorts of wildlife, but you'll knock his socks off! Let's surprise him — you stay quiet for a bit."

"Orite."

Pip slides Emmy into the breast pocket of his shirt and knocks on the front door. The door opens and framed in the doorway is the familiar figure of Mr Tom Wylder; he's a stocky, powerful-looking man, with a weather-beaten face and piercing blue eyes.

"Ah! Pip! Welcome! Come in! I'm home at last and it's good to be back and see the old place again."

"Hallo, Tom. It's nearly a year, isn't it?"

"Yep. This trip went on longer than planned. We had trouble, but we'll get to that later; let's have a cuppa and a catch-up."

Mr Wylder, wildlife cameraman, has been working in South America with a team of scientists, studying an area of tropical rainforest to film and record the wildlife. The scientists wrote reports to help governments plan for conservation. Well, that's what they hoped.

Mr Wylder talks about this for a while and then wants to know how Pip is getting on, and what's been happening around here.

Pip smiles. "Well, Tom, since you went away, something has happened that's changed my life."

"What? For heaven's sake, tell me!"

"I met this mouse."

"What mouse?"

"This one, in my shirt pocket."

Mr Wylder had already noticed the toy mouse in Pip's pocket, but now he looks more closely.

"'Allo, Mista Wylda," says Emmy.

"Good Lord! It spoke!"

"Mi name's Emmy n I's 'appy meetin' you, Mista Wylda."

"Hallo, Emmy, I'm happy to meet you too! Extraordinary. Pip, I need an explanation."

Pip begins to tell the story, with Emmy chipping in here and there, and they talk together all day and well into the night. Pip doesn't get any gardening done at all.

Tom is fascinated and wants to know more, and so Pip returns on another day with the orange ring binder and he reads the whole of 'Wot 'Appnd'. When they get to the bit in the story about Emmy's first purling, Tom asks where Emmy is now — at that moment, Emmy appears in front of Tom, purling.

"Astonishing! May I photograph you, Emmy?" asks Tom.

"Yip, I's 'appy."

Pip continues to read the stories right up to the recent meeting in the Glade.

"It's still happening, Tom. Every day — well, most days — I wake up to find a handful of written pages on the floor. I gather them up and put them in the ring binder. It's still a mystery how it gets written, especially the stories of Emmy's home world, and I wonder who the narrator is, because it certainly isn't me."

"I'm sure there'll be an explanation eventually," says Tom. "I'd like to meet your gang of friends, Emmy. But, Pip, something I don't understand — Emmy says he's been here for four winters, but you said he's changed your life and you've only just met him!"

"Yes, no, you're right, Tom. Emmy arrived four years ago, well, more than that now. He's been a big part of my life all that time, and LuLu's life too, but we haven't been introducing him to people. Now that 'Wot 'Appnd' is getting written and purling is happening, it's time for Emmy to meet everyone."

Tom and Pip are sitting on foldout chairs on the grass and Emmy is purling round the garden. Tom is wearing his usual outfit: tough boots, shorts, a greenish shirt, a greenish sleeveless jacket with lots of pockets, and a hat shading his eyes. Emmy purls back to join the two men.

"I want to meet your friends, Emmy," Tom declares. "Let's invite them all here for a picnic, right here in the garden."

"Good ideea, Mista Tom, they'sll be lovin' it," says Emmy.

"Yes, good plan, Tom," says Pip. "Some of the gang have been here before helping me with the gardening. They love being here. When shall we do it?"

"I'm away for a bit, so let's say, er, Saturday at 12 o'clock?"

"Perfect, I'll let them know."

"Excellent!"

~

Later that day, with Emmy purling at his shoulder, Pip walks around town visiting everyone they want to invite to Tom's picnic. The invitation is to come on Saturday at 12 o'clock, and to be their full size, not purling. This causes some excitement and some plans have to be changed, but when Saturday comes everyone turns up.

Tom introduces himself and explains that Pip and Emmy have been reading 'Wot 'Appnd' to him, so he knows that some of them have learned purling already.

"What's it like? Purling, I mean," he asks.

"Hallo, Mr Wylder, I'm Stomper Jack. I think purling's different for everyone, and some of us have had a really hard time and some of us make it look easy. But what's it like? It's the best thing, it's like swimming the wild web."

"That's a good image. Why do you think it can be so hard for some people?" asks Tom.

"'Cos you 'as to be wakin' up, 'n it 'urts," declares Billy.

"I think what Billy means," says Penny, "is that we are different when we're purling, and we aren't used to it, so it can make us feel ill. We see the wild web with all our senses, we feel it, and feel part of it, instead of seeing separate things. It can make us dizzy and sick."

"It's seein' wiv our 'earts," agrees Billy.

"It's brilliant, Mr Wylder," cries Larky. "You'll just love it, 'cos you know so much about Nature."

"Me?" cries Tom.

"Yes!" says Donna. "You just have to make a pouch. I'll show you, come over to our place sometime and you can make a pouch."

"Thank you, I will. But now I want to ask you all something. Pip told me what happened in the Glade, and that you are going to think of things that are good for Nature and things that are bad for Nature and get it all written down. I'd really like to help. Have you got much further with that?"

"We're waiting for more wild talk with creatures," says David.

"Well, I have an idea," suggests Tom. "While you're waiting, why not brainstorm it and really find out what you think about it and what you know and don't know, then you'll be ready to listen to the creatures."

"That's a good idea, where do we start?" says Penny.

"Well, you've learned a bit about the wild web already, and you'll be learning more from the creatures. What you can do now is to ask yourselves what you feel about Nature, and what you feel about what humans are doing. You could ask yourselves — what do you want, and what don't you want? That would be a good place to start, then we can look at what Nature actually needs."

The children begin to suggest things they care about, and ideas come faster and faster as they shout them out, competing with each other. It's hard to hear what's going on but Pip writes as fast as he can: 'stop killing animals', 'stop cutting trees', 'we want more wild places', 'put poachers in prison', 'don't kill badgers', 'stop climate change' and many more things. Tom tries to quieten things down and at last his voice can be heard above the racket.

"Alright, alright, good, good, but let's slow down a bit. Pip, are you getting this written down?"

"Some of it, Tom, but I can't keep up."

"Alright, everybody! Let's have a bit of order, let's go in a circle starting with you, David. You don't have to think of more than one thing at a time because your turn will come again as we go around."

"Erm . . . humans just take from Nature, and there's too many humans so Nature is hurting."

"Could we call that 'Give back to Nature', David?" asks Tom.

"Yeah, alright, but give what back?"

"What could we give back to Nature?" asks Tom.

"Freedom to be what it wants!" cries Penny.

"That's what we want too, isn't it?" says Larky.

"Exactly," says Tom. "Can you think of anything practical? To give back to Nature, I mean."

"Give land back to Nature, that's what I think," says Pip.

"Yes! That's what I think too," cries Stomper Jack.

"We want more wild places!" cries Larky.

"And leave Nature alone," says Billy.

"Pip, are you getting all this?"

"Yes, Tom."

"Next, let's go clockwise. Stomper?"

"I want wild places to be closer to where I live, not miles away."

"Alright, good, how about 'Rewild right into our towns'?"

"Good!" says Pip. "That's good for now, I'll write that down."

"What's 'rewild' when it's at 'ome?" Billy asks.

"It's what it sounds like, Billy," says Tom. "Leaving Nature alone to go wild by itself without humans meddling. There's a lot of arguing going on about it because people have different points of view. Some people want to see big herbivores and predators brought back — I do — but other people don't want that at all. But let's get back to our list, shall we? Donna, I think you're next."

"Thanks, Tom. What about the harm that's done in the name of progress and growth and there's nothing to stop it. They talk about 'sustainable growth', but that seems to be a contradiction, so what can we do to keep nature safe?"

"Thanks, Donna, that's good. We could think about what that means . . . safe from what?"

"Safe from climate change, for a start," says Donna.

"Safe from chainsaws and bulldozers!" says David.

"Safe from nasty chemicals," says Larky.

"We need Nature," Penny says, thoughtfully. "Nature should have rights, like people have rights."

"That's very good, Penny," says Tom. "We must develop that idea later."

"What do you mean, 'develop'?" asks Stomper.

"Well, we all probably have a different take on what 'Nature's rights' might mean. It's really important and we will talk about it much more, but now we need to build our list of ideas. Make sure it's on the list, Pip!"

"Right, Tom."

"There's too many people!" cries Stomper Jack. "We need monsters to eat people up."

"Good idea, Stomper," says Tom, laughing. "But the people with guns would just shoot them dead."

"Stop making guns!" cries Billy.

"We'll come back to 'population' later as well, it's really important," says Tom.

"Where's Emmy?" Larky asks.

"Purling around, I think," says Pip. "Probably talking with creatures."

"Why isn't he helping us?"

"We have to do it ourselves now, Larky," says Pip. "He's given us a good start, and it's up to us now."

"O-w-a!" cries Larky. Like everyone else, she's worried about how they will know what to do without Emmy. Tom breaks the silence.

"I've got an idea. Pip, have you written down the suggestions that everyone has made?"

"Yep, well nearly everything."

"Let's go inside, I want to show you something."

Tom's sitting room is arranged for him to do his film editing work. There are computers and various devices on worktables and on one wall is a large screen. Tom switches on the wall-screen and a computer, and as he types on the keyboard, words appear on the wall-screen. He types two headings: 'What we want' and 'What we don't want'.

"Alright, Pip, could you read out what you've got written down? I'll type it under the appropriate heading."

"Right-oh."

Pip reads out the suggestions and Tom types them into the computer. There's a buzz of excitement as the ideas appear on the screen. The words seem to become more significant now that they're typed and can be seen on the screen; they are no longer just sounds that fade away into the air — now they look solid and important!

What we want

We want everyone to know Nature's in big trouble
We want everyone to care more and do something about it
Make homes for wildlife
Give back to Nature, rewild and stop meddling
Make more wild places with wolves and monsters
Make more woods and plant squillions of trees
We want green energy
Make more animal hospitals
Nature's Rights: make hurting Nature a crime
Put them in prison when people hurt pets and animals
Bring wild Nature back into towns where people need it
Give us back our common land

What we don't want
  Stop climate change. No more smelly oil, coal or gas
  Stop too many humans happening
  We don't want our lives to be without wild Nature
  We don't want wild creatures being hurt or killed
  Stop slavery of humans and animals
  Stop poaching and hunting and all cruelty to animals
  Stop cutting down trees and woodland
  Stop covering Nature with concrete and roads and houses
  Stop making guns and bombs and wars
  Stop pollution
  Stop factory farming
  Stop machines smashing everything

  "Let's take a break now while I print this for you," says Tom.
  "Here's Emmy!" cries Larky, always the first to notice when
Emmy arrives.
  "'Allo, Larkee, 'allo, evree wun."
  Emmy purls slowly round the room, looking at every one.
There's a seriousness about him that makes them all attentive.
  "You's makin' good list, I's very 'appy," he says at last. No one
wants to break the silence as they wait for him to continue.
  "Creachaz iz askin' Emmy to be merembrin' to 'umans . . . wild
web iz dyin', n 'umans 'as to be changin' n listnin' to creachaz, n
listnin' to wild web."
  After a long silence, Tom speaks.
  "I think Emmy is reminding us how serious this is. Emmy, I'm
sorry if you feel that we're not being serious enough . . ."
  "You's all dun perfik, Mista Tom, fankz."
  Emmy purls slowly back out to the garden.
  "Oh dear," says Pip. "I've not seen Emmy so down in the
dumps for a long time. I'll have a chat with him later and see what's
wrong."
  "Why don't you go outside and be with him now, Pip?"
  "I know him too well, Tom, he'll need to be alone for a while,
but maybe we should all be outside."
  "Yes, I've got one more idea to share with the children, and then
we'll all go outside."
  "What is it, Mr Tom?" says Billy.
  "Well, I'm thinking about how you'll all be purling and learning
from creatures about the wild web, and I reckon you're going to be
having a great time this summer! What I want to suggest is that you
work on these ideas during the summer holidays, and when term

starts, you can make it a school project.

"Get your teacher to help you, you could make a questionnaire for all the school children to say what they think, and you could get parents to do it as well. Emmy tells me that there's going to be a big gathering in the Glade in the winter. You need to be ready by then with your ideas strong and clear!"

"That's all well and good, Tom, but what use is a list?" says Donna.

"Well, Donna, Pip has read me the story. I understand that you all feel very strongly about Nature and want to do something to help, but you don't know what. You've all agreed that the best way to find out what to do is to learn purling and to learn from creatures about the wild web. You are doing these things, and you are getting clearer about what the problems are, but you still have a lot of homework to do. When you've done the work, you must prepare a report, or list of suggestions or even a list of demands and present it to the government of the country."

"Mr Tom, that's frightening," says Penny, her voice strangely hushed. "You make it sound too big for us to do. We want to talk to the wild creatures and we want to do purling, but these lists make us feel heavy."

"You's right, Penny!" cries Billy. "Mr Tom, we doesn't want it like school!"

"I get that. Sorry to bring you down," says Tom. "What I mean is this: what we have just done today is to listen to feelings, feelings that we all have because we love Nature, and we've started to understand those feelings and come up with ideas. You'll be purling again soon and spending time with wild creatures, and you'll be able to talk with them. What a miracle! How amazing is that? With the wild creatures you can find out what really matters. The creatures will help you with that, but to really hear them you need to be as clear as you can possibly be."

"Thanks, Mr Tom, you've been a really great help," says Penny.

"So, what do *you* think really matters, Tom?" asks Donna.

"Ha!" interrupts Billy. "Like Mr Pip says, 'umans 'as to give land 'n sea back to Nature, 'n let it go wild 'n not take so much."

"Very good, Billy, yes, very succinct," says Tom. "Thinking about it like that is what the lists are for. I've been thinking about this for my whole life, working all over the world. I've seen wildlife disappearing, habitats disappearing, oceans changing, and climate changing . . .

"I've seen people losing their way of life and their homes because of these changes. I have seen people forced to migrate because the land where they live can no longer support them, and this is happening more and more. It's really hard to know what to do to help Nature, but every little thing we do is really important, everything, but the sad thing is that even though so many good things are being done to help Nature, the destruction goes on and is getting worse all the time.

"All we can do is find out what's going on and tell everybody; people don't know, except when they live where the horrible things are happening. Industry hides the truth, just look at advertising! Politicians hide the truth. That's why I make films."

"Have you got any films we could watch, Mr Tom?" asks Larky, yawning.

"I have, Larky, but not for today. I think we've done enough for today, and you should all get back outside. I'll just print these lists for you to take . . ."

The printer clicks and whirs, and Tom collects the pages and hands them round so that everyone has one. The children look at them with frowns on their faces. Their excitement of the last few days has become a scrap of paper that Tom is calling 'homework'. They fold the paper into small squares and stuff them in their pockets.

"Come on, everyone!" says Pip. "I can tell that you're all fed up with all this talk. Tom's given us some really good ideas and we don't have to figure it all out now. Come on! I'll count to ten, and anyone I find indoors after that does the washing up!"

"Yikes, let's get out of 'ere!" yells Billy, and after a moment's mayhem the children have all disappeared outside.

"Well done, Pip," says Donna. "I could feel their frustration."

"I hope I haven't put them off," says Tom, anxiously.

"They'll bounce back," LuLu says reassuringly. "All they need is to be outside running about."

"Tom," says Pip. "What you've been saying will serve them well when they go back to school, but now the last thing they want to think about is school, or anything to do with it."

"Hmm. You're right, I did lay it on a bit thick, didn't I?"

"Don't worry. I'd better get out there!"

Pip stands up, stretches, and goes out into the garden yelling: "Coming if you're ready or not!"

"Let's clear up the picnic things," suggests Donna.

"Tom," says LuLu. "Thanks for what you've done. I know the children seem a bit fed up now, but they needed to be given a way to face up to the big question 'what can we do?' It isn't going to be easy for them, or the grown-ups, and it won't all be fun. This wake-up call would be uncomfortable however it happened."

"I suppose that's true. It's hard for me to see how they can possibly do anything that will make a difference. But they have to try, just as we all have to try, and I'll help them in any way I can."

"Well said, Tom," LuLu agrees. "We'll all do what we can."

~

The children recover quickly from Tom's talk about homework, lists and school projects. Within a few days they've forgotten all about it and the summer holidays have begun. They meet often in the Glade, sometimes purling, sometimes not, learning how to call each other with their hearts.

The creatures of Tillings Wood lose their fear of them, especially when they are purling, and now the wild talk makes it possible for everyone to get to know each other. The children learn more of how creatures and plants feel about the harm done by humans to the wild web.

Sometimes the creatures will say something like, 'You must visit our cousins over the sea and hear what they have to say.' The trees too might say, in their slow way, 'You must visit our cousins in the jungles of the world and hear what they have to say.' But the children are not quite ready to purl so far away from their sleeping bodies. They practise every day, going a little bit further each time.

One day, when the sky is clear and blue above Tillings Wood, the purling children are playing chase with swallows and martins. LuLu appears amongst them and Larky shrieks with delight.

"LuLu! Hooray! Come and play!" she cries.

LuLu joins in, but not for long. She slows down, floating quietly, loving watching the children and birds playing. One by one the children gather around her — Billy and Larky, Penny and Stomper Jack, and David who was Dungl.

"LuLu," says Penny. "Where's Emmy and Mr Pip? We haven't seen them for quite a while and would love to; can we go and see them now?"

"I think they need to be alone for a while, they've gone away to have a think about things."

"Where, LuLu? Where have they gone?" cries Stomper Jack.

"They've gone to the sea, they'll be back in a few days."

"LuLu, can we go too?" says David. "I'd love to go to the sea!"

"C'mon, LuLu, we's just 'avin' to go!" says Billy.

"LuLu! We must all go!" cries Penny.

"Oh dear!" LuLu sighs. "I can see there's no stopping you now.

Alright, prepare yourselves for purling a very long way — are you ready for this? You will be purling further away from your sleeping bodies than you ever have before."

"We've been practising, LuLu," cries Stomper Jack. "We've learned from the wild talk that we have to purl far away to hear what the creatures have to say — we *are* ready!"

"Do you want to take anyone else with you?" asks LuLu.

"I's callin' Grandpa wiv my 'eart," says Billy.

"I'm calling Mummy!" cries Larky.

"I'm calling Nosey," says Penny.

"Ready now? All ready? Let's go!" cries LuLu.

The End

For release in the coming months . . .

The Adventures of Horatio Mowzl

Volume Three

The Great Rising

Chapter One

Creatures

Pop! Pop! Pop!

"Wha-at? What's happening?" cries Pip, swerving the car as purlers appear in front of his eyes.

"Purlaz iz 'appnin', Pippee!" says Emmy, laughing.

Pop! Pop! Pop! Pop! Pip's car fills with excited purlers, all laughing and whizzing about.

"Hallo!" says Larky.

"Where are we going?" asks Penny.

"Wait a minute," says Pip. "What are you all doing here? Wait, let me find somewhere to stop . . . Hey, don't purl in front of my eyes, I can't see where I'm going!"

Pip drives on, looking for somewhere to pull off the road.

"Phew," he says, when able to stop driving at last. "Alright you lot, what's going on?"

"Pip, I'm sorry," says LuLu. "I let slip that you and Emmy might be going to the seaside — we were purling over Tillings Wood and suddenly — here we are!"

"Are you really going to the sea?" Penny asks hopefully.

"Yip, we's visitin' oshn."

"Emmy! Please may we come?" Larky pleads. "Pleeeease?"

"May we come, Mr Pip?" says Stomper. "Please?"

"Is anyone else coming?" asks Pip. "Let's see now, who have we got here: Stomper, Billy, LuLu, Larky, Penny, Nosey, David . . . and who's this?"

"It's Grandpa, Mr Pip," Billy explains. "'Is name's Frank."

"Hallo, Frank, welcome to purling."

"It's the best thing ever, Mr Pip."

"Is that everyone? Anyone else?"

"Don't know, Mr Pip," says David.

Pop! "'Allo, Donna!" Emmy cries. "You's comin' too!"

"Hallo, everyone! No way I'm missing out on this trip, Emmy."

"Hallo, Mummy!" Larky is feeling very pleased because she has been able to 'call' her mum with her heart.

Pip greets Donna. "Hallo, Donna, I'm glad you're here. Now listen, everyone, I know you're all happy and excited at the moment but if we drive to the sea you'll get further and further away from your bodies and your wool pouches . . ."

"We'll be alright," says Stomper. "We've been practising a lot and now we can purl a long way, don't worry."

"Well, I don't think I could do it. Emmy, what do you think?"

"They'sll be orite, Pippee, n we'sll be meetin' lotz ov creachaz wot'll be teachin' 'uman cubz, so let's be goin'.."

"But what if something happens to your bodies back at home?"

"Pippee, you's nevva to be wurryin', we'sll be pulld wen we's pulld. Let's be goin' to oshn."

"Alright, if you're sure."

The purlers cheer as Pip restarts the car and drives back onto the road, heading west towards the hills. He opens the window a little and Stomper hovers on the edge of the slipstream, sucking at the opening.

"Ha-ha! This is fun," she cries. "Oh-oh — whoops!"

Suddenly the wind sucks her out of the car; she tumbles in the air while her pouch rights itself, speeding along to catch up. Pip slows down so the other purlers can jump into the slipstream too, joining Stomper outside; he opens the other windows and the purlers practise going in and out of the car, and soon they are purling round and around, through the car and up over the roof, chasing each other and laughing.

"Let's purl up to the top of that hill," cries Stomper. "We'll meet Pip and Emmy on the other side!"

"Alright, Stomper Jack!" calls Pip. "I'll find a track that goes up; see you up there!"

"Yeah! Come on!" yells Billy, and off they go.

Pip glances at Emmy. "Don't you want to go too, Em?"

"I's keepin' cumpanee wiv you, Pippee."

"Thanks, Emmy, I'll be fine. You go if you want to."

"You's 'appy?"

"I's 'appy, Em."

"Fankz."

"You're welcome."

"Bi."

"Bye."

Emmy disappears with a pop.

~

The hills below the purlers look soft and rounded except for the ridges where rocks stick out above the vegetation. Plantations of conifer trees, here and there, look like geometric patches sewn on to the landscape, like a patchwork quilt. Most of the ground is grass-covered, with moorland plants such as heather, bilberry and rushes

in patches here and there. Dotted about over the hills are white blobs, which seem to be moving.

"What's all those white blobs?" calls David.

"They look like maggots!" cries Larky.

"They're sheep, I think," Penny observes, peering down.

"Sheep! Let's go and say hallo to the sheep!" Larky suggests.

"Let's go to that funny patch of trees," yells Stomper. "Come on!" She's already moving fast, and the others follow, leaving Larky feeling a bit miffed.

"Don't worry, Larky," Penny calls back to reassure her. "We'll go and say hallo to the sheep later."

"Look out!" warns David. "There's a bird chasing us."

They turn to look, without slowing down.

"'E's a red kite," Billy shouts. "'Allo, red kite, don't try eatin' us, we'd be tastin' 'orrible."

The kite catches up and flies alongside; he's stripy chestnut and black, and his long wings have black, fingery feathers at the tips. He examines the purlers with fierce yellow eyes.

"Hallo, strange birds, or whatever you are. Don't worry, I'm not hunting, I'm not very good at hunting in the air, it's much easier for me to carry off carrion . . . ha-ha! Get it?"

The purlers exchange smiles. They've slowed down now, and the red kite circles round them, his wings spread wide, and his forked tail tilts and flicks as he turns.

"My name's Billy," says Billy. "What's yours?"

"I'm called Tricky," replies Tricky.

"N mi name's Emmy n I's a mouse," Emmy cries, appearing suddenly in the middle of the cloud of purlers.

"Emmy!" cries Larky. "Where did you spring from?"

While the purlers turn to look at Emmy, Tricky swoops under them, flipping over as he goes, plucking Emmy out of the air with his talons; he flies off at top speed towards the forestry plantation.

"Yiiiiiiiiikes!" cries Emmy.

"Oi, Tricky, you trickster!" yells Billy. "We's comin' for ya!" The purlers give chase, easily catching up with Tricky who, it turns out, hasn't hurt Emmy at all; even though his talons are sharp, they are not digging into the mouse.

Tricky flies over the plantation and down to the treetops, where two oak trees grow in a patch of land that was not planted with conifers. The foresters must have liked the oak trees and left them unharmed with a bit of room to grow. The conifer trees have grown more quickly than the oaks and are already taller, but the oaks still get enough light to survive.

Tricky flies to a nest near the top of one of the oaks where another red kite is busy building a nest. The purlers gather round, cautiously keeping at a safe distance.

"Where is he?" demands David. "Where's Emmy?"

"I's 'ere n I's orite. Trikkee 'azn't 'urt Emmy."

"Let him go now, Tricky," says Penny crossly. "Why did you do that?"

Tricky releases Emmy from the cage of his talons.

"Just can't help it, you see, collecting things, you know."

Billy glares at Tricky. "Emmy ain't a thing!"

"Sorry," says Tricky. "This is my beloved Pinch."

"Hallo, Pinch," says Donna.

"Krrk," says Pinch, ruffling her handsome rufous feathers. "Tricky brings me presents. Look at all these!"

She pecks at the things that Tricky has collected for her: bits of coloured string, plastic bags, an empty tuna mayo sandwich carton and an empty shotgun cartridge. She stands up to stretch, revealing her chick, a large fledgling red kite.

"This is Kirk."

"'Allo, Krrk," says Emmy.

"Krrk," says Kirk.

"That's why we call him Kirk," says Pinch.

"Did you collect all this stuff, Tricky?" asks Larky. "Did you catch Emmy to decorate your nest?"

"Yes. I'm sorry, Emmy, it's only a bit of fun," says Tricky.

"Trikkee, I's kno-in' you's eatin' Emmy 'xcept I's a toy mouse."

"But, Emmy, you're purling!" says Penny. "Tricky can't eat any of us when we're purling, can he?"

"You's rite, Pennee, I's forgettin'."

"Come on, you lot." Billy is impatient to get going. "We 'as to find Mr Pip."

"'Ang on a mo, befor we's leevin' letz 'ave a look about," says Emmy, purling to the ground, the others following. Tricky follows too, curious to see what they are up to; he perches in the oak to watch.

"Be lookin' n tellin' Emmy."

"Telling you what, Emmy?" asks David.

"Be tellin' wot you's seein' n 'earin' n feelin'."

The purlers look around. The oak trees shade the ground, and soft green light filters through the leaves. The branches of the oak trees are festooned with mosses, ferns and lichens, and on the ground are larger ferns and woodrush and bilberry.

"It's a bit like the Glade, only smaller," observes Donna.

"It's dark as night under the pine trees!" calls Grandpa, who's drifted off to the edge of the plantation.

"They's spruce, Grandpa," says Billy.

"I's wantin' you to be openin' yor 'earts n feelin' great wave," says Emmy. "Wot'z you feelin'?"

"I feel sadness," says Larky. "Why is that?"

"Sad? What's you meanin', Larks?"

"Don't know, Billy, just it feels different to the Glade."

"It's worse than sad over here," says David, who's followed Grandpa to the edge of the plantation. "There's nothing under these trees except needles, loads of them. It's dark as night in there, like Grandpa says."

Tricky flies down from his perch in the oak.

"What's all this about? What are you looking for?"

"We're learning to feel the unwords," says Penny, simply.

"Ah! Yes. Hmmm. The wave is very slow here, and quiet. You must be patient."

"Why's that, Tricky? Is something wrong?" Penny asks.

"We can feel the great wave here, where these oaks are growing, that's why we built our nest here; the great wave is slow, waiting, waiting on the mountain too, and in the dark trees."

"But the moorland looks so beautiful!" cries Donna. "Why is the great wave waiting?"

"I bet it's the maggots!" says Larky.

"I get it!" cries Stomper, excited. "Wildness can't grow, that's what it is. I've felt this before, at home, the very first time I was purling above the town. I can remember feeling the wildness trapped in the ground, squashed down into the ground because of the roads and buildings and machines and everything."

"The moorland would become covered with trees if the seedlings weren't eaten by the sheep," says Tricky. "It can never grow to be what it wants to be, and so the great wave waits."

"What about these dark trees?" David peers into the gloom.

"It's spooky in there, I don't want to go in," says Donna.

"I think the great wave is squashed in there too, look," says Stomper. "The trees are jammed in like sardines in a tin, there's nothing else!"

"Maggots n sardeenz! Ha-ha!" says Emmy. "Let's be findin' Pippee. Goodbye, Trikkee, fankz."

"Goodbye, Emmy, come back and see us soon."

Emmy purls up to the nest. "Goodbye, Pinch, n goodbye, Krrk, we's leavin'."

"Krrrrrrrr."

"Krrk."

Emmy rounds up the purlers.

"We's findin' Pippee!"

The purlers fade away, disappearing all at once with a loud pop.

"Hmm," murmurs Tricky. "I should've tried eating one."

~

Pip bumps along in the car following a track that leads up the hill, but a locked gate stops him. He's been looking for a way to get up the mountain, but with no luck so far. There's no room to turn, so he reverses back down the track. Suddenly the car is full of purlers, whizzing in all directions, blocking his vision.

"I can't see a thing! Help! Stop!" he cries, but he does manage to stop before crashing off the track. "All right, you lot, you'd better tell me, I can see that you're excited."

"Hallo, Mr Pip! You'll never guess . . ." cries Larky, and so begins the telling of Emmy's capture by a red kite on the mountain and all the other things that happened. Pip is relieved that Emmy is not hurt and he's amused by the maggots and sardines.

"I've got something to show you," he says, when they have finished their story. "Well, it's somewhere actually. I think you'll like it after what you've just seen. It's further down the track, I'll have to reverse down until we find room to turn."

Soon the track widens where the forestry people sometimes stack timber and load lorries; Pip turns the car and drives on down the hill, with the purlers lining up on the dashboard looking out of the windscreen.

"Please — I can't see — please keep low down or at the top of the windscreen, not in the middle! Thanks."

"La la la laa laaa! Maggotz n sardeenz la laa la laaa!"

"Emmy!"

Where the moorland comes to an end there's a cattle grid; the wheels of the car rumble over noisily.

"Drrrrrrm!" sings Larky.

"Drrrrrmm!" sings Emmy. "Laa la la! Maggotz n sar deenz!" The track ends at the main road, and Pip finds somewhere out of the way to leave the car.

"Come on, follow me!" he calls, as he sets off walking the path winding alongside a stream.

"Ha! Mr Pip! You'sll be followin' us!" cries Billy, as he and the rest of the purlers race ahead to explore the woodland.

After walking for half an hour or so, Pip finds a place to settle himself down to rest and have a good look at things — and a good listen. He closes his eyes, listening to the stream as it chuckles and chockles its way between rocks. He hears birds in the woods and nearby a dipper zinks and warbles, sounding like the water itself.

Opening his eyes, he sees the dipper bobbing his white bib, then flying upstream. He notices trees covered all over with lichens, mosses and ferns. The ground too is thick with plants and young trees. There are the big oak trees of course, and ash, birch, alder, lime, hazel and rowan . . . If you were to count the little things too, the list would go on and on. There are some dead trees still standing, stark and bony, and trees blown over in storms lying on the ground across the path and stream; these too are covered in growing plants. The older fallen trees are melting into the ground as they decay, feeding the fungi and creepy crawlies. One of the fallen oaks has recently shed its bark, which lies in a mess on the ground, either side of the trunk. Perhaps an animal peeled the bark off to get at the beetle larvae burrowing beneath. With the bark peeled away, the spiralling grain of the tree trunk is clear to see, the spiralling strength that once roped the tree into the sky.

Pip watches a family of tree creepers chasing each other around the oaks, in and out of tangled branches, hiding in clumps of moss and fern, chasing each other and catching insects as they go. Blue tits tease and chase each other up in the canopy. Pip might have gone to sleep if the purlers hadn't returned at that moment.

"Pip!" cries Larky. "Emmy and Donna have disappeared! What shall we do?"

"Don't worry, Larky," says Pip. "Emmy did warn me that purlers might be pulled back at any time. Emmy and Donna must have been pulled back; they'll be alright." Pip does feel a little bit disappointed that Emmy has gone, and a bit worried.

The purlers take a while to calm down and take notice of where they are.

"What a lovely wood!" cries Penny.

Pip clears his throat to speak. "Hrrum. I was thinking about what you said earlier about the plantation up on the hill and the moorland; the little glade where the red kites are nesting is a remnant of a wood like this. 'Remnant' means a bit leftover, a fragment that remains when the main part is gone."

"'Ere we go!" says Billy. "Mr Pips's talkin' 'abitat!"

"But this isn't sad, Mr Pip, not like up on the hill!" says Larky. "It's laughing!"

"You can feel it, then?" Pip asks.

"Oh yes, it's strong and clear," says LuLu.

"Right, good," says Pip. "But we have to remember that this lovely bit of wood we're in now is also a remnant — it's a remnant of the rainforest, or wildwood."

"Rainforest?" cries Larky. "That's in Brazil and hot places!"

"Yes, you're right, Larky, but that's tropical rainforest and this is temperate, or 'Atlantic' rainforest, but still rainforest. Once it covered all this land, all the hills and all the mountains, up to the treeline. Once there were big herbivores that browsed on the trees and plants, and big predators that hunted and ate the herbivores, keeping their numbers down. We've lost all that, for the sake of a few sheep."

"Do you mean that if there weren't any sheep or humans, it would all go wild again?" says David.

"I don't mean no sheep or humans!" cries Pip. "What I mean is there could be big areas of land that humans don't meddle with and these wild bits could be all connected up, with no roads or fences."

"What about the magg . . . er, sheep I mean?" says Larky.

"It's not their fault, is it?" says David. "It's humans that put the sheep there!"

"Right," says Pip. "We humans could choose not to put sheep on the hills, so we could have woodland and big animals again."

"Farmers wouldn't be 'avin' it, Mr Pip," Billy comments.

"No, you're right, Billy, they wouldn't. But the wilded land could be worth more to them than the few sheep these barren hills support. The hills would be less prone to wildfires and would absorb more rain, so reducing flooding in the valleys. The farmers can make a better living in other ways than sheep farming. Oh dear, I'm getting into words again — come on, let's go to the sea!"

"Hooray!"

Pop! Pop! Pop! The purlers disappear, leaving Pip to walk back down to the road; when he arrives back at the car, he finds them there, but not quite all of them.

"Mr Pip!" cries Billy. "Grandpa's gon' missin'."

"And I haven't seen Nosey for a bit," says Penny. "Has anyone seen Nosey?"

"Nope," replies Billy.

"He's been very quiet," says Stomper. "Is he alright?"

"I hope he's alright," says Penny. "He didn't get snatched by Tricky, did he?"

"No, he was with us a minute ago," says LuLu. "I saw Nosey when we came to the woods."

"They've both been pulled away somewhere," Pip says. "Remember, you're purling because of the magic that Emmy brings and it's to help you to learn from creatures. You never know where purling will take you next— it might be back to your body or it might be to somewhere far away.

"Don't worry about Frank or Nosey, they'll be all right. After all, the invisible ones are looking after them. Now, shall we go to the sea?"

"Yes!"

"Yes!"

"You bet!"

"Come on then, let's go."

They drive on with the windows open enough for the purlers to practise their flying skills. An hour later they crest a hill and see the gleam of the sea.

"The sea!" cries Larky. "The sea!"

"We won't be long now," says Pip.

They go through a few towns and villages on the way, where people stop and look curiously as the car goes by, thinking there's something a bit odd about the birds flying along with the car, or are they huge bees? People stare, without knowing what it is that they have just seen.

Pip drives to a place he knows, near the sea, where there's a car park in a field especially for people who want to catch the ferry to a nearby island. At this time of day, the field is empty and there's no one around. He parks the car, dons his backpack, and sets off on foot for the beach with the purlers high above him. They race about, excited by the cliffs and seabirds, the wind and the sound of the waves breaking on the rocks below the cliffs. Pip walks across the shingle to a narrow strip of sand at the edge of the sea.

"Mr Pip, I want to get in the water!" cries Larky.

"Larky, you can go into the sea, of course, but you won't get wet. The invisible ones will bubble you," says Pip.

"Bubble me? Let's see!" says Larky, waiting for a gap between the waves before she dips into the water. Her pouch goes under, then her arms, and then her head; in another moment out she pops, dry as a bone. "Hey, this is great! Come on, Billy, come on, David!"

The purlers disappear into the sea like shadows slipping down. Pip squats down on the sand, looking and listening for them to come back. Closing his eyes, he lets the sounds and smells fill his senses. The purlers are gone for a long time; he decides to walk up to the cliff top above the bay to watch the sunset. He climbs to the top of the headland where the grass is closely cropped by rabbits; tufts of sea-pinks grow near the edge of the cliff. He sits to watch the sun until it disappears over the horizon, the sea and sky blazing with light.

"I wonder where the purlers are?" he says out loud, just to hear the sound of a voice, but no one answers. "Let's go down and make a fire."

He walks back down to the beach to find a sheltered spot amongst the rocks, gathering twigs and driftwood from above the high tide line. None of it will burn easily, he knows that, because everything is salty from the sea and salty things are always a bit damp, but eventually he gets a fire going. Settling down beside the little fire, he opens a tin of beans and pushes it into the embers at the edge of the fire to warm.

"Hallo, Pip, we're back!" says LuLu, purling out of the twilight.

"Ah! There you are! I was beginning to think you'd all gone away to a magical place at the bottom of the sea!"

"Well, we did!" says Stomper.

"We've seen some wonderful things, Pip," says Penny, wistfully. "We've talked with fish and dolphins, gannets and other creatures, and they've talked to us about the wild web. They want to show us more and invited us to return.

"The dolphins told us that humans have been taking too many fish for a very long time and many species are extincting. They showed us the bottom of the sea where the trawlers pull nets along the bottom with weights, and everything is dead for miles and miles. They showed us the horrible rubbish that kills creatures, because they get stuck in it, or it blocks their gills or their tummies, even a little plastic bag can kill a creature that eats it thinking it's a jellyfish, and the noise is terrible with ships' engines and propellers all the time, and the water's poisoned with oil and chemicals . . . it's really horrible!"

"I hate us!" says Larky, sobbing. LuLu purls to her side.

"It's true," says David, quietly. "The sea creatures say it's getting really bad, there are huge 'dead zones' in the oceans, and the worst thing of all is the sea is getting warmer . . . everything's changing too quickly for creatures and plants to adapt or move. Things are dying. It's really sad."

"That's climate change, David, you've been learning a lot purling in the sea!" says Pip. "Climate change is the thing that humans don't want to talk about or admit to. It's the elephant in the room. That's why what you are doing is so important. There isn't much time."

LuLu comforts Larky; no one speaks for a while. Pip pokes at the fire, sending a stream of sparks into the air; they burst into more sparks, cascading down like fireworks in the dusk. The purlers move, about avoiding the sparks and the smoke but then realise that the smoke doesn't make their eyes water or make them choke.

Larky begins to get over her upset. She gives LuLu a hug, well, as close to a hug as is possible for a purler in a pouch.

"Mr Pip," she says. "I really want to get wet in the sea, but I can't. I can't even make myself cry properly in this smoke. I want to be in my body! I'm fed up with this, and it's all so sad anyway, and I felt so sorry for the dolphin with the propeller wounds on her back."

Larky does actually begin to cry now, not because of the wood smoke but because she is so upset. LuLu purls close to her again, putting an arm around her shoulders.

"We all feel it, Larky," whispers LuLu. "It's horrible. But there's a reason why we are purling and that's so that we can find out for ourselves about the wild web. It's time to get back to our bodies and recover so we'll be strong enough to go back to the dolphins."

"Thanks, LuLu, I want to go back now."

"You're right, Larky!" says Stomper. "Let's all go back and get wet and dirty and eat something!"

LuLu has known all along that purling would be difficult for the children. It is fun and it's exciting, it's miraculous! You can understand the wild talk, even feel the unwords, but you can't get muddy and wet, you can't get sweaty and hungry, you can't cut yourself or bleed or fall over a cliff. The purlers are missing the creatureness of their own bodies, creatureness that they have never thought about because it's just normal — you take it for granted.

"I want my body back!" declares Stomper. "I want to smell the sea properly and taste it and get wet in it."

"You'll have to travel here in your real body to do that, Stomper," says Pip. "Purling allows you to see what's behind things, the deep Nature, but you need your body to experience these things with your senses."

"Is it real then?" asks Penny.

"What's that, Penn?" says Billy.

"Purling."

"It's real, Penny," says Pip. "Imagine the invisible ones — they are formless and have no way to taste or feel thrill or to hurt; they are the unwords, the deep Nature."

"So why are we purling?"

"Wildness is the wild web and the great wave; it's not something imagined. You can know deep Nature when you are purling, which humans have separated themselves from and forgotten. Now that you know this, you can truly be wildness in your bodies. That's why you're all longing to be in your bodies."

"I know what you mean, Mr Pip!" cries Stomper. "My first purling was brilliant, and when I woke up my body was a hundred times wilder!"

"That's right," says Pip. "It's different levels of seeing and feeling, it's different levels of awareness. What do you say to going home to your bodies, recharging, and purling back tomorrow — if you want to?"

"Can we do that? It's so far," says Penny.

"Yes, Penny, you can, it's not far for a purler. You've probably been further than that just now, under the sea."

"I'm for doing that, Mr Pip," says Billy. "See you tomorrow!"

"Goodnight, Mr Pip!"

"Goodnight!"

The purlers disappear, each one making a little pop as they vanish. Where the firelight had a moment ago shone on their tiny faces, the air is now empty and black.

Pip finds a spoon in the backpack and sits back to eat the beans; he gazes at the embers of the fire, listening to the waves whispering on the beach. The evening is still, the sea is calm. The shrill piping of an oyster catcher echoes from the cliffs, reminding Pip of the other trip to the sea with Emmy, when he found out that Emmy comes from the future — where there are no humans . . .

To be continued . . .

Mowzl's family tree

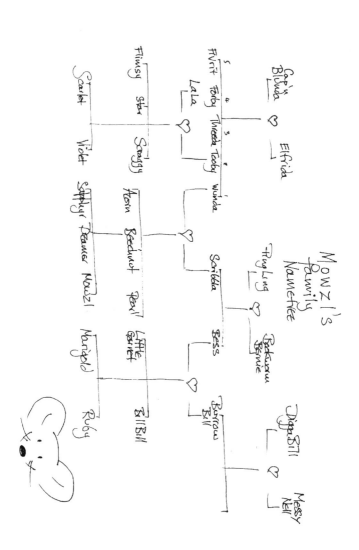

Crochet Pattern for Making Pouches for Purling

Double knitting wool and a size 8 hook makes an Emmy-sized pouch
Do not turn at each row, continue with right side facing

Row 1: make loop
Row 2: ch 2 (these count as first dc), dc 6 into original loop
Row 3: ss, *ch 3, dc into next stitch*, repeat ** throughout row forming a flower shape
Row 4: ch 3 (these count as first tr), tr 2 into ch loop, tr 3 into each remaining ch loop, ss into top of first tr
Row 5: ss into top of next tr stitch, *ch 4, miss 2 tr, dc into next tr (this is the middle tr of each group of 3)* repeat ** throughout row, anchoring remaining ch stitches into base of first ss with ss
Row 6: ss, ch 3 (these count as first tr) tr 2 into ch loop, *ch 1, tr 3 into each ch loop*, repeat ** throughout row, ss into top of first tr
Row 7: ch 3 (these count as first tr) tr in each stitch throughout row, ss into top of first tr
Row 8: *ch 3, miss 1 tr stitch, dc into top of next tr*, repeat ** through row, anchoring remaining ch stitches onto base of first ch loop with ss
Row 9: ss, *ch 3, dc into next ch loop*, repeat ** throughout row, anchoring remaining ch stitches into base of first ss with ss
Row 10: ss, ch 3 (these count as first tr), tr 2 into ch loop, tr 3 into each ch loop, ss into top of first tr
Row 11: ss into top of next tr stitch, *ch 3, miss 2 tr, dc into next tr (this is the middle tr of each group of 3)* repeat ** throughout row, anchoring remaining ch stitches into base of first ss with ss
Row 12: ss, *ch 3, dc into next ch loop*, repeat ** throughout row, anchoring remaining ch stitches into base of first ss with ss
Row 13: ss, *ch 3, dc into next ch loop*, repeat ** throughout row, anchoring remaining ch stitches into base of first ss with ss
Row 14: ss, *ch 3, dc into next ch loop*, repeat ** throughout row, anchoring remaining ch stitches into base of first ss with ss
Row 15: ss, ch 3 (these count as first tr), tr 2 into ch loop, tr 3 into each ch loop, ss into top of first tr
Row 16: ss into top of next tr stitch, *ch 3, miss 2 tr, dc into next tr (this is the middle tr of each group of 3)* repeat ** throughout row,

anchoring remaining ch stitches into base of first ss with ss

Row 17: ss, *ch 3, dc into next ch loop*, repeat ** throughout row, anchoring remaining ch stitches into base of first ss with ss

Row 18: ss, ch 3 (these count as first tr), tr 2 into ch loop, tr 3 into each ch loop, ss into top of first tr

Row 19: ss into top of next tr stitch, *ch 3, miss 2 tr, dc into next tr (this is the middle tr of each group of 3)* repeat ** throughout row, anchoring remaining ch stitches into base of first ss with ss, tie off

To make the tie:

Row 1: ch 90 stitches, tie off

Row 2: tie back 8 stitches from each end of the ch to form loops

Finishing:

Sew in all the ends

Thread the tie through the loops made by row 17 (2 rows from the top)

Crochet stitches and terms:

ch = chain stitch, pull a single strand of wool with the hook through your previous loop, making a chain of single stitches

dc = double crochet, pull a single strand of wool with the hook through the stitch on your existing row (2 threads are now on the hook), then pull a new thread through both of these stitches

tr = treble stitch, wind the thread around your hook, pull a single strand of wool with the hook through the stitch on your existing row (3 threads are now on the hook), pull a new thread through 2 of these stitches, and then another new thread through both the remaining stitches

ss = slip stitch, pull a single strand of wool with the hook through the stitch on your existing row and pull it straight through the stitch already on the hook

** = repeat. Example: *ch3, dc into next stitch* = repeat these stitches to the end of the row. Repeat the stitches indicated between the * . . . . * until the end of the row.

A space for your Mowzl notes

Author's notes:

Being outdoors in Nature has been essential to me since childhood; I have spent my working life as much as possible outside. As a student in the 1970's studying biological sciences and ecology, it was clear even then that Nature is in big trouble. Species decline, and habitat loss has escalated since that time to become the industrial scale destruction of the natural environment that we now see happening globally.

Meanwhile, human beings, particularly children, have less and less opportunity to access Nature. These changes have been accompanied by ever more sophisticated means by which children are enclosed, and separated from wild Nature, including the increase of technological substitutes. As successive generations of children and parents benefit less from contact with Nature, they know less about it and hence care less for it, and the continued degradation of the environment goes mostly unchallenged, even unnoticed.

Nature conservation is not an easy subject to make into a story, but when the rewilding of the natural world is extended to include the rewilding of children's hearts and lives, anything can happen!

This novel, to be published in three volumes, is devoted to bringing these issues into the children's domain, inviting children to ask the questions, and to see for themselves — see what it is that is missing that their hearts yearn for, and to support them in creating a platform for rebellion.

Paul Thornycroft. Stroud, Gloucestershire October 2017

~

I wrote the above in October 2017 when preparing the Mowzl manuscripts for publication. Since then there have been exciting developments — Greta Thunberg has triggered global protests by children who have become aware that their futures are being sold for immediate profit by indifferent politicians and wealthy minorities. She began alone, with a simple placard, sitting on the ground outside her school demonstrating against climate crisis inaction. "I have done my homework," she says. "Our house is on fire, you should panic." Now, millions of children all over the world have found their voices, thanks to Greta, and the movement expands everyday.

The floodgates have opened, as though we now have permission to admit what we feel and to speak out. There are many organisations and people finding their voices and shouting truth to power. Notably, Extinction Rebellion, appearing almost overnight during the winter of 2018, shows unprecedented clarity of purpose, tenacity and scrupulous codes of conduct. This is rolling out around the world. It is time! We must all shout louder and yet louder, doing what we can, when we can, how we can. Every tiny detail matters, every action; and every species matters, every fragment of habitat damaged or destroyed matters, however apparently insignificant.

The Mowzl trilogy is written to give support to this wave, and to encourage people young and old to look and taste the wild in order to understand what ecological collapse looks like — what it feels like — and all this while reading adventure stories exploring the implications of there being no quick fix. We find ourselves in a dilemma: we are the dominant species on the planet yet seem to be unable to stop ourselves from destroying life on Earth. What to do? This conversation must happen, is it at last taking centre stage?

It is important to remember that ecological breakdown is not caused solely by climate change and global warming, it is the result of human activity destroying the natural world — on an industrial and global scale in every corner of land, sea and air — by mechanical and chemical elimination of Nature for exclusive human use of land and resources. The changes required to reverse this trend go far beyond reducing carbon emissions, yet even that one thing we seem to find impossible to achieve.

The ecological emergency is real, clear and present. Climate Breakdown is real, and is happening now. These headlines are the only headlines worth talking about. Children know this, and we must all take heed. If we are not alarmed, we should be.

Paul Thornycroft Stroud, June 2019

www.mowzl.co.uk

Printed in Poland
by Amazon Fulfillment
Poland Sp. z o.o., Wrocław

61228167R00132